Author and anthologist **Mitzi Szereto** has more than a dozen books to her credit, including *Erotic Fairy Tales: A Romp Through the Classics*; *Dying For It: Tales of Sex & Death*; *The World's Best Sex Writing 2005*; *Wicked: Sexy Tales of Legendary Lovers*; the *Erotic Travel Tales* anthology series, and several erotic novels penned as M. S. Valentine. She has also pioneered erotic writing workshops in the UK and Europe. Her work as an anthology editor has earned her the American Society of Authors and Writers' Meritorious Achievement Award. Originally from the USA, she now lives in England, where she occasionally seeks revenge.

D1078212

Getting Even:
Revenge Stories

Edited by
Mitzi Szereto

First published in 2007 by Serpent's Tail
an imprint of Profile Books Ltd
3A Exmouth House
Pine Street
Exmouth Market
London
EC1R 0JH
www.serpentstail.com

Typeset by FiSH Books, Enfield, Middx
Printed in the UK by CPI Bookmarque, Croydon, CR0 4TD

ISBN 978 1 85242 961 4

10 9 8 7 6 5 4 3 2 1

Contents

Acknowledgements

To all those women who have
ever been wronged

To all those who have ever
wronged a woman

And to the certain belief
that what goes around
comes around

(even if we have to do the
job ourselves)

✝

Introduction

Mitzi Szereto

A woman goes into a pharmacy to ask for some cyanide. The pharmacist is shocked by her admission. 'May I ask, Madam, what you intend to do with this cyanide?'

'I'm going to kill my husband,' she replies.

The pharmacist takes a step back, on the verge of panic. 'Are you insane?' he shouts. 'We'll both end up in prison!'

The woman calmly opens her purse and hands him a photo of her husband and the pharmacist's wife frolicking naked on a bed.

'Oh,' the pharmacist says calmly, 'you didn't tell me you had a prescription.'

As human beings we've all thought of things to do to those who have caused us harm or grief – from the perverse and twisted to the downright murderous, but how many possess the courage to actually do them?

Revenge. It evokes fear in the sturdiest of us, especially if there's a chance we might be made the recipient of it. Yet for some reason this fear seems to be amplified when it comes to the revenge of women. Is this a cultural stereotype? Are there members of the delicate sex without the desire to exact vengeance on those who have wronged them? Not according to the stories in this collection, anyway! However, revenge can take many forms, and not always the most obvious ones.

I knew I'd hit on a good theme when I received a number of irate emails from a gentleman lambasting me for encouraging what he considered highly dangerous and inciting content, dubbing me and whoever might contribute to my project 'man-haters' – the erroneous presumption being that every story in this anthology would have as its object of revenge A MAN (now that would be a bit predictable wouldn't it?). To placate those who might level such accusations, this collection not only contains revenge against those who are NOT men, but includes male writers as well. I'm nothing if not an equal opportunity revenge-seeker!

From the Bible to Shakespeare to contemporary cinema, our times have been filled with those getting their own back...and often loving it.

Who says revenge isn't sweet?

✝

Glazed

Danuta Reah

Anthony Richardson woke up in the spare bedroom, aware that the mattress was not the well-sprung one he was accustomed to. His back was aching. He climbed out of bed and opened the curtains, looking out onto the grey November day.

He pulled on his dressing gown and tiptoed barefoot to the marital bedroom. He pushed the door open silently. Molly was asleep, her face hidden, her red hair spilling across the pillow. Her hair had lost its brightness over the years, and her face, though it still had its delicate prettiness, was creased from sleep. At one time, seeing her like this would have been a powerful incentive for him to climb back into the bed they had shared for over twenty years, but not any more.

Quietly, he collected his clothes from the wardrobe. He would shower in the other bathroom rather than risk waking her. He'd stayed too late the night before with Olivia, falling asleep next to her perfumed softness. 'You see,' she'd whispered as he climbed reluctantly out of her bed, 'it's time to let Molly know. It's for the best, darling. *I* wouldn't want to keep you in a dead marriage if it was me.'

He sighed. He still cared for Molly. Of course he did. But... The image of Olivia, fair-haired, beautiful, and most of all *young*, rose up in front of him.

Anthony Richardson had met Molly when she was twenty-one.

He was handsome, in his thirties, sophisticated and successful with his own chain of exclusive designer stores. She was a graduate from St Martin's College, with a degree in ceramics and a talent for design that was yet to be fully recognised. She was beautiful, of course. She had to be. Anything less than beautiful would not have done. And she wasn't just beautiful, she was one of the most talented ceramicists he had ever met. Her designs had a quality he had never seen before, designs that her current employer had dismissed because people who want cups with feet on them and smiling teapots tend to be limited in their appreciation of style. It was an added advantage that she was very young and not very confident.

It was serendipity. Molly needed a Svengali. Anthony needed her talent. His business, though successful, had reached a plateau. He worked by finding good designs and importing them, but a lot of other people were doing the same thing and there was nothing to distinguish his company, Richardson Design, from the mass. The continuing success of his shops depended on his having something new, something distinctive, something that no one else had. And in Molly, he had found it.

Molly Norman Ceramics became the cornerstone of his company, Richardson Design. RD, the discreet silver logo that marked his company, became a byword for the best in fine china.

Anthony was a good husband. He kept the business running well and provided a comfortable, even luxurious, home for her. And though any man has a need for variety that even a young, talented and beautiful wife can't entirely fulfil, he kept his infidelities low-key and away from home.

The marriage was a success. Except that they didn't have children. Not really. Molly had got pregnant a few years into their marriage but the child was born defective – Down's Syndrome, the doctors said. A Mongol. Anthony believed in calling a spade a spade. He had made sure that there were no more children. He wanted no more defectives in his family.

Molly made a reasonable job of raising the boy who was now fourteen, a lumbering presence in the house. She insisted on private schooling, which was an irony Anthony found hard to bear. A real son would have gone to Eton of course, but Dominic... 'He's a lot more able than you give him credit for,' Molly had said sharply. 'I want him to be able to earn some kind of a living.' In fact, the youth would be a drain on his resources forever.

And then, just a week ago, Olivia had hit him with the bombshell of her pregnancy. 'Don't worry, darling,' she'd said briskly. 'I can deal with it. I know you've got problems with...' Her eyes, dark-lashed, flickered sideways to the photo of Molly that stood where it always did, on his desk.

And he realised what the dissatisfaction with his life was. He had achieved the material success he craved. Now he needed the personal fulfilment of knowing there was someone to carry on that success. He wanted a son, a proper son, not one with a lolling tongue and an incoherent voice, one that only a mother could love. He wanted a son he could be proud of. He finally understood why men of his age took up with younger wives. They achieved success with their first wives and raised a family with their second and it was an unfortunate trick of nature that prevented women from doing the same.

'You were late last night.' Molly came into the room, tying the cord on her dressing gown. Her hair was untidy and she looked pale.

'Yes.' He didn't elaborate.

One thing that had been holding him back from the final decision was that once he'd asked her for a divorce, the company would lose Molly's talents and – at a time when he was planning a major expansion – he would have to give a large part of his wealth to her. He had discussed this with Olivia, who happened to be a lawyer specialising in the divorces of the wealthy and powerful. The company, she suggested, was his. Molly was an employee, not a joint owner and she had earned a good income through the years. As for her leaving, well, the company was more than the Molly Norman range of ceramics and anyway, Richardson's had the copyright on the Molly Norman name and all the designs she'd done for the company over the years.

He could find and promote another designer. Molly was probably getting a little passé now, a little past her prime creatively as well as physically.

He'd have to get his lawyers on to it. He didn't want a prolonged fight.

He realised he hadn't heard what Molly was saying. '... Start training Tim as an assistant today. He's really very...'

'What?'

'Tim. He's been with us for six months now. He loves the pottery – he knows the work – he's helped me often enough and...'

A few months ago, she'd taken on a youth from some charity she was involved with that looked after people with so-called 'learning difficulties'. The young man was another Dominic, another flat-faced defective with a protruding tongue that stumbled and spluttered over the few words he could manage. The pottery needed a general dogsbody – someone to make the tea and sweep up, the kind of work he was fit for and there were grants available for companies who took these people on, so Anthony hadn't argued.

But now Molly was planning to spend good money training this man, this Tim, as an assistant in the pottery, letting him load the kiln, even letting him switch it on and keep an eye on the firing. 'No,' he said.

He saw Molly's puzzled frown. 'I told you last week. I've already promised...'

He vaguely remembered her mentioning something. It was typical of Molly to drop something important into her general chat. She probably did it knowing he wasn't paying attention.

'Then you'll have to un-promise.' He saw her open her mouth to argue – she could be stubborn sometimes – and said, 'I'll see you later.'

He left the house, intending to go straight to the office. Instead, he drove to Olivia's. It was time they made some decisions.

Tim Sergeant was cleaning up in the workshop. Every morning when he came in, he mopped the floor to clear up any dust that had settled in the night. At the end of each day he cleaned up all the dropped clay, all the spatters of glaze, all the wood ash and bone meal for the colours that Mrs Richardson used on her pots, leaving everything clean and scrubbed for the next day. Then in the morning, he came in early and mopped everything again so that the decks would be cleared (Mum) and ready for the beautiful things that Mrs Richardson made.

He liked the pottery in the early morning. It was quiet with no one to distract or confuse him. He liked the wheel with the seat where you could sit and make it spin with a treadle. He did that now, pretending he was throwing a pot and making it grow under his fingers like Mrs Richardson did. When he'd first started, he'd been afraid of the kilns, especially the big gas one. The first time he'd seen flames come shooting out of the little hole in the door, he'd gone away and hidden, but Mrs Richardson had explained the kiln was supposed to do that.

There were rows of pots on the table waiting to be glazed. At first, Tim hadn't understood about the glaze. Mrs Richardson had shown him a bowl of pale sludge, and she'd dipped the beautiful, fragile bowl into it, then she'd swirled her brush along the side. It didn't look like anything special to Tim. Just sludge.

But then it had gone into the kiln with all the other pots, and when it came out, it had been the most beautiful yellow, bright as the sun. 'It's like Mum's canary,' he had breathed. 'It's magic.'

Mrs Richardson had laughed, but not in a mean way. She'd been pleased. 'Yes, like canary feathers. You're right.' After that, she'd let him help with the glazes. She'd taught him how to use the ball mill to grind up the materials, and he helped to mix the glazes she wanted to use, carefully adding the wood ash, the flint, the feldspar, the bone meal, making something ugly that somehow, miraculously, became beautiful in the fire.

And today was a special day. For weeks now, he'd watched her as she'd packed the kiln and closed the heavy door, sealing it shut by turning the wheel on the outside. He'd been allowed to turn on the gas tap as she wielded the flaming wand that made the gas ignite with a *whoof.* And she'd taught him how to keep checking the temperature gauge hour after hour as the heat crept up and up. 'Red hot,' she'd say, then 'White hot,' as it reached the magic number: 1300. And the last time they had done this together, she had nodded to Tim and, not able to keep the grin off his face, he had turned off the gas. Then the kiln would have to be left for a day and a night to cool down. 'I think you're ready,' she'd said to him, the last time they'd fired the kiln together.

Today, she was going to let him pack it by himself. She would be there in case he needed help, but she was going to let him do it, and she was going to let him use the wand to light the gas and then she was going to let him watch by himself until the time came to turn off the gas. He wouldn't be the cleaner any more. He would be Mrs Richardson's assistant. He would be a potter.

He watched from the window as Mrs Richardson's car pulled into the car park and went to make her a cup of tea in one of the teapots she designed. His hand hovered over the yellow one, but then he decided to use the one with the deep red glaze that was so fine and delicate that you could almost see the tea as you poured in the boiling water. He put a cup and saucer on the tray, and some biscuits carefully arranged on a plate.

He carried the tray through, keeping his eyes fixed on it so that it stayed level, and put it carefully down on the table in Mrs Richardson's room as she came through the door. 'Tea,' she said. 'Just what I wanted. Thank you, Tim.' But there was something in her voice that worried him. She was frowning as she poured the tea as if she was thinking about something else. She needed to be left alone to work.

'I'll go and finish sweeping,' he said.

Molly watched Tim leave, cursing herself for being a coward. She should have told him that his days of working as her assistant were over. Anthony wouldn't tolerate it. When he looked at Tim, he saw Dominic and he couldn't forgive the boy for being less than the perfect son he had envisaged. She used to fool herself, tell herself that his distance from the child was self-protection, that he didn't want to be too close to a child whose health was giving them concern. But she couldn't do that any more.

She had stayed because, for a long time, she had loved him. Later, she had stayed because Dominic needed the long-term security that money could buy. He wasn't like Tim who was able to earn money and have some independence. Dominic's disability was much more severe and he would need caring for all his life. She dreaded what would happen to him if she died, if she hadn't managed to make provision for him. She had to make certain that his future was secure.

She put on her overalls and went into the pottery to finish the designs on the new Molly Norman range. Her mind focused on her work and her worries faded into the background.

It was late morning before Anthony arrived. She was just putting the finishing touches to a special commission, something that would bring a great deal of business into the firm, if it went right. She was making a set of long-stemmed cups, fragile and beautiful, which she was glazing to try and capture some essence of the fire that would create them. She could see the colour in her mind – a clear, translucent glow. She hadn't quite managed to get that in her various experimental firings, but this time – maybe this time she'd got it right.

'What's this?' Anthony's voice broke into her thoughts.

'It's the De Clancy commission.'

'Haven't you got that done yet?'

'It's got to be right.' She swivelled her chair to face him. 'Anthony, about Tim . . .'

He interrupted her. 'Olivia's pregnant,' he said.

She felt as though something had kicked her in the stomach. 'Pregnant . . .'

'I want a child,' he said.

She could feel the anger growing inside her. 'You have a child.'

His jaw set. 'I meant a proper child. You can't give me one. Olivia can. I want a divorce.'

She could only think of Olivia pregnant, about the children she hadn't been able to have because there was only her looking after Dominic. Deep down she had always known that Anthony would be no father to his son.

He was still speaking. 'You'll want to leave the firm, of course. You'll get a generous pay off, I'll make sure of that.' A generous payout. That wouldn't be enough to keep Dominic, not for the rest of his life.

'I'll fight,' she said.

'Then I'll fight back and we'll all lose.'

Molly watched him leave and felt a black wave of despair wash over her.

Tim felt a jump of excitement as Mrs Richardson came out of her office. He'd been getting more and more worried. It took twelve hours to fire the kiln. He'd told Mum it was one of the nights he would be late, but the day went on, and Mrs Richardson stayed in her workshop, painting the pretty cups she'd been working on for days.

When he saw her, his heart sank. She had changed out of her overalls and was carrying her bag. She was going home. She'd forgotten. 'Come and sit down in the kitchen,' she said. 'I want to talk to you.'

Slowly, he put down his brush and followed her. 'Tim, you've been an excellent worker. I'm very pleased with you, you know that, don't do?'

'Yes, Mrs Richardson.' He looked at her, willing her to tell him he was still her assistant, waiting for her to smile at him, but she didn't.

'I'm very sorry,' she said, 'but you can't be my assistant any more. Not just now. You'll still do your other work, of course you will. But Mr Richardson doesn't think you're ready. And . . . Tim, listen. Things are changing round here. I might be leaving.' Her voice was odd and far away, and he got the impression she wasn't really seeing him at all.

'But . . .' He couldn't imagine the pottery without Mrs Richardson. He wanted to protest but the words wouldn't come. His tongue felt big and unwieldy in his mouth.

'I'm so sorry, Tim. You go home now. Take the rest of the day off and enjoy the weekend.' She smiled then. 'Don't forget to lock up.'

She still trusted him to do that, but Tim's bubble of happiness had burst. He watched her as she left the pottery. He saw her walk across the car park to her car and get in. He dropped his mop on to the floor and sat down. He could feel the disappointment inside him like a knife. He'd told Mum that he'd be late tonight because he was working overtime. 'I'm promoted,' he'd told her.

'Promoted!' she'd said. 'I'm proud of you, Tim.' And now he'd have to go back and tell her, and she'd think that he'd got it wrong because he wasn't clever and he did make mistakes.

The pottery was quiet. Everyone had gone home. It was a long weekend and they wanted to get away for their holidays. There was only Tim, sitting there in the gloom, and he wasn't crying, not really, because he was grown up now, and grown-ups didn't cry, but something was making his face wet. He sniffed and wiped his hand across his nose. He might as well go home.

Instead, he went into the room where the big gas kiln stood, its door open, waiting for the pots that Tim would no longer be loading in there. He'd got everything ready, the supports that would keep the shelves secure, the shelves on which each layer of pots would stand and he'd planned exactly where each pot would go.

And then he had his idea. When it popped into his mind, he couldn't believe he was thinking it, and it made him so frightened that he found it hard to breathe. He hid his face and waited for it to go away. But his mind wouldn't let it go and the more he thought about it, the less scared he became.

All the pots were ready. There was no reason why they shouldn't be fired. The weekend – the long weekend with a holiday – would be wasted otherwise. He would stack the kiln. Mrs Richardson wouldn't be there to watch him, but he would do it as slowly and as carefully as he could. Then he would light the kiln – when he thought about the flames of the gas wand, he had to hide his face again for a while – but he would switch on the gas, light the gas wand, and listen to the *whoof* as the burners in the kiln ignited. After that, he just had to wait. Then Mr Richardson would know that he was good enough to be the assistant.

When he went into the workroom, he saw the pots for the firing were on the table, all carefully glazed, all covered with the dull, dry film that the magic of the fire would turn into glorious colours like canaries' feathers and butterflies' wings. And there, on Mrs Richardson's own work table were the long-stemmed cups that she had been working on that day, using the new glaze that Tim had ground and mixed and ground and mixed again as she tried to get it right. When they were fired, they were going to be more beautiful than anything, and Tim couldn't wait.

But if he didn't get today's firing right, then he wouldn't be allowed to assist Mrs Richardson again. He turned away from her table, and began to load the pots onto the trolley.

'What the hell do you think you're doing!'

The voice came from behind him. Tim jumped and dropped

the pot he was holding, a tall jug with a delicate handle. It shattered on the floor and Tim wanted to weep. He'd never broken anything before.

Mr Richardson was standing behind him. 'Where's my wife?'

'She's gone home,' Tim tried to say. He could feel his legs shaking and he wanted the toilet.

Mr Richardson turned on his heel and went into the kiln room. When he came back, his face was dark with fury. 'Were you going to load that kiln?'

Tim nodded.

'Does my wife know what you're doing?'

Tim always told the truth. He shook his head. He couldn't speak.

Mr Richardson's lip curled. 'You're fired. Get out before I kick you out!'

Tim felt his nose clog up as his eyes filled with tears. He'd done it wrong. Mum had been so proud of him being an assistant, and now Mr Richardson had fired him.

As he stood there, Mr Richardson started shouting. 'Well? Did you hear me? Are you too stupid?' He grabbed Tim's arm and started pushing him towards the door. They were near Mrs Richardson's table and he was going to knock into it and make the beautiful long-stemmed cups fall over and shatter. He panicked. He pushed Mr Richardson away, hard. The grip on his arm loosened and he waited with his eyes screwed shut tight, waiting for Mr Richardson to start shouting at him again.

Nothing happened, and cautiously, Tim opened his eyes.

Mr Richardson was lying on the floor. There was blood on the corner of the stone table, and blood on the floor coming out of Mr Richardson's head and ears. Tim felt sick. Mr Richardson would tell the police that Tim had attacked him. He was going to go to prison. He watched, frozen, and then as he saw Mr Richardson's face turn blue and bubbles come out of his mouth, he realised he was in even more trouble than he knew.

Mr Richardson wasn't going to get up at all.

Tim sank down to the floor and forgot about being a grown-up. He cried.

After a long time, he mopped his eyes. It was no good crying over spilled milk (Mum). He screwed up his face, trying to think. That was the trouble with not being clever. It took him a long time to know what to do. Usually, he asked Mum, but this time, he couldn't. And eventually, he worked it out.

It was a good job he had the trolley. Mr Richardson was heavy. He wheeled him into the kiln room, and, grunting slightly with the effort, he slid Mr Richardson into the kiln. A leg flopped out, and then another. Tim stood there, perplexed. He bent Mr Richardson's leg and then the other, and wedged it against the kiln wall. He had to try several times before Mr Richardson was safely folded in.

But now, there was no room for the pots. They were all big, heavy ones. 'We'll start you off on the basic stuff,' Mrs Richardson had said.

Tim screwed his face up as he thought. When the idea came, it scared him as much as when he'd thought about doing the firing on his own. He wished, now, that he'd just gone home, but it was too late for that. Look before you leap (Mum). But he didn't have time to hide his face and wait for the idea to go away.

There was just space in the kiln for one shelf of pots. Very carefully, he set the supports. Bits of Mr Richardson kept getting in the way, and he had to remember that Mr Richardson wouldn't be there all the time to prop up the shelf. It was an hour before he'd got it right and he was confident that the shelf would stay in position by itself. Then, his tongue clamped between his teeth, he picked up the long-stemmed cups, one at a time, and placed them on the shelf. He felt as though he hadn't breathed in all the time he was doing it, and when the last one was on the shelf, he had to sit down for a while.

Then he swung the heavy door of the kiln shut, and turned the wheel to seal it. Everything was ready. He turned on the gas, lit the gas wand – he wasn't even a bit scared of it now – and slipped it into the ports where the burners were waiting to be lit. *Whoof!* The kiln ignited.

He went into Mrs Richardson's office to phone Mum. He was going to be out all night and he didn't want her to worry. 'Will you get a lift back?' Mum asked.

'Yes.' Tim didn't like telling lies, but he knew the early bus would get him home safely. All he needed to do now was wait. He sat on the floor watching the temperature gauge. It was going to take a long time. After a while, the smell of something cooking began to fill the room and Tim realised he was hungry. He went to his locker to find the sandwiches that Mum had made for him that morning.

Anthony didn't come home all weekend. Molly hadn't expected him to. When she went into work on Tuesday morning, she expected to find him there with the details of the divorce all worked out. She was going to fight him. She wanted every penny that he owed to her to secure a future for their son, and she wanted what he owed her for other children, the ones he would never agree to and now she would never have.

His car was in the car park when she arrived, but there was no sign of him.

Puzzled, she went into the pottery. Tim was already there, down on his hands and knees scrubbing the workroom floor. 'There's no need to do that,' she said. 'Just mopping it is fine.' He muttered something, and she realised that he was rigid with tension. She looked round the room and saw at once that a jug was shattered on the floor.

'Don't worry if you've . . .' and then she saw that the long-stemmed cups were missing.

Her eyes went back to Tim's. He dropped his gaze.

'Tim,' she said. 'What have you done?'

He didn't answer, but the way his eyes moved towards the kiln room told her all she needed to know. She ran through, hoping that she was wrong, but when she got there, she saw the kiln door closed. She touched it. It was still warm. 'Oh, my God, Tim!' Anger fought with guilt. She should never have let him think he could do this. She should never have left him alone in the pottery. She'd have to start from scratch, the commission would be delayed...

She checked the temperature then spun the handle and dragged open the door of the kiln.

And what she saw silenced her.

She was aware of Tim, a nervous presence in the entrance behind her, but all she could see were the cups. She'd never seen such a quality in a glaze. The colour had the deep translucence she had been dreaming of. Scarcely breathing, she lifted one out and held it to the light as she turned it in her hands. They were the best things she had ever done.

'Tim,' she said. 'What did you do?' For there had to have been something in the firing that gave it this extra quality, a quality she had never planned because she didn't know it existed.

Then she noticed that there was ash in the bottom of the kiln. She leaned forward and studied it. It wasn't just ash. There were lumps of charred...

'What's this?' she said, straightening up.

His face flooded red. 'Just...stuff...'

There was a pool of metal on the kiln floor, something melted beyond recognition, something about the size of a man's watch... Her eyes met Tim's. His face was wretched with guilt. She remembered him scrubbing the workroom floor, his face tense with effort...

She looked at the pots again and found herself wondering what the effect would have been of very high levels of carbon in the kiln during the firing, carbon from...

'Fine,' she said slowly. 'I'll get rid of it.'

No one ever found out what had happened to Anthony Richardson. The investigation into his disappearance went on for several weeks. His car was found in the car park at his office. His secretary said that he had left shortly after six. As far as she knew, he was going home.

His wife told them that her husband had been having an affair and that they were planning to divorce. His mistress told them the same thing, but both women had alibis for the evening he had last been seen.

No one really asked Tim any questions at all. No one knew that Mr Richardson had visited the pottery before he went home, no one knew Tim had stayed late, apart from his mother, and no one asked her. Tim was pleased about that. He didn't like telling lies. He knew the best lies were the ones you never had to tell because nobody ever asked you the question.

And the long-stemmed cups that he'd fired were the best things that the pottery had ever produced. But Mrs Richardson decided to keep them. 'These are special,' she said. 'I'm going to give them to the people I think should have them.' To Tim's surprise, she gave one to Mr Richardson's lawyer, Olivia. 'For drinking a toast when the baby's born.'

And she picked out one for herself and one for him.

'Let's celebrate you becoming my assistant,' she said. 'Champagne, Tim?'

†

Parvati

Umi Sinha

The dream came again last night, as it comes every night now. The patch of light on her face gets smaller and smaller as the bricks rise. First the mouth disappears, then the nose, until it is just the eyes, framed by black shadow and this is when I start to scream . . .

My name is Thakur Pratap Ransingh Deogarh. I am the Maharajah of Raniganj. My family goes back for thousands of years in a direct line. Until the British came, we were a law unto ourselves: we made the laws, we judged the people, we claimed the taxes. We were the lords and masters of this land. And now I, *I* – Thakur Pratap Ransingh Deogarh, twenty-seventh in line of the Thakurs of Raniganj – have to answer to a pink-faced clerk for my actions.

My grandfather despised the British, my father ignored them and was deposed. They took me from him young, educated me at Harrow and Oxford, and allowed me to ascend the throne on condition that I swore allegiance to the British Queen; I will not call her Empress. The clerk – who titles himself Resident – is here to ensure that I keep my oath, despite the fact that the word of the Thakurs of Raniganj is sacred. One might argue, however, that an oath sworn under duress is no oath at all.

Be that as it may, my relationship with the British is amicable. We have good hunting in our country. Tigers, wild boar, deer –

the land is rich with wildlife – and European princes and other nobles are often invited to play shikar with us. It is useful to keep the ear of those with influence and it seems all the royalty of Europe is connected, by blood or marriage, to the Old Sow.

It was while I was playing shikar with a minor English nobleman – a baronet, who was visiting Raniganj – that I first saw Parvati. We had been hunting a tiger which had killed several villagers, but the beaters failed to flush it out that day. A pity, but no matter. There would be plenty more opportunities. We were riding back past the home of my Chief of Police, Rai Bahadur, when a servant emerged, bowing and scraping, and begged us to honour the family by accepting some refreshments. I declined and said we would press on, but before we could move off a small girl of about eight or nine came running out of the house carrying a tray of sweetmeats and some glasses of sherbet. She had a pink dupatta over her head which almost covered her face but as she stopped by my stirrup I saw two sparkling black eyes peeping at me over the rim of the tray. I leaned down and took a sweetmeat and pinched her cheek. The baronet refused one. I toyed with the idea of insisting, just to watch him squirm, but abandoned the whim and turned back to the child.

'What is your name?'

'Parvati.'

'An illustrious name for so small a girl,' I said, smiling, for Parvati is, of course, a goddess – the wife of Shiva and the mother of Ganesh, the elephant-headed god.

She smiled back at me and her dupatta fell away from her face. She was not going to be a beauty. Her skin was too dark and her mouth too wide. But there was something dancing in her eyes and in her curving mouth that was better than beauty – mischief and a love of sensation.

At first, I did not realise how deeply she had got under my skin – an English expression, but a good one. I simply thought that she was a rather charming child, even though I had never been particularly interested in children. My wife, Shakuntala, was barren – a misfortune for her, because I was duty bound to produce heirs, and therefore would have to take another wife. But there was time for that and for now I was well supplied with courtesans and dancers.

But I found myself thinking of Parvati at the oddest moments. I began to drop in at Rai Bahadur's every time I returned from shikar. Delighted by the unexpected honour, he offered me everything of the best, as was only to be expected. Parvati usually served me. Her mother was too modest to appear in front of a strange man. I could have insisted, but it suited me not to. As Parvati got to know me she began to lose her shyness. She sat beside me, prattled to me about her nursemaid and her friends, and allowed me to put sweetmeats in her mouth. I brought her little gifts – balls dyed in various colours, dolls, miniature cooking utensils, a cage with a mynah bird in it. While at Harrow I had read a much talked of translation of Vatsyayana's *Kama Sutra* by an anonymous Englishman, which was passing round the school. It gave advice to a man, among other things, on how to 'gain over a girl from her childhood to love and esteem him'. One of the older boys had managed to borrow the book from his father's library and I earned considerable kudos from this latest fashion because it was assumed that I, as an Indian, would naturally be an expert in sexual matters, although in fact I had never heard of either Vatsyayana or the *Kama Sutra*.

At first Rai Bahadur was flattered by my interest in his daughter, but as the weeks passed I noticed him start to wonder. I laughed up my sleeve, for what could he do without risking offending me? Soon after this Rai Bahadur's wife made an appearance with her sari wrapped closely around her head and face. She touched my feet, offered me sweets and sherbet and then took a seat in a corner where she closely watched me as I teased her daughter. Parvati had gained enough confidence to sit on my lap or allow me to tickle her but after her mother appeared she became coy, lowering her eyes, smiling shyly and refusing to come near me. I relished this as a good sign for, according to Vatsyayana, 'a girl always shows her love by outward signs and actions ... she never looks the man in the face, and becomes abashed when she is looked at by him; she hangs down her head and answers in indistinct words and unfinished sentences ...'

But the next time I visited Parvati did not appear. After some time I asked Rai Bahadur casually where she was.

'She is visiting her in-laws,' he replied.

I rose to my feet. 'What do you mean?'

I could see I had frightened him. He begged me to be seated again, offered me more sherbet, which I refused, started to stammer. 'She is b-betrothed, Huzoor, since birth, to a b-boy from our caste – a Shrivastav. He is from a g-good family and they were promised to each other as infants. Naturally they have never seen each other, but his p-parents wished to meet her now she is nearly old enough ...'

'Old enough for what?' I shouted. 'Don't you know the British laws about child marriage?'

He blinked. Everyone knew that child marriages, and suttee too, went on under the Resident's nose just as before.

'W-we will not m-marry her off until she is old enough, Huzoor. We will wait ... until she is a w-woman ...'

'Who is this boy?'

'He is from a g-good family, M-Maharaj Ji, a fine b-boy ...'

'His name!'

Trembling, he told me.

It was easily taken care of: the work of a few minutes. An effective ruler always has a few men around him who can be trusted to keep secrets, even from his Chief of Police.

A week later I entered the house to the sound of weeping and wailing. Rai Bahadur came to meet me. His face was grey.

'Please excuse me, Huzoor, we have received bad news. It would be inauspicious to receive you today.'

'A ruler is always interested in the problems of his subjects.'

He raised his eyes and I saw anger in them. I held his gaze until he looked down.

'Parvati's betrothed husband . . . he died suddenly two days ago. We received the news only this morning.'

'A tragedy. How did it happen?'

This time he did not look at me. 'Someone had given him a mango in the marketplace. He ate it and became sick. He died the same night. He was the same age as Parvati.'

I said again, 'A tragedy.'

He said bitterly, 'Yes. But not only for him.'

'What do you mean?'

'Parvati is his widow. She will wed the fire tomorrow.'

'No!'

He raised his head. 'It must be so. She is a widow. She cannot live when her husband is dead.'

I said violently, 'Suttee is against the law. It has been banned by the British.'

His face twisted and he glanced at me. As he knew only too well, I had always maintained that British foibles could not be allowed to interfere with our beliefs.

'I will not allow the law to be broken. I forbid it. The British are looking for an excuse to annex native kingdoms. An official of mine breaking such a law will give them that excuse.'

'It is the reputation of my family, Huzoor. It will bring shame on our name . . . and what will happen to her if she lives on? A widow – dishonoured, impure?'

'Be careful. My mother was a widow.'

'Maharaj Ji, I meant no dishonour. It was different in your case. When your most respected father died you were still in England. The British made your mother Regent. She could not have committed suttee – they would not have allowed it. And she had a duty to perform: to guard your birthright until you came of age.'

'Parvati too has a duty to perform.'

'Yes, Huzoor, the duty of a loyal wife – to die with her husband. Anything else would bring shame upon her. No man would marry her.'

'You imagine that these beliefs we hold are sanctioned by tradition, Rai Bahadur, but according to Vatsyayana – an ancient sage – a virgin widow may remarry.'

'What man would marry her and bring such dishonour upon himself?'

I waved my hand. 'Times are changing, Rai Bahadur. We must change with them or we will be left behind. I need another wife. As you know, my wife is barren. Parvati will bear my sons. That will be her duty.' My words astonished even me. I had never intended to marry the girl.

Now he looked stricken. Before he had not shed a tear at the prospect of his daughter being burned alive. 'Sh-she is not worthy of such honour, Excellency. You are far above her.'

'That is for me to decide. Let her come to the Palace tomorrow.'

'Tomorrow! But she is too young, Huzoor.'

I smiled. 'I am a patient man, Rai Bahadur, as you know. Parvati will live with my wife, Shakuntala, who will care for her like her own mother and train her up in all she needs to know. I will not marry her until she is old enough – you have my word on that.'

He bowed his head but I could see that it was fear, not joy, that had silenced his protests. A strange father, I thought, as I rode away, who welcomes his daughter being burnt alive, but grieves to see her become the consort of a king.

I sent for her the same day. I could not take the chance that they, obsessed with their insignificant family honour, might smuggle her out to be burnt on her husband's funeral pyre.

Her arrival at the Palace was discreet. I had made it clear that my new bride's past was not a subject for discussion. I knew there would be whispers, but no one dared to speak their criticism aloud. But in the following weeks as I rode around my kingdom I thought I detected something like scorn in the eyes of my lowliest subjects.

So far as Rai Bahadur was concerned, his daughter was dead. Neither he nor his wife spoke of her again and I naturally ceased my visits to his house. In fact I gave up many of the pastimes that had previously afforded me so much amusement. I hardly played shikar unless I had important visitors to entertain. The courtesans lost their charm for me; Shakuntala had lost hers years before. Celibacy suited me now – it added to the sexual excitement which consumed me at the thought of Parvati. And what made it much, much better was that I knew it would be two or three years before she was old enough to satisfy my desires.

I visited her the day after her arrival. She was red-eyed and pitiful, still crying for her mother, still terrified by the death of the husband she had never met and the fate that had awaited her on his funeral pyre. She was confused, not understanding why she was here. I had, naturally, forbidden Shakuntala to tell her, afraid her jealousy would make her want to turn the girl against me. I did not want her to understand her future relation to me until I had won her over. For the moment I simply pinched her cheek and told her she would be safe. No one would harm her and I would come to see her every day.

She looked more composed the next afternoon and even tried to smile at the wooden doll I brought for her, although her lips were quivering so much she could hardly manage it. Patience, patience, I told myself. It was like stalking a doe – though this was the most exciting shikar I had ever played. I found myself wanting to clasp her in my arms and had to control myself by an effort of will. Over the next weeks I visited her daily, sometimes with a doll, or some sweetmeats, or flowers for her hair, which she allowed me to plait into it, and gradually she became at ease with me and greeted me with smiles and laughter, even feeling in my pockets to see what I had brought her.

My fears about Shakuntala proved unfounded. She treated Parvati like the daughter she had never had and sometimes looked at me as though it was I, not Parvati, who was stealing the object of her desire. But, dutiful as always, she prepared for us a pleasure garden, as recommended by Vatsyayana, in which to while away our afternoons, for affairs of state occupied me in the mornings. We met daily in this special pavilion, draped with richly coloured fabrics like a tent, which opened onto a private inner courtyard filled with flowers and a fountain in the middle. Here we sat and played and talked, on a bed suspended with chains from the ceiling, lying back against silken cushions.

The *Kama Sutra* had now become my bible. I consulted it daily, following its advice faithfully. I bought her little presents, played games in which she searched my hands for gifts, unclasping my fingers one by one, putting her little hands into my trouser pockets to grope for playthings. We played blind man's buff and she laughed shrilly in delighted terror as I cornered her and ran my hands over her body, pretending not to recognise her through my blindfold. She was still so innocent then. Often when I arrived I would find her sitting on Shakuntala's knee or playing with her hair and she would pout and sulk when I asked Shakuntala to leave us.

One day, while playing shikar, I shot a monkey by mistake. I was aiming at a leopard camouflaged in a tree and the bullet hit the monkey which was on a branch above. This caused consternation amongst the beaters because among these ignorant and superstitious people it is considered very bad luck to harm a monkey – all monkeys being followers of Hanuman, revered devotee of Rama and rescuer of his wife Sita when she was abducted by the monstrous Ravana.

When we went forward to look at the corpse we discovered a baby monkey still clinging to its mother's fur. It had been stunned by the fall from the tree. I took it home and gave it to Parvati who raised it by hand on bread, milk and mashed bananas. It was a pleasure to watch her gentleness with the tiny creature and imagine her one day feeding my children with the same motherly tenderness. I had a cage made from solid gold, which she hung in our pleasure garden from one of the pillars of the swinging bed. Her gratitude was most touching for she said he kept her company in the mornings when Shakuntala was busy with household matters.

So two years passed and Parvati was eleven and beginning to show signs of becoming a woman. It was time to move on to the next stage of Vatsyayana's instructions. Parvati was now too shy to sit on my knee, but I sat close beside her as I told her a story or hid some precious gift in my hand. I would put my foot as though accidentally upon hers and press it slightly, or hold her close just that little bit too long when I caught her in blind man's buff. When she washed my feet, as she always did when I removed my shoes on my arrival, I would catch her fingers and press them between my toes. Sometimes I would pretend to have a headache and ask her to rub my head. Each time I found it harder to restrain myself and would go away burning with passion.

There were, of course, always courtesans available for my relief but they suffered from my neglect and pouted when they saw me, for I did not want to consummate such excitement as no other woman had ever aroused in me, with anyone but her. I walked around in a state of exaltation so profound that my courtiers began to despair of me, because I had begun to make decisions whimsically, and had freed a woman accused of poisoning her husband because her eyes reminded me of Parvati's.

I was now at the next stage of Vatsyayana's instructions: having gained Parvati's trust, it was time to awaken an awareness of sexual pleasure. I entertained her with stories of love and danger and saw the wonder in her eyes as she began to think about the relation between men and women. I ordered for her ivory carvings of entwined lovers; I employed musicians to sing ghazals in which lovesick fellows pleaded with their mistress to grant them her favours. All went to plan. The only fly in the ointment was Parvati's fondness for her pet monkey. As she became aware of my desire for her, she began to use the wretched beast as a way of avoiding my attentions. She would be playing with him when I arrived, chasing him round with peals of laughter, trying to catch him as he swung from cage to lamp to the cords which tied the tent hangings, and refuse to stop when I asked her to. She would pout when I put him back in his cage and refuse my gifts sulkily. His chittering as we talked began to irritate me. He would sit there watching us with his round black eyes and then draw back his lips and imitate the sounds I made until Parvati laughed out loud. But because of her fondness for him I dissimulated and smiled.

The time came at last when my wife informed me that Parvati had become a woman. And indeed, although she was still only twelve or thereabouts, she had begun to develop womanly ways. She was now old enough for marriage although, strictly speaking, it was no longer necessary for me to marry her, for Rai Bahadur never asked about his daughter. It was as though she had indeed been cremated with her husband. But I had given my word, and the word of the Thakurs of Raniganj is sacred.

Now began the period I had anticipated for so long. According to Vatsyayana, for the first three days of marriage the man and his wife should sleep on the floor, abstaining from sexual pleasures, and eat unseasoned food. For another seven they should bathe to the sound of auspicious music, decorate themselves, dine together and mingle with relatives and friends who have come to celebrate the marriage. On the tenth day the man should begin to win her over with words to dispel her fears. But Parvati was not afraid of me. On the contrary, she regarded me so much as her playmate that when I began to speak to her romantically, to sigh, to tell her how I could not sleep for thinking of her, as Vatsyayana recommends, she tittered, ridiculed me and encouraged her monkey to imitate my sighs.

I then began the next stage, which was to embrace her with my upper body, place paan and betel nut into her mouth with my fingers, following this with a soft kiss upon her lips. And here I practised all the types of kiss recommended by Vatsyayana – the nominal, the throbbing and the touching kisses. I was determined to be patient and tolerate her wriggles and protests. Next I began to caress her gently, first her arms and hands, then her breasts and waist. Parvati still giggled but allowed me to do so and gradually surrendered herself to my manipulations without resistance. She ceased protesting and pushing my hands away and began to relax and a dreamy look would come into her eyes. She even began to ignore the monkey, which took a great interest in our proceedings and often clapped its hands together as though in admiration or ridicule.

On the advice of my doctor, my wife had for some weeks been administering to Parvati at night a drink made from poppy and other herbs, which made her pliant to my wishes. Gradually, as the days passed, I grew closer to my objective. She made no objection to my fondling her feet, then her calves, until my hands could rove around 'shampooing', as the English translation has it, the area around her thighs and thigh joints. But still I held off from consummation, for I could not bear that so much patience and waiting should come to an end. I wanted to show her the pleasure a woman could experience, the pleasure that brings forth the cries from her mouth that the *Kama Sutra* describes as follows: 'The sound *hin,* the thundering sound, the cooing sound, the weeping sound, the sound *phut,* the sound *phat,* the sound *sut,* the sound *plat*... and those that are expressive of prohibition, sufficiency, desire of liberation, pain or praise, and to which may be added sounds like those of the dove, the cuckoo, the green pigeon, the parrot, the bee, the sparrow, the flamingo, the duck, and the quail...' At the conclusion of congress, according to Vatsyayana, the sounds that should be forthcoming from the woman are those of the quail and the goose.

Over the following weeks I attempted to elicit these sounds from Parvati. I used all the techniques described by the sage: kissing, pressing, striking, marking her with my nails, shampooing her breasts and thighs, but though she often sighed or moaned, she failed to produce the sounds described. This worried me.

I had also begun to introduce her by touch to my lingam, which happens to be of the 'horse' – the largest – type. Parvati's yoni, I suspected, would be of the smaller types – the 'mare' or possibly even the 'deer', thus making our union that of the 'high' or 'highest' category. During these days I was like a man possessed, leaving her, each time, sweating, maddened with desire. I felt as though I could mate with a tree, or a peacock, or indeed any living thing which happened to cross my path. But I was determined not to weaken.

On the morning of the appointed day my self-control failed. The previous afternoon I imagined I had heard her make some faint sounds suggestive of a sparrow or a dove, and had had to tear myself away before excitement overcame my resolve to follow Vatsyayana's every step. I knew she would not expect me till the afternoon but I could not wait a minute longer. I left the munshi – who was by now accustomed to my inattention – tut-tutting over the figures, and rushed through the women's quarters to Parvati's own room. Surprised at not finding her there, I made my way through a rear door into the courtyard where our pleasure garden was situated. As I closed the door behind me I heard sounds which puzzled me.

Peering round one of the hangings which formed the tent, I saw Parvati lying on the swinging bed, her head tilted back, her eyes closed. She was moaning, and as I watched in puzzlement, her cries mounted until she began to emit sounds like those of a wild bird. It seemed she had reached the 'green pigeon' stage of her own accord!

I was so overcome with lust that I could no longer control myself and was just about to throw myself upon her and reap the harvest of years of careful sowing and nurturing, when I noticed her skirt moving in a strange way. As I stared, astonished, I saw something like a furry black snake emerge from under her skirt and coil itself around her ankle. I recoiled in terror, imagining I don't know what, but in the next moment I realised the golden cage was empty.

With a cry of rage I stumbled towards the bed, but it was too late. Before I could reach her, her body convulsed, her voice rose and – unmistakably! – I recognised the cries of the quail and the goose mingled in celebration!

I reached her side in a moment and seized the tail, which was still oscillating to and fro. In my rage, I wrenched the monkey away from her, swung him through the air and crushed his head against one of the pillars which supported the swinging bed. The corpse fell to the bed next to Parvati, spattering her with blood. She screamed and recoiled in terror and grief and as she looked up at me I saw undisguised hatred in her eyes. Like one possessed, I fell upon her and consummated our marriage with all the violence of three years of self-denial.

Afterwards Parvati was ill and for a time we feared that she would die. The doctor had been called to stitch her wounds. Her yoni had indeed proved to be of the 'deer' – the smallest type. Shakuntala nursed her day and night, but after her wounds healed she developed a brain fever and became terrified and screamed hysterically at the mere mention of my name. Despite my pleading, Shakuntala would not permit me even to see her.

The doctor advised me to give her time. 'Women are very delicate-natured, Huzoor. It is necessary to utilise patience.'

Such an undeserved reproach incensed me. Had I not been a very monument of patience? I saw contempt in his eyes and longed to chastise him for his impudence, but I bit my lip. It was impossible that I – Thakur Pratap Ransingh Deogarh – should admit to being cuckolded by a monkey!

I returned to the courtesans, took up shikar again. In the next few months I exceeded the total of tigers shot in my father's and grandfather's time. The fame of my balls spread throughout the country. I bought two Rolls Royces and a Bentley. The Resident joined the munshi in shaking his head and clicking his tongue in disapproval.

But none of these distractions served their purpose, which was to take my mind off Parvati. I thought of her night and day, of her laughter and teasing playfulness and, especially, of the excitement of those last few months.

I decided to travel – to go to Europe for a while, visit Monte Carlo and Nice, London and Paris. I could not stay in one place, could not allow myself to think, to remember what I had lost...I moved constantly and when my mail caught up with me I refused to deal with it and returned it all to the Resident. Let him earn his money for once, I thought. For six months I tried to bury the memory of Parvati in girls with plump pink bodies and yellow hair. But it was no good and in the end I decided to return home.

I arrived in April, as the hot season was reaching its peak, on the day of Hanuman Jayanti, the festival of the monkey god. Loyal crowds lined the streets to greet me, waving peacock fans. I was pleased to note that the cheering had improved. Parvati's father was evidently taking his job seriously. I rode on the state elephant back to the Palace, carrying the absurd clipped poodle which I had acquired in Nice as a present for Parvati. Unfortunately the voyage had not agreed with the creature. He looked bedraggled and was so weak that he could hardly stand, but I knew that Parvati would enjoy nursing him back to health.

At the banquet held to welcome me, famous musicians had been summoned from Lucknow to sing ghazals, beautiful new dancers swirled and languished at my feet, singing of their unrequited love and breaking hearts. And I felt nothing, as I had felt nothing throughout my stay in Europe. Gambling at Monte Carlo – losing thousands on one throw of the dice – my heartbeat had not even quickened. The poodle enjoyed it however. He gorged himself on the luxurious dishes and expensive sweetmeats prepared for the occasion, although he regurgitated them all soon after.

I was just about to halt the celebrations and retire to bed when the doctor approached me, grinning and bowing. He looked tired and rather dishevelled, but before I could reprimand him for appearing before me in such a condition, he said, 'Maharaj Ji, on this doubly auspicious day, I have the honour to announce to you that your wife has given birth to a child... A son, Huzoor! An heir to Raniganj!'

The blankness of my expression must have struck him for he faltered and stopped. I said slowly, '*Shakuntala* has had a child?' I had been so sure she was barren. Anyway I could not remember the last time I had had congress with her. A terrible suspicion entered my mind. The doctor saw it there and said hastily, 'My Lord, not Rani Shakuntala. It is Rani *Parvati* who has given birth to your son. He was born earlier than expected. As soon as she heard of your arrival her pains started, as though she could not wait another moment to present you with an heir. Maharaj, he is small, but he is a healthy boy!'

He waited for me to express my delight but I could say nothing, think nothing. Parvati... giving birth to a child? It was inconceivable.

'Why did nobody inform me that she was expecting?'

'Maharaj Ji, I wrote to you many times, reporting her progress.'

'I must see her.'

'She is weak, Huzoor. Her opening was small and she has lost a lot of blood. I hope she will pull round, but tonight she needs only rest.' He saw me hesitate and added, 'Her joy on seeing you may be too much for her.'

A brilliant explosion signalled the start of the fireworks on the bank of the lake and the sky filled with colour which obliterated the stars.

The next day my son was to be presented to me and acknowledged as my heir before the whole court. A small procession from the women's quarters carried the child through to the Durbar Hall. Shakuntala held him in her arms as though he was her own and, close behind her, came Parvati, thin and pale, leaning on a maidservant's arm. I approached the group and spoke directly to her.

'Parvati, are you well?' I tried to intimate, in my loving tone of voice, that all sorrow was in the past, all transgressions had been forgiven. She was, after all, the mother of my son – twenty-eighth in line to the Thakurs of Raniganj.

She looked at me with an odd smile and gestured towards the infant which had been placed in a cradle. I looked down at my son and heir, who was lying silent. He was small and dark and wizened-looking. Soft downy fur covered his face; his eyes were round and black. As he returned my gaze, he drew his lips back from his gums in a familiar grimace. I started back with a shout of terror.

The doctor's hand gripped my arm, 'Huzoor, what is it?' Lowering his voice he said softly, 'There is no necessity for anxiety, Maharaj Ji. Black hair on the face is a feature of a premature baby. In a few days it will be gone.' He hesitated. 'Huzoor, the people are waiting for you to name the child.'

I felt dizzy. How could I give the name of my illustrious ancestors to this creature? I looked from Parvati's blank face to Shakuntala's. She smiled. Why did I feel she was on Parvati's side and not mine?

'He was born on Hanuman Jayanti, my Lord. What better name than that of the god on whose holy day he entered the world?' The astrologer, who had been waiting to prophesy the good fortune which surely lay in store for the child, stepped forward eagerly, 'It is a most auspicious sign, Huzoor!'

The courtiers around us exclaimed with enthusiasm, 'Yes, yes, *most* auspicious. For the Prince to be born on Hanuman Jayanti! JAI HANUMAN! JAI HANUMAN!' The cry was taken up within the hall and passed to the crowd waiting outside. And so my son was named for Hanuman, the Lord of the Monkeys.

Like an elephant, I do not forget. A week later, when I judged Parvati had had time to recover, I paid her a visit. I took with me, as a love gift, the French poodle, who was unfortunately looking more sickly than ever. I seated myself upon the swinging bed in our love pavilion and awaited her arrival. She entered with her eyes lowered and held out a tray of sweetmeats. It was a master stroke, surely intended to remind me of that first occasion upon which she had stood by my stirrup with her tray of sweets. As I took one, I said her name softly. She raised her eyes to mine and I saw the mocking brightness in her eyes. In a fury, I threw the sweetmeat on the floor. She lowered her eyes and backed away. The poodle snapped it up before following me from the room. The next morning the dog was dead.

'Unaccustomed heat and rich food, Maharaj Ji,' the doctor said. 'This type of dog has a very delicate constitution.'

Shakuntala insisted that she herself had baked the sweetmeats, but I knew better. I had seen it in Parvati's eyes.

There is only one fitting punishment for a woman who tries to poison her husband. She must be immured alive.

Rai Bahadur had not seen his daughter since she entered my household, but he made no protest when I ordered him to carry out the sentence. Perhaps he felt her death was overdue. I, in my turn, overlooked it when he chose to deputise someone else to do the actual deed; I am not totally without pity. But I knew I would have to be rid of him afterwards.

She did not beg or scream as the bricks grew higher. If she had, I swear I would have forgiven her, embraced her, made her once more my wife, my queen, my lover. She simply stood and watched me with those dark, mocking eyes as the hole grew smaller. I dreamt of them that night and every night since. The next morning the pains started.

Since I have realised that I can trust no one, I have come to appreciate Shakuntala's devotion. At her instigation and that of the priests, I have offered sacrifices to the gods, undertaken penances, fasted – to no avail. Knowing the pain I suffer, she waits upon me day and night, preparing all my food with her own hands. She allows no one to approach me, not even the doctor. But despite all her care, my health worsens daily.

Meanwhile my son and heir flourishes, growing stronger every day. The people worship him as a god, and I dare not touch him, but when he looks at me I see the mockery in his round black eyes. One day last week I walked past his apartment and saw him mimicking me, ordering his servants to bow before him, swaggering round the room, his servants overcome with laughter. But in my presence he pretends obedience. So we circle each other warily.

All this I bear patiently. But the dream comes every night and wears me down. The shadow of the rising bricks crept over her mouth, her nose, until only the eyes were left, staring, as I imagine them now... still staring, even through the wall behind which she was entombed alive.

Her eyes follow me by night and *his* by day, while the fire in my belly consumes me.

Acknowledgements: All quotes in the story are from The Kama Sutra of Vatsyayana, _Translated by Sir Richard Burton and F. F. Arbuthnot (1883), George Allen & Unwin Ltd, 1963._

Payment in Kind

Stella Duffy

Four o'clock in the morning and I am wide awake again. As I have been since one, since two, since three. As I have been for a year. Since he left me. Ducked out, chickened out, was pushed, forced, fled, jumped away from me. Jumped indeed. Four hundred feet down. You know they really mean it when they jump off a cliff. No cry for help this one, no chance to get him back, claw him back, bring him back to life when the leap is four hundred feet onto rock and what life there was has been broken into shards and splinters and sand. I'm not sure they ever did find all the pieces. Of him. Me. Pieces of me went too, with him. Maybe he didn't know that, didn't think he'd take away some of me when he jumped, landed, badly. Landed very badly. But he did.

The love part, that was taken. The hope part. The sleep part. I could maybe cope with the first two if I had the last. Grief does what it does, I've had grief before – not this bad admittedly, not this close, not day-to-day change to my routine close – but grief, yes. I know it ebbs and flows, it changes with time and tide and it doesn't get better, really it doesn't, time does not heal. Unusually as clichés go, that one is definitely not true. Things need to be left alone to heal, need quiet and stillness to heal, ticking hands ticking past keeping on moving on are not still. They agitate and irritate and the wounds do not heal. But you do get used to it, grief. Did get used to it. I was used to my other griefs, became accustomed to my losses. Cut them, counted them, lived with them, carried on. Not this one though. Not him. Too much of me went with him. My sleeping went with him.

He and I would lay together, sleep together, we could sleep for England, Olympian sleepers we were, we loved to sleep. Now I know better. I know that I loved to sleep beside him, dream beside him, rest in the luxury of our bed. How stupid I was not to realise the precious nature of that sleep. I slept with him for the joy of sleeping with him. The sex was good, of course it was, we were a long-together couple. Longer than many of our friends, heading for a good-sized anniversary, a fine trip away to celebrate at least. We had our good times and bad times and always we came back to the bed. Great sex to start, that spark that ignites any good relationship, then good sex on occasion, and adequate sex on several more, and fine sex on holiday in someone else's clean white sheets, someone else's laundry, someone else to wash and clean and tidy away. But beyond that part, the euphemism that is 'sleeping with', there was also the act, the actual event of sleeping with, being asleep beside. I loved to sleep with him. Because I was with him. I was not always able to fall asleep with ease but, once I did, I was happy to stay there. He, on the other hand – as I know now – he slept to escape. Sleep was his place to hide. From everything that was going wrong. From all the very many things that were going wrong. None of which I knew of. None of which he shared with me. None of which he told me were keeping him awake as I lay beside him in my blissful ignorance. But I know now.

In the first week after he died, after he killed himself, while I waited on police report and autopsy and investigation – jump not slip, leap not fall – I searched everywhere for answers. He did not keep a diary, there were no secret messages on his computer, nothing hidden at the back of a drawer or cupboard. His shoe boxes contained only shoes. In that first week I had no idea at all. But death notices are checked and understood, acted upon by any number of businesses and companies and, seven days since he hit rock bottom, the responses began to arrive. Slipped through the letterbox and twisting in their own fall to the mat, mixing themselves up with condolence cards, slipping between letters of sympathy, the halting phrases in uncertain handwriting, so hard for our family and friends to work out what to say. 'I'm terribly sorry that your husband killed himself.' Well yes, that would do. The financial companies and credit card companies and banks and mortgage people though, they knew exactly what to say. We are sorry for your loss. These are our terms. You have thirty days to pay.

I had no idea.

Thirty days to pay the outstanding balance on his credit card. The first card I knew about, the other seven I did not.

Thirty days to pay the unpaid demand on a second mortgage when I thought the first was nearing the end of its useful life, when I'd believed we were soon to be mortgage-free.

Thirty days to make a delayed payment on this account and that account and this telephone – a number I did not recognise – and that online casino. The man I married, was married to for almost twenty years, did not even like to play Monopoly. The man who killed himself that day was, it seemed, excessively fond of blackjack and poker. And not very good at either. And an eBay account where he had bought a kitset car. A car. We didn't even have a garage. I have no idea where the car went, if he sold it on again. I had no idea.

A month after the funeral the house was sold. Our house. The one he'd forged my signature on the papers for, making it his house. The one I no longer had the right to live in. Good of him really, the forgery meant I wasn't entirely culpable for his debts, his uncovered lies proved my innocence of his crimes. As if defrauding a massive financial company can really be considered a crime. When hounding a man to death with red-letter bills is perfectly acceptable. My assets were frozen for another six months until it was proved I truly knew nothing about his debts. I moved in with a friend for a few weeks, another friend for a few weeks more, then another. I ran out of friends who were able to cope with the twin pillars of my grief and my fury. I stayed with friends who didn't feel they needed to cope and left me to get on with it. I became very very dull, mired in anger and bitterness, and no chance to just get on with it. Whatever it is that widows are supposed to get on with. I wanted to wear mourning, picked up a hat of hate instead. Not him, not much anyway. I could not hate him, he was too weak to hate. That was something else I had not known. His weakness. His soft, pathetic fear. Scared to tell me, scared to face the facts, scared to acknowledge the mess he had made of it all, scared to look at himself and his truths. Chicken. Why did the chicken cross the road? Because it saw a truck coming. My husband was a coward and my husband had killed himself and I cleared up the mess. Got on with it. Did my duty as wife and lover and gave up on sleep.

Eventually things cleared a little, I suppose they always do. I was allowed access to my accounts again. My empty accounts. I took a new job, the pay was far less than I had been used to, but the responsibilities were less too. I took a studio apartment in an ugly part of town. I went to work and came home. I had a small television, no cable. I didn't have much to do and I did it well. Doing little was far easier than I had expected it to be. Until he died I had been one of those women who likes to do it all. The high-powered job and the high-powered husband and the great cooking and the amazing garden and the ongoing charity project because, after all, we are so fortunate, we must find some way of giving back. It did occur to me in one or two or thirty of my empty, sleep-free nights, that perhaps I am in need of charity myself, of care, of love. Perhaps I could have been someone's project. I had friends who would take me on, one or two members of family who could care, but I preferred not to answer the telephone and did not want to Talk About It. And anyway, I had a plan of my own.

I had a list. The bank manager. The person who founded the online casino company. The other bank manager. The credit card bosses whose firms offered zero per cent interest for the first three months and then insane amounts thereafter and no way to back out of the deal. The woman who answered the phone for the company that took his money for the enormous dark green leather sofa he bought that arrived four days after his death and who would not allow me to tell her I did not want it. It sat outside our old house for three days and was only taken back when my father got on the phone and screamed at them for half an hour. Even then they did not refund the full sum. The advertising companies and the housing companies and the banks and building societies and mortgage advisers and debt collectors and bailiffs. I had their real names. Their home addresses. There is much that can be achieved with one small, second-hand home computer, broadband access stolen from the woman who lives next door, and night after sleepless night of time to kill.

I had another small project. The charity was myself.

My husband killed himself because our bank manager realised I knew nothing about the second mortgage on our house and the bank manager threatened to tell me the truth. I know this because the bank manager very kindly explained it in the softly spoken words of one syllable that a grieving widow might understand when the man in charge is foreclosing on her mortgage and alerting her to the fact that she has fourteen days to vacate the premises. He was very sorry. He is now. He is sorry that he has been having an affair with a sad widow he has been comforting for the past three months. He is sorry that his wife has seen evidence of the affair with her own eyes. He is sorry that the sad widow he has been comforting took photos and videoed much of their sexual activity in order to send the evidence later to the bank manager's wife. The bank manager thought he was being kind to the widow. And had the bank manager, even once, spent the night with the widow, allowed her to fall asleep with another warm body in the bed, then there is a chance – slim, but there nonetheless – that the widow might not have followed through with her plan to screw up his marriage. But he didn't. So I did.

My husband killed himself because an online betting company, an online gambling company, an online company that was born into the dotcom boom and managed to escape the dotcom cull, took his money night after night, day after day, took his credit card number and our money, and turned my husband into an addict. This took a little more effort than simply screwing the bank manager. But not a lot more actually. These dotcom millionaires are always in the press. They cannot help their grinning joy, hold back their self-satisfaction. They love to give interviews about how well they've done. They find it very hard to turn down another opportunity to tell the story of their great success. And who better to tell that story to than a group of disaffected youth? Who better to request the dotcom millionaire's speech about her 'council estate via trading estate rise' than the youth leader who has recently retired from working with the disaffected youth, the untimely death of the part-time youth leader's husband having meant she found working in the shallows of youthful despair just too upsetting? And who better to ask than the four most dodgy, smart-mouthed, quick-fisted lads she's ever worked with to welcome – in their own, very individual way – that dotcom leader?

I always rather liked the kids from my little charity project, my little bit of giving back. They quite liked me too, put up with me at least, the do-good, want-to-help manner I had. Don't have now. Certainly don't have now. But in truth they preferred – they far prefer – beating the shit out of arrogant arses that lie about coming from a hard background. They love it when the 'I come from the streets too you know' turns into 'Fuck!' and 'No!' and 'Please!' and 'Please!' again. I promised them there'd be at least a Rolex and a good quality sat-nav in it for their time and effort. I didn't necessarily expect them to go for the diamond ring and earrings as well as the car. Stupid bitch shouldn't have been wearing the rocks round there though, should she? Still, if she'd understood that area even half as well as she said she did, she'd have known better. The kids down there can tell diamond from paste at forty feet. And they're too cool for gold.

Two different credit card bosses have recently been arrested on child pornography charges. It may come to nothing, probably will. But by the time that nothing comes the fire will have been smoking for long enough to cause trouble, the stain set. The warehouse those sofas come from burned down last month. I do love a good fire. And Bonfire Night fires are the best. So many otherwise-occupied firemen, so many calls on the same night. Anywhere that a fire takes hold on Bonfire Night it has such a good chance to really get going. And after all, as long as no one gets hurt, as long as it's only property, right? Absolutely. Only property. And that nice lady's job, the one who wouldn't let me cancel my husband's purchase. After all, she's trained in customer service, when there's nothing to serve the customers with, and only a melted telephone to answer, no point in employing her any more, is there? The little town's local paper had some amazing pictures the next morning. All the sofas and chairs charred but still standing, great evidence of their fire-proofed stuffing. Just the warehouse that came down, heavy timbers sitting comfortably on water-logged leather. And all for the princely sum of a quick shag with a friendly security guard. Men so often fall asleep once they've come. I never do. I like to get up and get busy. It used to be work late at night, or cooking sometimes. The beloved husband upstairs asleep and me downstairs getting on with our life, storing up preserves and biscuits for us to nibble on in the long winter months. As long as he was up there in bed, I knew there was a warm place to return to. The furniture warehouse was a very warm place. I will not return.

His parents have been dead for some years, but they too shared some of the blame. The overly high expectations, the demands

41

they placed on his too-narrow shoulders. The way they always thought he could have done better. Better than me. It was childish I agree, but I took some pleasure from defacing their portraits in his family albums. Cutting out his father's face, drawing moustaches on his mother. When I gave the albums to his sister I apologised. Told her she might want to look through the albums privately first. She might be upset. Explained that her brother had attacked the albums a week or two before his death. Of course he had, the man was a suicide, we now knew. I explained that I'd never have wanted her to see what he'd done to the pictures, but that she had, fairly persistently it must be said, kept asking to have them back. As she'd so clearly put it, they were photos of her family after all. Her dead parents, her dead brother. She got what she asked for.

She called me in tears when she finally was able to bring herself to open those albums. What had happened, where were the pictures of herself and her brother? All those happy family pictures. Why was she in none of them, any more? What could possibly have happened? How could she not have known he felt this way? That he despised her so? How indeed. She went on to ask what had she ever done to hurt him? In truth, I had no idea, nothing about her in particular I mean. But she's always been a boring woman, I assumed she was a boring girl too. I told her he thought her so dull he didn't think she deserved to stay in the pictures. That was why he hadn't left her a letter saying goodbye. He hadn't left me one either, but I didn't need to tell her that. What he had left, in a pile of creditors' letters, was her own card to him reminding him that she'd loaned him several thousand pounds last year and that if she didn't get it back before Christmas she would tell me exactly what had been going on. What a liability he was as a brother. How he had cheapened himself and their family name. I thought she'd like to know he'd kept it, taken her so seriously. Taken it all so very seriously. She hung up on me. Good.

The list of creditors was comprehensive and detailed, intricate as grief. I worked my way through, paid them all back. A very few with money, most of them in kind. Like to like, ashes to ashes. Imagine if someone, anyone, just once, had been kind to him. Had told him gently to take care. Had not threatened him with revelation and recrimination. Had helped him find a way back. I do not say he wasn't to blame. He made the mess he was in, he chose to keep it from me, chose to keep himself from me forever. But grief is exhausting and not sleeping is exhausting and getting on with it is exhausting. And when you only have yourself for company, and your own thoughts to think, then it is inevitable that you begin to think hard thoughts. I thought hard thoughts, and followed through with solid action. Rock solid.

The list is done now. Almost done. They have all been repaid in some way or another. All the people that hurt him and cheated him and worried him and frightened him. The people that drove him to the edge of the cliff and the companies and firms and creditors that helped him leap out and into the thin air. When they finally gave him back to me and I put the pieces of him into the box and laid that box in the ground, I promised him I would get them all back. Every last one.

I am the last one. The wife who couldn't be told the truth. The wife he didn't trust. The wife not lovable enough to make him stay alive.

The sea is cold and grey today. A high, strong wind calling our names. I told you, my dear, I would get them all back, make them suffer, make them pay. My turn.

It's late at night. My skin is cold. It is warm beside you, always has been. I cross off the last on my list.

Coming, darling.

✝

How to Kill an Aries

Tony Fennelly

Chaucer described the pilgrimage to Canterbury as occurring in 'the time of the Ram'. Back when Astrology was a new science, during the first third of spring, the time of Aries, the Sun was in fact passing through the constellation of Aries the Ram. But the fixed stars keep moving ahead in the sky and now, during most of that period, the Sun is actually travelling through the constellation of Pisces, the Fish. The course of Aries, though, never changes. It's that thirty degrees of sky the Sun traverses after the Vernal Equinox.

My husband Ronald's character flaws were mostly due to his being born one hot spring morning when the Sun was in Aries.

Aries is a fire sign ruled by the red planet, Mars, which was named for the god of war. Astrology books give such key words as 'arrogance, aggression and impatience'. And 'accidents'. Mars's influence gave Ronald a surfeit of energy, not always constructively harnessed.

When he filled out our tax forms, in the blank labelled 'Spouse's Occupation', my husband always identified me as a 'housewife'. But what I really was is what rehabilitative counsellors call a 'co-alcoholic'. That is, a faithful helpmeet who enables her partner to spend all his leisure time drinking, without care or interruption.

Ronald's lively and adventurous Martian energy was actually what had attracted me when we met. And of course he was handsome. (Since Aries is the sign that rules the head, most Aries people are good-looking, with perfect noses.) The first time I saw him, he was riding a motorcycle, a red one naturally. He spotted me waiting alone at a bus stop, made a U-turn, headed straight for the kerb where I was standing and braked to a screeching halt.

'Hey, pumpkin!' he called out. 'How about climbing aboard and going for a ride!'

And so I did that one reckless thing, just hoisted myself up on the seat behind him and let him carry me hurtling down the highway with the wind whipping by us. I loved the excitement of it the first time. But whenever he rode with me after that, he would persist in speeding over a hundred miles an hour, leaning and swaying as he careened in and out of traffic. I screamed in terror and begged him to slow down, but he only shouted back that he wasn't going to let my cowardice interfere with his fun. If I couldn't take it, he shouted, I could just ride the bus or stay home.

I had no say in the matter. After all, I was just a dumb seventeen-year-old nobody when we met and he a twenty-five-year-old 'man of the world' with a brilliant future at a top insurance firm. My only chance of really making it in life would be to latch onto Ronald and do as he said. He explained all that to me and I understood it well.

The winter after we met, almost inevitably, Ronald totalled the red motorbike. I remember that day well. He had attempted to ride off without his helmet but I had stopped him and insisted that he put it on. In those days he wanted me just enough to accede to my wishes and the helmet saved his life. He came out of the accident with nothing but a scar on his chin.

(Most Aries people have a scar somewhere on the face because they attack everything head-first like a ram.)

Now, thirty-three years later, the once-handsome face was

bloated after decades of heavy drinking and riding in the car with him didn't feel much safer.

I buckled in tight then cringed against the door as Ronald darted in and out of traffic, covering all three lanes. I held onto my shoulder belt with both hands.

'The speed limit on this road is sixty miles an hour,' I would remind gently through gritted teeth.

'Don't try to tell me how to drive! I'm only keeping up with traffic!'

When some motorist even more foolhardy than he shot past us, Ronald erupted. 'Look at the way that ass is driving! He must be some damn foreigner!'

Ronald liked to sound off about foreigners at the top of his lungs, especially those who lived right on our block, commonly calling each race or nationality by the most pejorative term assigned to it. It was a wonder our home hadn't yet been fire-bombed.

'Myra! I'm *home*!'

After three decades of marriage, I should have been used to that loud bellow but it was so unsettling that I still winced when I heard it. I tightened up and hunched my shoulders as always when Ronald burst through the front door after work, hollering my name. I was on duty now and would be at his beck and call every minute until he left the house again or passed out, drunk.

As he came barging down the hall, I rushed to turn off the space heater but it was too late. Walking into the living room, he could still feel its warmth.

'What the hell did you have the heat on for?!'

'Well, I just wanted to take the chill off the room.'

'*I* ain't cold.'

'It's January and it's forty degrees out, so I was feeling...'

'There must be something *wrong* with you then.'

Aries is the first sign of the zodiac, the sign of self-awareness, and boasts the motto 'I am', so it's not unusual for an Aries to think of the world around him only in relationship to himself. During a 98 degree spell last summer, I wasn't free to turn on the air conditioner because Ronald wasn't hot. Of course it helped that he was always holding an ice-cold beer.

He slumped into the recliner and pulled off his wingtips. 'Hurry up and get me my athletic shoes!'

'Right away!' I sprinted into the bedroom to face a wall-length line of identical-looking athletic shoes. I picked up the closest pair and carried them back out to him.

'No! Not those!' he roared. 'Those pinch in the toe! I want the shoes that fit right!'

'But they all look alike. I can't tell which...'

He flung an arm in disgust.

'Never mind; I'll get them myself! You can't even do *that*.'

He was too impatient to be very specific about what he wanted. Then when I guessed wrong, he hollered about my stupidity and how I was never competent to make my own way in this world and so very fortunate that he was kind enough to marry me.

After dinner, I was enjoying a mystery on Lifetime, the women's channel, when Ronald barrelled back into the living room wearing only briefs, with his pot belly ballooning over the waistband. (He stopped wearing clothes around the house about the same time he started losing his looks.) He gestured with his can of snuff.

'Are you watching that?!'

'Well, yes,' I admitted, popping up to give him the recliner. 'I thought it was an interesting programme.'

'No, it's not. It's stupid.' As always, he pulled shut the curtains so he wouldn't have to look at any foreigners who might be walking down the street before he settled in the recliner, picked up the remote and began flicking through the channels. 'Nothing good on!' He spat his tobacco chew into the wastebasket. 'I pay thirty dollars a month for this damn cable and the son-of-a-bitch never has anything good on!'

'Well, since you're not watching, I can tell you something funny that happened today. I was talking to Mrs Schwartz about the...'

'Get me a beer!'

'All right.' I bustled down the hall, into the kitchen, got one of his 16-ounce cans out of the freezer, washed and wiped the top and brought it to him. He didn't feel the need for a glass.

'As I was saying, Ronald, Mrs Schwartz noticed that the...'

'Boy, what a day I had.' He spit in the wastebasket again and took a long swig of his beer. 'The damn copy machine broke down and the repairman didn't know his ass. He's a damn foreigner; that's why. I must be unluckiest bastard on earth.'

My story about Mrs Schwartz was yet another conversation attempted and ignored. Maybe my husband heard me at the moment I said 'I do' to the preacher over thirty years ago, but nothing I've said since has been worth listening to. I tried to get through to him yet again.

'You think you're unlucky, Ronald? I just saw a TV show about an Indian woman of the Untouchable caste whose lifetime job is cleaning out the human faeces in a public latrine with her bare hands. I think *she* is unlucky.'

'A "lifetime job"?' He flung his hands out. 'See, *she's* got job *security*. I don't have that. If I ever screw up, I could get *fired*.'

He continued channel-surfing and swearing at all the foreigners who are allowed on television these days until at last he stopped at the Stag Channel to watch two pretty young women being inordinately nice to each other. I left the TV to him and retreated to the back of the house with an astrology book.

I'd long given up trying to sit in there with Ronald. On those rare occasions when he let me watch a programme I liked, he would lie back in his recliner and repeat: 'Oh, my aching ass! Oh, my aching ass!' all the way through it so I couldn't hear the dialogue.

After reading for an hour or so, I stole into the kitchen, spread some peanut butter on a piece of bread and was about to lift it to my mouth when Ronald banged open the door and stuck his head in. 'Is that for *me*?'

I froze. 'Well, no. I just thought I'd have a piece of bread and peanut butter.'

'You're always so selfish! You could have fixed me some.'

'Right away.'

I tried always to eat out of sight of Ronald because whenever he saw me with anything at all (it could be a plate of *paint* chips), he decided that he was terribly hungry for that very thing and I had to stop and hustle to get him some.

I delayed having my hot meal until he was in bed for the night. It was impossible to enjoy my dinner when I could be interrupted at any moment with a bellowed 'Myra!' That may be why I was so thin. I'd never join those contented women who can savour their food and get pillowy around the middle until I achieved blessed widowhood.

After I served him his peanut butter, the phone rang and I ran to answer it as it was always for me. (Ronald had no social life; he was a solitary drinker.) The caller was my sister in California.

'Hi, Myra. How are you getting along?'

'Things have been a little tight, Julie. It was a bad year for hops and the price of the local beer has gone up. I wish I had a way to earn some extra money.'

'You should advertise for astrology clients.'

'Where would I bring them? Here?! How can I make people believe I have the wisdom of the stars to impart when the man of the house is lurching around, drunk in his underwear?'

'Yes. I've experienced his personal charm.'

'Unfortunately.'

Julie came for a visit a few years ago. She was supposed to

spend the week in our guest room but Ronald drove her out after only two days, raging in the most vulgar terms about the breach of his personal space and the sanctity of his home. (He was angry that he couldn't have the run of the house in his underpants and watch the Stag Channel.) So Julie spent the rest of her visit in a hotel and I had to sneak out to meet her.

'Hey! Myra!' I heard him from the back of the house. 'Hey, Myra!' he kept shouting while he made his zigzag way down the hall to the living room.

'I can't come now!' I called back. 'I'm talking to my sister!'

He leaned into the doorway and burped. 'You're *always* talking to your sister. What am *I* supposed to do? I need my pyjamas!'

I covered the mouthpiece. 'They're in the top drawer of your dresser.'

'Well, *get* them for me. I don't have all night!'

Julie hmpfed. 'I hear him raving in the background.'

'He needs his pyjamas, Julie – just a minute.' I put the phone down and ran into the bedroom, got his pyjamas out of the drawer, tossed them to him, and sprinted back to the phone.

'Here I am!'

'Welcome back. Why do you put up with that boor? Is he so great in bed?'

'Are you kidding? Those days are over.'

'You mean you even don't do it any more?'

'Not in years. The only curve Ronald wants to put his hand on is a beer can.'

'Then tell me. What's the attraction?'

'Simply that he's been a good provider.'

'He's providing stress, if you ask me.'

'He's just impatient. That's his problem.'

'Impatient? Is that what all his shouting is about? Have you considered an intervention for Ronald?'

'An intervention?'

'Yes. That's where you gather all his friends and relatives

together like a surprise party to tell him how he is hurting himself and his loved ones with his drinking.'

'All my husband's relatives are drunks themselves, he has no friends, and he doesn't love anybody.'

'I can believe it. So why don't you just divorce him?'

'Because I'd lose everything; that's why not. Since we don't have children, I wouldn't be awarded any financial support. And the house is in his name, so I'd have no home.'

'You would just get a place of your own.'

'With what?'

'You could make it, Myra. That lout has you brainwashed into thinking you're not competent to take care of yourself.'

'But I'm not, really. Imagine me looking for a job at the age of fifty without any experience. No, I don't want to be a divorcee.'

'Well,' she admitted, 'it would be a struggle for a while.'

'But, on the other hand, Julie, I wouldn't mind at all being a widow.' I let myself consider that and smiled. 'I'd get the house, the insurance and the nice little pension. This place would be so blissfully quiet and I'd have my days free. And people would feel sorry for me to boot.'

I heard a long sigh on the other end of the line. 'Don't count on ever making it to widowhood, dearie. Most alcoholics like Ronald out-live their co's.'

'But how could he? He gets stumbling drunk every night of his life and I don't do anything unhealthy at all.'

'You think not? You're dealing with him and all his problems while, as a non-drinker, you don't even have the solace of booze.'

'Oh, dear. Well, maybe I could find some practical way to become a widow.'

She lowered her voice. 'You can't just kill him, you know.'

'Of course not. That would be a sin.'

'I don't mind that it's a sin, Myra. Our problem is that it's a *crime*. Under the law, if you knocked off your husband, you couldn't inherit any house or get any pension. And I don't want to have to send you cigarettes in prison for the next thirty years.'

'Don't worry; I won't have to commit any crimes. The eclipse next week will square Ronald's fourth-house Mars.'

'Is that good?'

'It can be. Will you lend me some money?'

'I'd be happy to. What do you need it for?'

'A present for Ronald.'

'Are you crazy?'

'No.'

The following Saturday, I headed for our mailbox as soon as I finished the breakfast dishes but Ronald beat me to it, so all I could do was wait till he finished with the day's mail. He held it in both hands then sat back in his recliner with elaborate ceremony and slowly sorted through the envelopes, as I waited with my hands clasped. I couldn't tell him I was expecting a check from my sister so just stood patiently while he made a show of examining every piece, even the bulk mail ads.

'Lookie here. Toyota is having a sale on brake pads.' He looked up at me. My knuckles were getting white with tension but he didn't notice. 'Well now, here's the utility bill.' He tore open the envelope, unfolded the bill and read. 'Forty-nine dollars! I knew you were using too much gas.'

'I use less than any of the neighbours.'

'I don't care what those damn foreigners do! I'm gonna lose all my money just heating this place.' Then at last he held up the envelope I was waiting for. 'What's this?'

'A letter from my sister.' I put my hand out.

'What the hell is she *writing* to you for? You're always on the phone with her.'

'We're sharing our poetry. Do you want me to read some of it to you? It's very poignant.'

He snorted and tossed the letter at me. 'Poetry is *stupid*.'

★

When I was a girl, I always looked forward to weekends because they were my time off from school. But now I dreaded them because Saturday and Sunday, Ronald was home all day and I had to be on duty even when he was sprawled out in his bed, reading the sports section.

'Myra!' His shout rang down the hallway, so harsh and thunderous that I cringed. I jumped up and ran into his room.

'What is it!?'

'Don't you hear those son-of-a-bitch foreigners next door?! Their damn music is so loud, I can't even read!'

'I have no trouble reading.' I held up my news magazine.

'Then there's something *wrong* with you. Come in here and listen through the wall.'

Obediently, I joined him at the wall. 'I can't hear anything but you.'

'Oh, you're on *their* side!' His nose turned a deeper shade of red. 'Why don't you go live with *them* if you like them so much!'

'I don't really know those people. I hardly think they'd just let me move in.'

He looked down at the magazine in my hand. 'Why do we still subscribe to that?! I told you I don't like it.'

'Well, *I* still like it.'

'Look!' He pointed. 'They got another damn foreigner on the cover. A regular American doesn't have a chance any more.'

Back in the kitchen, I gathered up his beer cans, rinsed each one, crushed it and dropped it in the blue recycling bin which was already filled to heaping. (Every year, my husband went through enough aluminium to build a DeLorean.) Unfortunately, he caught me doing it.

'Hey! What are you washing those cans for?'

'You know that everything that goes in the recycling bin has to be washed first so they don't draw rats.'

'All you're doing is using up water that *I* have to pay for. Forget the recycling. Just throw all that stuff in the trash.'

'Recycling is important to the planet's future.'

'What do I care about the planet's future? *I* won't be here for it. And I'm tired of doing everything for other people.'

Tired? Try as I might, I couldn't remember a single thing Ronald ever did for anyone else.

I dropped the last can in the bin and announced, 'I'm going out.'

My preferred form of exercise was a daily walk around the circumference of the neighbourhood. Ronald couldn't complain because it didn't cost anything. The main advantage was that he would never rouse himself to go with me and I could have an hour all to myself, far out of range of his booming voice. Heading towards the river, I pondered Julie's warning. It was a chilling thought that widowhood might be denied me. Don't wives look forward to that the way people with jobs look forward to retirement? We have earned those few years of peace and solitude after a lifetime of serving a man.

That afternoon was quite warm for January and old Mrs Stoddard was sitting out on her porch in her rocker, petting her tabby cat which lay purring on her lap. I bid her my customary 'Good afternoon' on passing, but then turned back and called over her fence, 'Excuse me, Mrs Stoddard. Are you a widow?'

She smiled. 'Yes, I am. Why do you ask?'

'No reason really. You just look so . . . content.'

'Griselda is good company.' She stroked the cat, the nice quiet cat, which stretched languidly and twitched the end of her tail.

I decided that when I got to be a widow, I was going to have a cat too. Ronald had vetoed the suggestion early in our marriage. 'A cat?! We don't need any stinking cat; they're *selfish*. All they think about is *themselves*.'

'But the people I know who have cats say they're very affectionate.'

'What crap! All those things do is eat food that *I* would have to *pay* for.'

On the way back to the house, I picked up a half-gallon of milk, not without some trepidation. Ronald got angry when I didn't buy the more economical gallon jugs. But the gallon was just too heavy to carry the whole mile home. I considered pouring the milk into the open gallon jug already in the refrigerator so he wouldn't realise I'd paid more per ounce. But since he insisted upon drinking his milk right out of the jug, I was afraid it would sour too quickly.

It was nearly midnight by the time he grew tired of watching TV and lurched off to bed and I got the living room to myself. But first I had to open all the windows, though it had turned chillingly cold, and air out the room. Like many gluttons, Ronald had prodigious amounts of intestinal gas and considered the emission of it an expression of wit.

I must not be a typical patron of Iggy's Cycle World on Judge Perez Drive.

The young denim–clad salesman looked puzzled at the sight of me, wondering perhaps if I had just stopped in to ask directions. 'Yes, ma'am? Can I help you?'

'I hope so. I'm looking for a motorcycle for my husband. It will be a surprise for our anniversary.'

'A surprise?' He looked me over. 'I don't mean to be inquisitive but is your husband . . . ? An older man?'

'Older than I, even.'

'Then he isn't likely to have the reflexes to handle anything too racy. Most older men would like a utility highway machine like this Royal Gold 2000 here. It's heavy, so it'll hold the road and the rider's got a lot more defence. As safe as a motorbike can be.'

'I can see that.' I walked right past it. 'But my husband would like a trim racing machine like this red job back here.'

'Oh, no, ma'am.' He rushed to intercept me. 'This Quicksilver model is only for speeding around a track. You wouldn't take it on the highway; it's too fast and too light.'

'I understand that. But this particular bike is just what Ronald needs.' I opened my purse. 'I'll write you a cheque.'

He was probably used to haggling over the sticker price but I didn't have enough mental energy to oblige him.

'We're not supposed to argue with the customers.' He shook his head. 'And what about the helmet?'

'There has to be a helmet, of course.' I rummaged for my chequebook. 'No one would buy a motorbike without getting a helmet too, would they?'

'No, ma'am. They sure wouldn't.'

'Then I'll buy a helmet too. It has to be red.'

'Red it is. What size?'

'Size? Oh . . . Extra large.'

'So glad you're home, Ronald. I cooked your favourite dinner, corned beef and cabbage.'

'Good.' He opened the refrigerator to get his first beer of the evening. 'What's this? You bought the half-gallon jug of milk instead of the gallon?! Don't you know it's forty cents more that way? I'm going to go broke just buying milk!'

I picked up a slotted spoon and began loading his plate. 'Tonight is a special occasion.'

'Huh?' He popped the can open and took a swig. 'What's so special about it?'

'It's the anniversary of the day we met.'

'Oh – sure.'

It was no such thing, of course. We had met in the summer. But making this a happy occasion for me required celebrating on a freezing night in January.

I served him small portions of the food but kept the beers coming. After he finished his custard dessert, I looked at my watch. 8.05 p.m. It was the Mars hour, time for the surprise. I took his dishes away.

57

'And now for the best part of the evening, Ronald. I've bought you an anniversary present.'

'Yeah?' He burped. 'What?'

'It's out in the garage.'

'Okay.' He worse-than-burped.

I had set his present on display on its kickstand directly beneath the light bulb so that it was the first thing he saw when we opened the garage door.

'Oh, wow! A new motorbike! This is great!'

'It's no more than you deserve, dear.'

He hurried over to it and whistled low. 'Looks just like the one I used to have.' He turned the key in the ignition and revved the engine. 'But I can hear that it's got much more power.'

'I know you'll love the helmet too. It's red.'

By now he was astride the machine. 'Sure, where is it?'

'I have it on special order. They promised to deliver it in no more than two weeks.'

'Two weeks?!' He shouted loud enough to make the concrete walls vibrate. 'You expect me to wait two damn weeks to ride my new bike!?'

'Well, you can't very well ride without a helmet, dear. It's against the law.'

'That's a *stupid* law!'

'You mustn't think you can get away with it just because it's dark and no one will see you.'

'Never mind. I'm going out for a spin.'

'But you shouldn't take that kind of risk, dear. It's not like when you were twenty-five and you could just tear down I-10 in the middle of the night with the wind in your hair.'

He set his jaw. 'You think it's not? Just *watch* me!'

'And most important, you can't go out riding after you've been drinking.'

'Don't try to tell me what I can't do. I ride *better* when I'm drinking because I'm more *careful*.'

So Ronald wheeled his 'Happy Anniversary' present out to the street, started the engine and zoomed away to 'be careful while drinking' with the wind in his hair and I went back into the house and turned the heat up to a comfortable level. There was no point in putting on my pyjamas, so I picked up a romance novel to read but then couldn't concentrate on the pages.

Ronald had been off on his new bike for an hour and fifteen minutes when the awaited phone call came. I didn't answer till the third ring, so as not to seem too eager.

'Is this Mrs Ronald Johnson?' asked a sober masculine voice.

My heart was pounding. 'Yes.'

'Mrs Johnson. This is Officer Tom Stoaks. I'm afraid I have very bad news for you. Your husband got in an accident on his motorcycle.'

'Oh, dear! How could that happen?!' I sounded properly shocked. 'He's always... (I strove not to giggle.) ...so *careful*.'

'As the police reconstruct it, Mr Johnson had to have been going a hundred miles an hour down I-10 outside La Place.'

'La Place?!' (He'd got *that* far?)

'Yes, ma'am. Then he hit a patch of ice. Unfortunately, he lost control of his machine, was thrown from the motorcycle and landed head-first on the embankment.'

(How appropriate. Aries people do *everything* head-first.)

'Oh, my goodness! Where *is* my poor husband?'

'He has just been taken to the St Bonifice Emergency Room.'

'St Bonifice. Thank you, Officer Stoaks. I'll get there as soon as I can.'

In the hospital's emergency wing, the bearer of the terrible news was a cute boy in scrubs. He looked like a high-school kid to me, but he must have been a resident physician. His name tag said 'Dr Mendez'.

'There was massive head trauma, Mrs Johnson. We've had the

patient on a respirator all this time, but he can't breathe on his own. You see, your husband's EEG is flat.'

(Brain dead.)

His voice remained low and sympathetic. 'I'm sorry to say there's no hope at all.'

'No hope at all,' I repeated with my handkerchief up to my nose.

'The sad fact is that Mr Johnson would have survived if only he had been wearing a helmet. I can't understand why he didn't have one on.'

'I don't either, doctor.' I shook my head, the very picture of desolation. 'Ronald's helmet is sitting on the hall table at home right this minute. It's a red one.'

'All the more tragic. I'm afraid there's no point in continuing with the respirator and other heroic measures.'

'No point at all.' I had said that too quickly, so amended, 'My dear husband would not have wanted those extreme measures continued. We discussed the issue many times.'

Another young man in scrubs came up behind Dr Mendez and tapped him on the shoulder.

'You've got to ask her now.'

'Ask me what?'

'Mrs Johnson,' Dr Mendez coughed. 'I'm so sorry to bring this up in your time of grief but it has to be done right away.'

'What has to?'

'This evening, an eighteen-year-old boy, Duc Tran Ng, was working at a convenience store when a hold-up man, some scum-bag on crack, shot him for the money in the cash register.'

'Ng? A Vietnamese boy?'

'Yes. And he's still alive at this moment but the bullet nicked his heart.'

'His heart?' I clutched my own.

'And the boy is bleeding out. He only has a chance, a small chance, if he could have a heart transplant right now.'

The second doctor stepped forward. 'You see, Mrs Johnson, we've cross-matched your husband and he's the right blood group.'

'So you want to take Ronald's . . . ?'

'We want permission to harvest his organs, yes.' Mendez said. 'If we could have given you more time to think about this, we would have. But every minute is vital.'

'The OR is ready,' his colleague prompted. 'Dr Kovacs is ready to scrub in.'

'He's the cardiac surgeon.' Mendez reached into his jacket pocket and drew out a two-page form and a pen. 'Would you sign a permission slip?'

'Oh, yes.' I accepted the papers and put my signature on the 'Next Of Kin' line. 'Ronald always had a special feeling for friends from other nations. Take it all.' (Though I shouldn't think the good doctors would like the liver much.)

'Thank you, and God bless you!' The second young physician snatched the form from my hand and took off down the corridor at a dead run.

Dr Mendez stayed a moment longer. 'If you will wait, we'll locate Mr Johnson's personal effects so you can take them home with you.'

'Certainly.'

I sat in the visitors' room, happily drinking watery hot chocolate out of the vending machine, while the TV stayed tuned to CNN, and I considered whether to continue signing my name as 'Mrs Ronald Johnson' or perhaps make it just 'Myra Johnson'. I could even go back to my maiden name. 'Miss Myra Murphy' as though Ronald had never happened to my life. But in that case I would be thought a spinster and wouldn't get proper credit for all the years I spent putting up with him. No, it was a widow I wanted to be.

Also, I had to think of a good name for my new cat which I was going to pick out at the SPCA. Though since I was getting a grown cat, a middle-aged lady cat, it would probably have a name already. I didn't care about the colour or the markings, so long as it would be the kind of cat who enjoyed rocking and purring on my front porch.

I planned for my first day alone to be a leisurely one. In the morning, I would call the cable company to cancel the Stag Channel and replace it with the Romance Channel. And there would have to be a few phone calls to share the 'tragic' news with our insurance firm and some distant in-laws. Then I would take a long hot bath, undisturbed. The afternoon schedule would involve four hours of television, uninterrupted. My 'stupid' movies about handsome, gallant men wooing spunky ladies in designer wardrobes.

In the interest of delicacy, I decided to wait a day or two before gathering up all of Ronald's double-extra-large clothes and dumping them in a recycling bin.

Time went by quickly in my perception, though the whole *Larry King* re-broadcast had played, before a young nurse came in with Ronald's watch and wallet in a plastic zip envelope. 'I'm sorry you had to wait here so long, Mrs Johnson. We were backed up in Intake.'

'That's perfectly all right. Miss...' I read her name tag. '...Washington. I actually had no place else to go tonight.'

'I understand.' She looked sad about my situation. (That made one of us.) 'And thank you so much for your generosity in making the donation. Would you like us to call about the er... final arrangements?'

'You mean the funeral?'

'Yes, ma'am.'

'There won't be one.'

She misunderstood. 'I realise that it's difficult when it's so sudden. But all the funeral directors know what to do, so if you have a particular one in mind...'

'Ronald wouldn't want an elaborate funeral,' I explained. 'He was a very frugal man and would have preferred a simple cremation.'

'Since you're allowing all his organs to be harvested, we can make that sort of disposition. At no cost to you, of course.'

'That will do very nicely.'

Dr Mendez stepped into the room behind her.

'Oh, Mrs Johnson,' he said earnestly. 'I was hoping you would still be here.' He came to stand in front of me and clasped his hands. 'You may want to know the transplant went well. The new heart is functioning and we have every hope the boy will recover.'

'I'm glad, doctor.' A grin would have been inappropriate here, so I just nodded solemnly.

'What's more . . .' He stole a glance over his shoulder. 'There's someone here who wants to have a word with you.'

'Who?'

'I would like you to meet Mrs Ng, the boy's mother.'

He turned and beckoned to a tiny, grey Asian woman tented in an old coat that looked like a hand-me-down from a fisherman. She had tears in her eyes as she clutched my right hand and bowed over it. 'Mrs Johnson, I don't know how to thank you for saving my son's life.'

'No need to thank me at all, Mrs Ng.' With my free hand, I patted her bony shoulder. 'I know your son is going to do very well with my husband's heart.'

It had never been used.

Never Die

Niall Griffiths

Her first thought on waking was: *I'm still alive.*
And her second was: *Oh for fuck's sake.*

She's not even a good suicide. Can't even top herself properly. She can imagine Robbie saying that, the usual smirk on his lips, his entire face contorted in a sneer: *Lie down on the railway tracks and do it properly,* that's what he'd say. Or something like that. The prick.

She lay on the bed for a while, staring into the darkness. The red numbers on the clock were flashing 00:00, so evidently there'd been a blackout or a surge of electricity or something while she was knocked out. For how long had she been out? It was night-time outside, she could see stars and streetlights through the uncurtained window, and it had been night-time when she'd taken the pills, but that gave her very little to go on, really; this could be the same night, or the next, or some other. How could she tell?

Bad smells. There were bad smells around her. She'd been sick. There was a puddle of it on her chest, she could feel its wet weight. She turned her head to the left and saw the empty pill bottle and the empty vodka bottle on the bedside table and the envelope containing her suicide note propped up against it. There was a damp crunching sound as she turned her head and the movement felt odd to her, as if her entire neck had moved – not as if her neck muscles had acted as a pivot for her head but as if her whole neck – muscles, spine, everything – had shifted to the left. It was unsettling. She tried to sit upright too and on the fourth attempt she managed it and doing that felt similar; not as if she'd used her muscles to propel her up into a sitting position but as if she'd forced her body up out of the horizontal by an incredible act of will. As if by mind-power alone she'd dragged a dead weight upwards, bone-become-stone and mushy, moribund muscle up into a sitting attitude. Something thick and moist like porridge came out of her somewhere and smelled terrible. Maybe she needed the toilet. Or maybe she'd just gone.

An entire bottle of sleeping pills. She hadn't been messing around. Could anyone survive that? Enough to fell a bull. She must be stronger than she thought. Stronger than that cheating bastard Robbie thought, anyway.

She'd show him. She'd prove her strength to him. Show him how strong she could be. *Look,* she'd say. *I'm still alive. I don't need you.*

There was a buzzing in her head and she scratched her skull and her fingers came away entangled in clotted hair. She couldn't tell for sure in the quarter-light but it looked like there was a bit of dripping scalp attached too and the buzzing in her head stopped and a few flies passed in front of her face – she heard and felt the little wind off their wings. The buzzing in her head was replaced by a squirming. Maybe she was getting ill. It had become a hot summer, this, after a cold winter, and maybe the sudden change in temperature had given her a chill. She'd have to see a doctor. She could feel sweat on her skin, all over, a thick and clammy wetness from head to toe.

She wriggled to the end of the bed and stood. Spinning, dizzy, sick. A midden somehow becoming vertical. She shuffled over to her dressing table, the place where she'd tried so many times to make herself look attractive, and she jiggled her hand over the bin until the clump of hair fell in. She had the uncomfortable feeling that one of her fingers went in, too. The bed, moon-illuminated, held the impression of her supine body shape in the mattress, some dark and dully gleaming patches in it which suggested flayed skin. She studied that shape for some time. The mark she'd made on the world, was this it? Was this the imprint of her passing, this rank and sunken image? Herself in negative? Was this all she'd leave behind? Robbie would say it was. He'd say worse.

All those years of humiliation. She couldn't cook, sing, shag, tell jokes. She couldn't earn money. She was ugly. Useless. She was lucky that she'd met him, Robbie, because no other man would be stupid enough to put up with her. Who'd look twice at a fat classless bint like her?

That's what he told her. Every day for over two years, a relentless chipping away at her spirit and her self-respect, pushing her little by little towards a bottle of sleeping pills and a bottle of vodka and a bed. He'd murdered her, basically. Or *tried* to, at least, and now it was *his* turn to fail because here she was still, look, moving around, walking.

There was a blaze in her soul that wouldn't rest, that wouldn't accept the deaths he seemed to wish on her, neither the ego-death nor the cell-death. Some burning inside her somewhere that would not rest nor let her rest. She'd show him.

Her dressing gown hung over the bedroom door and she put it on. Went downstairs and as she moved she seemed to slosh and flop inside as if most of her had liquefied. Must be the vodka. She'd drunk the entire bottle. She worked her feet into slip-on clogs and picked her bag up off the kitchen table and slung it over her shoulder and was glad of the gloom that prevented her from seeing the mess she lived in, the dirty plates everywhere, the piles of unwashed clothes, the general garbage. The darkness couldn't mask the stink, however. Most of it seemed to be coming out of her, cloying, sweetly rancid. She'd clean up tomorrow. Couldn't be healthy to live like this.

God, her head spun. How long had she been out for?

She left the house and stepped out into the warm night. The street was deserted except at its foot by the row of unlit shops where a scruffy little dog came up to her with its tail wagging then suddenly raised its hackles and began to growl. Its owner – crusty type in a camouflage jacket – grabbed its collar and told it to be nice but then his smile quickly died as he looked at her face and he backed slowly away from her, staring at her face then turned and bolted, the dog after him in a brown blur. She heard him scream as he turned the corner by the shut chip shop.

Jeez, she didn't look *that* bad, did she? Dishevelled, sure, hair like a bird's nest, eyes bloodshot, crusted vomit on her ... not nice, no, but did she warrant *that* reaction? From the dog, even. The bloke, that crusty, had been no bloody oil painting either. This was doing nothing for her self-esteem. What was wrong with these people?

Eyes down, she scurried through the side streets towards Robbie's house. Let her hair be a matted curtain. People passed her and she saw their shoes and didn't look up, not once, not even when they asked aloud what that awful fucking *stink* was. Mad hag in a dressing gown scurrying in streetlight, that's what she was. Glad that that bastard lived nearby.

At his door she stopped, delved in her bag, pulled out the house keys. He'd asked her for them back when he dumped her and she'd obliged but not before she'd had copies made, ho ho. No light behind the windows and she let herself in quietly, closed the door very gently behind her. Stood in the familiar hall. She heard a hiss. Robbie's furry rugby ball of a cat was spitting at her from the third step up. Never did get on, the cat and her. She flicked a hand at it and what looked like a nail shot out and pinged off the cat's face and it yowled and ran up the stairs and into the bathroom.

She climbed the stairs. Very softly, carefully, stepping over the one that creaked. There was a bubble in her chest that felt like it might contain a chuckle, along with a pocket of fetid gas. At the top of the stairs she stepped out of her shoes so as not to make a noise on the uncarpeted floor in the bedroom and, it seemed, out of her feet-skin too and she opened the door slowly and crept into the bedroom. She could hear two deep breathings and in the weak light she saw two heads on the pillows, Robbie's agleam with hair gel next to a fan of blonde hair. I *knew* it wouldn't take him long to find another woman. Probably had her on the side all along. Well, they were about to be rudely awakened. About to get the shock of their lives.

There'd be trouble; breaking and entering, some kind of assault charge, maybe others. But she didn't care. There'd be revenge.

She moved to Robbie's side of the bed and leaned over his sleeping face. His thick and ever-wet lips whiffled with each exhaled breath. She leaned further and got the impression that things were leaving her face – an eye, both lips, some teeth. She must've been out longer than she thought. Terribly groggy. Was that one of her lips there, lying on Robbie's chest like a dead earthworm? An eye next to it like a dried fruit? She delved in her handbag again, felt around, took out the lighter he'd given her a couple of years ago on the first anniversary of their meeting. She traced the engraving with the tip of her thumb, ran the tip of her thumb over the familiar words four, five times until she was tracing them with the stub of her thumb: OUR LOVE WILL NEVER DIE.

Well. *Hers* wouldn't.

She leaned further. It seemed most of her nose slid off. Her face but six inches from his and his sleeping slut's. Oh they were about to get a fright. A big, big one.

She'd make a noise to wake them up. A scream. A screech, the loudest she'd ever made. Make them shit themselves with shock.

She spun the wheel on the lighter, held the flickering flame up next to her face. Took a deeeeep breath.

A Cake Story

Josie Kimber

Imagine a woman eating a cake.

You'd be surprised at how many variants there are to be found on the reliable theme of cakes plus women. Maybe you dismissed a skinny phantasm in favour of Mrs Middle-Aged Hearty, but you didn't fully and thoroughly consider the delicious options available to you, confectionarily, fleshily or otherwise.

So. Imagine a woman enjoying the cake she is eating. And as this woman is bound by the terms of a possible charter concerning cakes (the eating of) and her gender (the cultural impositions of), she is a masochist: loving what she does and latently hating herself for it.

Any closer? Of course you are. You've taken the easy, pre-packaged notion. You shouldn't; there's really no reason why you should. But you did and there you are, you're right.

Jennifer diets. She isn't fat; she's certainly not thin. She'd tell you she wants to lose a few pounds. Or, half a stone to her friends and ten pounds to herself. Temptation doesn't come in many guises, it approaches in a straightforward, honest sort of way, announcing itself boldly and without guile. If you eat me, I will taste good. I can promise you that and I do not lie. No, you will not lose ten pounds if you chew, swallow and digest me. Madam, you confuse me with running. You are making a category error.

It's the type of category error a girl might make.

She doesn't merely diet, either. Jennifer also works as hard as she has to. She is a magazine editor. Hers is a monthly style mag: one of those sharp little numbers that point us to the right entrance of the right club in the right shoes, which is useful to just as many people as you would think. How else might we have committed ourselves so loudly to sushi, or Ben & Jerry's ice cream?

Let's see: Jennifer doesn't preside, she mingles with the worker bees. Jennifer has, must and needs to do lunch. Her landscape, with its rolling accessories and sweeping parties, is a seasonal thing. Down go the hemlines and out come the credit cards. Into the gallery to schmooze beside the art. Invites to openings to do a quick headcount. Is everyone there? Important this: everyone?

To return to the cake. Imagine fresh vanilla lips stained cherry. Picture a tongue tip shyly dipped in cream. Then reserve the soft-focus, placing it carefully to one side, and cover a face in custard. Bring back the soft, mix with the ridiculous and strike a balance between the two. Jennifer at play, or Jennifer at worship.

I work for Jennifer. Although a freelance journalist, I have to admit that a good eighty per cent of my revenue comes from that magazine. As such, my labour is subject to Jennifer's tweaking and pruning. It's okay. I guess she's a competent editor. Yes, I work for her, and for my sins, I buy her cakes. Many cakes, lots. You see, I would like to hurt Jennifer. Not with a sudden, dramatic, murderous fist of hate; more a treacherous, gentle-fingered stroking. A smoothing, relentless caress. You might almost call it love. You would of course be wrong.

It goes like this and that, but boils down to missed deadlines. The deadline quite obviously suggests death, doesn't it? Judgement day. Accountability and the fear of being found wanting. To my mind, the reason that missing a deadline whips up storm and tempest is that it proves there is no God. You're still here, you're just being shouted at. Chastised. In a more imaginative world, being late would cause revolutions. But as the world still clings to its need for a good beating, being shouted at is often, pathetically, enough. We should weep, and we do.

To the crux then: if you miss a deadline, Jennifer will wave aside temporal punishment if you give her a cake. You have bought an indulgence, knowing damn well what an ephemeral pardon it is. The long-term solution has to be getting back on the path or starting something new. Atheism doesn't work. No one takes it seriously any more, and let's face it, even atheists have to eat, pay the bills and make rent. Voltaire has a lot to answer for. Only the brave resist redemption and it wouldn't be too modest to admit a lack of bravery. So you could conclude that my prolonged, exacting, torturous plan for revenge is almost Miltonesque.

I'm writing book reviews at the moment. That's what she's got me doing. It's meant as a kindness; a 'thank you' for all my recent hard work. I've had at least two features in each of the last three issues and although the money's been welcome, trying to arrange interviews with infantile 'It' stars and tired old style-mongers has worn me down. It's not the interviewees so much as their agents. You might think you'd had a good evening if you'd hung out with friends, watched a movie, did some pills or split a bottle of bourbon with your loved one. Agents, over their morning coffee, pat themselves on the back if they've caused a journalist to commit suicide the night before. I hate agents. Hate them all.

Well, I had three books to review in one night. This was last Tuesday. I'd pretty much finished one of them (the author's a friend), but hadn't so much as opened the other two. Sometimes I think it would be helpful if publishers provided reviewers with detailed summaries of their books; a sort of illicit York Notes system to help us along. I was thinking on this, lazing on the floor with a glass of red wine, when I became aware that something was happening which can reasonably be described as unusual. I was experiencing the prickling, pointed sensation that seems to precipitate a fully-formed thought. Now I don't know, you might have gorgeously circular ideas without beginning or end all the time. But I'm not like that. Chains of thoughts, each knotted into the next, sometimes fluidly, most often jarringly, like a knee in motion lacking enough lubrication – that's how it goes with me. Very rarely does a thought sneak its way undetected along my synaptic pathways, covert and silent, only to deliver itself into consciousness whole and replete. Still, it does happen from time to time, like then. Last Tuesday.

It was so simple and perfect, I jolted, knocking over my glass of wine. How to kill Jennifer. I remember laughing, stunned. You see, it wasn't the 'how' so much as the 'why'. Or rather, the lack of 'why'. Prod the thought as much as I could, it proved almost impenetrable on this front. I just wanted to kill her. All my idea yielded so far as reasons went was that I had most likely wanted to kill her for some considerable time. How about that, I thought. I wanted champagne, cocaine, hurricanes. I wanted to celebrate, with Hitchcock directing. I wanted to dance with James Stewart and Cary Grant all night long. I felt suddenly other than me; the sort of person who makes grand plans and gets things done. I was besotted and beside myself.

As I say, this was last Tuesday. I still had three books to review, so I flipped through the two I hadn't read and typed some scanty pieces on how 'refreshing' they were and as one of them was a first novel, I was able to add that the author was obviously a 'startling new voice'. Who cares for accuracy: I was feeling generous and distracted. However, when I came to start the last review of the book I'd almost finished, I got stumped. Maybe it was some secret bit of innate goodness, but I didn't want to let my friend down by turning in a half-baked hack's job. It was, after all, an engaging read, but I was fizzing with glee, don't forget. I was a potential murderer.

Everyone has different ways of dealing with a psychological

inability to finish their work. I understand that most people walk away, occupy themselves with some (hopefully useful) task, then try again. I know others who will stare for hours at a space needing to be filled with productive endeavour, wishing and dribbling their work to completion. I suppose you have a fifty-fifty chance of getting things done if you use this method. The way I deal with such moments is to stop altogether. I don't mean that I just stop trying to work in order to trick myself into working again. I just stop. All right, this has absolutely no positive effect in terms of finishing the job, but it is wonderful for clearing the mind. The important thing is to stop definitely and immediately once the decision has been made; none of this hand-wringing nonsense. By taking charge so swiftly, you are still the one calling the shots, which is a blissful tonic for the work-shy everywhere. I can thoroughly recommend it.

The next step is to immerse yourself in something pleasant, which must rule out any type of chore or good deed. If you imagine that tidying a desk drawer or writing that long overdue letter to your aunt will get you off the hook – albeit temporarily – you are mistaken. Take a step back and assess the situation. That's right, you're being productive, which is exactly the state you sought to remove yourself from. I won't be cruel about it; it's an easy enough trap. But it has to be said that if you can accomplish something as worthy as writing to your aunt, then you're more than capable of returning to your work. All you're guilty of is evasion, which is always ignoble when patently obvious. So have a bath, get drunk, smoke some cigarettes.

Well, it works for me.

A rose-scented bath and a bottle of wine later, I reached for my second packet of Marlboro Lights. There wasn't much planning to be done, as the muse had pretty much taken care of everything. All I needed were opportunities for implementation, and they wouldn't be hard to find. Jennifer was my editor; I saw her at least twice a week. I remember scrawling some notes down: equations, really. As I started in on the next bottle, I realised it was going to take some effort after all. For a minute or two I was discouraged; not on any ethical grounds, of course. It was the sheer sweep of my project that daunted me. More than anything else, it needed the long-term approach in order to come to fruition. I wasn't sure quite how long, but five years seemed a sensible estimation. Five years is a very long time in the media. Celebrity can be nurtured and neutered in less. I comforted myself with the knowledge that journalists, and indeed all manner of cultural stage-hands, are a hardy bunch. Still, Jennifer could, probably would, be working for someone else before I could bring her to an unarguable end. 'You're a freelance,' I repeated. 'You could follow her.' Well, yes, in theory I could, but stalking my victim didn't have quite the touch of finesse I was looking for. And then it hit me. There was one way I could ensure a modicum of contact with Jennifer for the foreseeable future. I could make myself one of her closest friends. I mean, why not? I could do that. Keep your friends close and your enemies closer, and so forth. Keep them so damn close they won't even see you when you strike.

It would have to be a rare and special friendship, as the locus of my plan demanded that Jennifer maintain a regular annoyance with me. I had to make myself both irritant and balm. Difficult, certainly, but not impossible.

I slept well.

'But the deadline's today. You've had a whole week.'

'I know, I'm sorry. What can I say? Here's two of them.'

'Fantastic. No, really. Jesus Christ.'

Wednesday then, and with the calming effect inherent in repetition, I was being shouted at.

'I'm sorry, Jen.'

She gave me one of her looks. It was unlike me to apologise twice and unheard of for me to call her 'Jen'. Only her favourite people addressed her thus.

'Just get it done, will you? Use Tony's computer — he's out all day.'

Tony is the assistant editor. No doubt he was out and about slurping platitudes all over some record company's foot soldier.

'All right, but let me get a coffee first. Do you want one?'

'Yeah, whatever.'

My, the right side of bed clearly hadn't been an option for precious this morning. I slithered away to the make-shift kitchen.

Waiting for the kettle to boil and fiddling with a spoon, I thought, why not start right now, as I mean to go on? I checked my bag for loose change. More than enough for a cake. Enough for at least three cakes. Good. I slipped out of the office and into the lift. Luckily, there was an excellent patisserie three shops along from the building. If I hurried, I'd be back in five minutes.

I was actually back in ten, but the cake I bore was beautiful; a lovely bit of work. What craftsmanship, I mused. What precision. Cake makers are the much underrated heroes of consumerism. I wondered fleetingly if I should write a short piece about consumable art, remembering all the little sponge cakes adorned with rice paper pictures I'd eaten as a child. Just a short article, to sell to some other publication. Jennifer wouldn't be interested. In point of fact, I don't mind telling you, it's a rotten magazine. It intimidates half its readership and leaves the other half insufferably smug. The zeitgeist pounds like hypnotic dance music through every page, threatening to reduce us all to the pulse of its beat. That's fine and gorgeous in a club, but nauseating in something of so little substance. It's all hot air and treble; no bass line to hook on to and no groove to anchor against. This would be the difference between dancing and being told what club to be seen dancing in.

I returned to Jennifer's desk with the cake held behind my back. She pretended not to see me for at least five seconds too long to be convincing before slowly looking up.

'Uh-huh?'

'Coffee's almost ready,' I said, 'but you know what the kettle's like.' I rolled my eyes to initiate a small feeling of camaraderie between us.

'And?'

She was almost unbearably uptight today. I wondered when she'd last had sex.

'Look, I know things are hectic at the minute, but I'll get that review done by three, so don't worry about it.'

'Oh well, that's all right then. It's not as if there's anything else to think about. God, you'd think one stupid little book review was all the worry I had.'

She does this, she undermines me. She digs and she snaps, then finishes it all off by reminding me how unimportant my work is in comparison to absolutely everything else.

'Back off, Jennifer. I'm only trying to help.' Then I do that. I assert myself, which always works, but somehow leaves her more distant than before.

'I know, all right. Sorry. I've got to get on, though.'

This would be the moment where I'd sigh, obviously swallowing my indignation and then turn to go. Either that, or I'd get churlish. But not today.

'Fair enough, but I've bought you something to eat. I figured you wouldn't get out for lunch today.' This was a lie, as Jennifer always found time for lunch. I placed the cake on her desk and smiled. 'I'll get you that coffee, then.'

I could see the devil on her shoulder as she regarded my peace offering. I visualised thousands of magnified saliva droplets flooding her mouth. Her fingers twitched like a spider's legs as she reached out for all that joy and cream. A job well done, indeed.

She smiled almost sweetly. 'Thanks.' Her lips were already a mess of froth as she added, 'I really shouldn't, you know.'

Oh Jennifer, you don't know how right you are.

★

So here we are, a week later. Three cakes down and a possible million to go. Yes, it really is the perfect crime. All I need is time and maybe preferential discount cards for five or six purveyors of fine pastries. I've already cut back on non-essentials (food) in order to start up a cake fund. Of course I'm aware that three cakes in one week is, quite frankly, feeble, but have a little faith. Successful ventures nearly always have two things in common: a small beginning and a solid concept. And my concept has everything – breathtaking confidence, epic proportions – and let's not forget that necessary touch of madness that skims the top of all great ideas. Phase two will obviously see me upping the cake quotient dramatically. At least two a day seems realistic, but only after I've established myself as Jennifer's confidante. If only I could force-feed the bitch. Never mind. It's better this way, watching her march willingly towards her demise. We're partners, she and I. She has become the centre of the universe in my eyes, for the rest of her life. And when the march becomes a waddle, I'll be right there, to help her cross the road.

We're in a bar in Soho and she's buying. She's had a bad day, no, a dreadful day. The man she's seeing, Philip, has told her he needs some space, he's not ready to commit, it's moving too fast and all the other stock phrases relationship-shy media boys come out with. She's been on the verge of tears since this morning at work and fortuitously, I've been spending more and more time in the office, using the computers, pretending that mine's broken. Come six-thirty everyone else had left, but I'd been spinning out a flimsy piece concerning Northern indie bands. Some unwritten rule dictates that every four issues or so we peer myopically past London to prove that we're a national magazine. It's tokenism, that's all. Apart from Scotland (and then, only Glasgow and Edinburgh), the rest of Britain might as well not exist for these Islington-loving idiots. Regardless, at six-thirty, she wandered over and asked me if I'd like to get a drink. She asked me. This was a turning-point and a definite coup. We could make like proper friends for an entire evening.

She's at the bar, getting the drinks and I'm feeling a lot more relaxed than I did half an hour, minus two whiskys, ago. This is my first time in a social situation with Jennifer alone, after all. Oh yes, there have been many gatherings and 'let's pat each other on the back for all our hard work' scenarios, but this sets a precedent. There's just her and me. She with her crisis and me with a constantly replenished tub of sympathy. She's been spilling it all, pounds of pain, out of shallow duck-pond eyes and all over me, her drink and some tissues. I've met Philip a few times and he's an irritating little bastard, but next time I see him, I think I'll kiss him, or buy him chocolates. There are two barometers here and as hers sinks lower so mine threatens to burst its mercury into the sun with joy.

She returns with straight whisky for me and a Sea Breeze for her. I can't believe she's still drinking Sea Breezes. I thought we'd all moved on. Maybe she's slipping. Don't get me wrong, I love cocktails, but Jennifer never did. It's a silly, flouncy cocktail, anyway. I have often speculated that the rise in popularity of the Sea Breeze was directly linked to the fact that most ordinary pubs didn't stock cranberry juice, especially pubs in the provinces. This provided a laughably easy way to ascertain which drinking establishments one should frequent.

'Cheers,' I say, raising my glass nominally as she settles herself. She's certainly put on weight, these last three months, thanks to me, and I'm sure I see the swelling of a new baby chin under the old one.

'Cheers. Can you spare a cigarette?'

'Sure.' I pass her my packet, outwardly calm. Damn. She's smoking. This is not good. The last thing I want is for Jennifer's appetite to diminish.

She pulls that nervous, please-think-everything-is-just-fine face. 'God, look at me.' Cue tinkling half-laugh. 'Cigarettes, yuck.'

Now this is just plain rude. You don't say 'yuck' about cigarettes to a seasoned old smoker like me. It's a subject I'm sensitive on.

'When did this start?'

She waves her hand through the smoke. My smoke, from my cigarette. 'Oh, I haven't really started. Just one now and again. It helps, you know?'

Christ, I swear her lip trembled. I nod gently. I understand, Jennifer. You can trust me. I even lower my lashes to signify that her pain is my pain.

'I can't believe he's done this to you,' I venture. I'll be rolling them out in the hours to come. I'll be calling him a fool, I'll be telling her he's the one losing out, I'll be wrapping her up in second-hand ribbons of wisdom all evening.

'I know. I just don't get it. If he felt suffocated, he should have said something. We could have talked about it, sorted it out.'

Talking. That's everybody's answer to everything. Nobody acts any more. Except me and unusually, Philip, on this occasion. He'd hooked up with Jennifer last night to see some band in Camden, they'd had a minor disagreement about the proficiency of said band and then, bang. From apparently nowhere (to hear Jennifer tell it), he'd rattled off how he felt and then, despite protestations from her, strode away into the night, without looking back.

'Well, yeah,' I agree. 'I mean, what was he thinking? Typical fucking man.' Cheap shots work too.

'I guess.' She stares into her glass. She bites her lip. She smokes some more. 'I don't know.'

No, no, don't clam up now. 'So tell me again how it happened exactly,' I say, looking bemused, rubbing my forehead. 'One minute you're discussing the band and the next, he just goes right into it?'

'Yeah. From fucking nowhere, the arsehole. I say, "Well, they're just another sub-Pixies," and he's like, "Look, forget it," you know, all tight-lipped, so I'm thinking, okay, and then he looks straight at me and says, well, you know what he said.'

This is better. Keep her angry for a while. Keep her ranting.

I'm shaking my head. 'It's unbelievable. 'God, it's unbelievable. Just like that?'

'Just like that.' She leans back, triumphant. 'So he comes out with it, how he needs space, how a serious relationship isn't on his agenda right now—'

'He actually said "agenda"?'

'Yep. And then he said he needed time for himself, yeah? So I'm totally thrown, I mean, are we breaking up, were we even really together, and he says he has to go and he'll give me a call in a few weeks. And then he just fucks off.'

'So basically, he's left you hanging. You don't even know whether he's finished things for good or not.'

'Exactly. Can you believe it?'

Of course I can believe it. Just as these dolts can never affirm that they're actually part of a couple – they're perpetually 'seeing someone' – so they don't have the backbone to end relations definitively. They live their lives by the comma, these people, never the full-stop.

'No, I can't,' I say, eyes widening and head shaking. 'God, it's outrageous. What a bastard.'

'I just, I just—' she stammers, one plump tear rolling down the semi-sphere of her cheek.

'Hey, it's all right, Jen,' I say, reaching across the table and squeezing her arm. I am bold; I seize, risking rejection.

She forces a pitiful smile. 'Thanks. You're being really nice.'

Oh bliss, oh euphoria, come unto me.

'No problem, Jen. Really.' I sip my drink. 'Look. He's the one losing out, right? He's a fool. You're better off without him.' I stop short of referring to fish and the sea.

Jennifer's face looks wobbly; it's on the turn. This is a make-or-break moment. She'll either flood the bar or compose herself. Either is fine by me. I am mistress of the situation. I can play it any way she wants.

'You're absolutely right.' She wipes her eyes and clears her throat. 'Fuck him. Do you want to get something to eat?'

What sudden courage, I muse, and what a marvellous idea. 'Sure, that'd be good.'

'Right,' she says, draining her glass. 'Drink up. I know a good Thai restaurant round the corner.'

'Okay.' I neck the whisky and pull on my coat. 'Let's go.'

I could skip, I really could. Tonight is Jennifer's night. She won't have to count a single calorie. That's part of my job remit.

As no higher power has intervened on my behalf, we find ourselves in something of a quandary. A year into my grand scheme, Jennifer went to work for another magazine. A magazine that I don't freelance for. She's adapted well, as her job is the same, all the people look and act the same and the magazine itself is pretty much identical to the last. It uses a slightly different typeface, but you'd be hard pressed to discern any major distinctions between the two. The only consolation is that I've pretty much clamped myself on to Jennifer's heart and she's promised me some work 'once she's settled in'. That was two months ago, but I couldn't bear to doubt her word. I'm her best friend, if not her favourite person. Remember, I still had a year of missing deadlines to honour, but I always came through when she needed me. I don't think I've ever been so reliable.

At night, I dream of her. She's standing by a stream, encircled by empty cake boxes, one chubby hand squashing another pastry into her custard-smeared mouth. It always starts this way; only the cake changes. Last time it was an apple turnover. Two weeks ago, she was binging on an enormous Eccles cake. I'm sure we shall end on 'Death By Chocolate', but I hope not. That would be too obvious. Anyway, I'm watching her, but she doesn't see me. I have concluded that we all eat differently when we're alone. We don't care how messy we are, or how much we slobber. It's quite disgusting. An unfortunate side-effect of this dream is the cooling relationship I have with food. To begin with, a cutback was necessary (recall the cake fund), but this last year has seen a resurgence in my fiscal status, so I could, in theory, gorge myself if I wanted to. But I don't want to. Sometimes I feel that Jennifer and I are engaged in some kind of symbiotic, night-time embrace, whereby she draws the flesh from my bones – swelling it like cooked rice – and assimilates it into herself. There is a part of me hiding in the shadows of her bulk.

I dream on, watching her feed, horrified and fixed by the relentless motion of hand, mouth and jaw, then I step forward and whisper her name. She turns and smiles, wiping crumbs from her lips and opening her arms, inviting me in. But I hold back till I hear the piano and a low croon echoing, 'Give me the moonlight, give me the girl.' And then we dance lightly, a moonlight meringue. We have never been so close.

I've lost a stone, but she's gained two, so I win.

Since Jennifer's career move, opportunities for slowly murdering her have dried up somewhat, but I still get to see her a reasonable amount. Unfortunately, our rendezvous are generally limited to book launches and the like, which doesn't provide me with the best circumstances in which to jam and sponge her. I have to admit it, I'm getting desperate. I've even considered poison, but I was so against that in the early days. It was of paramount importance that the project be left unsullied by such low blows. Poison felt like cheating and there was always the threat of discovery. It just wouldn't do. As the months draw on though, and the woman shows no signs of dying, it becomes a terrible temptation. I'm weakening, I can feel it in my spine. I have to resist. I will resist.

I've been writing about new and exciting fashion designers for Jennifer's replacement at the magazine. He's much nicer than she was. I've even slept with him, hence my increased workload and sprightly bank balance. So you can see how vital it is that I don't prostitute my plan. Some things must be sacred. I'll bend and contort for my career, but I mustn't compromise where Jennifer's concerned. I want to lead her gently to the ground. She deserves it.

Tonight, I'll be seeing her alone. I have to keep reminding myself of that. It's my hook and my hope. Tonight is one of those all too rare occasions when she comes to my flat to unwind after a stressful day. Oh, she uses me. It's so blatant. I hate her with such purity, such vigour. I was cooking for hours last night. Anything that can be deep-fried has been. Everything else is steeped in sugar. I want her so full of saturates she can barely roll herself home. Maybe I can get her to stay the night, only to greet her with a generous fried breakfast in the morning.

But for now, it's midday and I couldn't be more irritated. I've been trying to find the perfect cake all morning. I wanted something beautiful, resplendent, irresistible; something flawless. I'm sure you understand. Could I find anything worthy, anything that measured up? No. I've witnessed customer upon customer quite happy with some sadly dreary purchases: can't they see how sorry their flat little flapjacks and bruised Bakewell tarts look? Standards, standards. Nobody cares.

So I'm sitting here chain-smoking, scratching imaginary itches, knowing full well I'm going to have to bake a cake myself. Honestly, what I'm forced into. Just to make things right.

Half-past one and the kitchen's a mess. Every surface, every object, is covered in flour. It's like a brilliant white sandpit. I'm attempting to make a Walnut Spice cake, but no matter how carefully I follow the instructions in my severely under-used cookbook, I don't seem able to prevent a blizzard of ingredients flying in all directions.

'Flour, salt, cinnamon... flour, salt and cinnamon,' I chant, roughing them up in a soup bowl and roughing them up some more. God, I could do with a drink.

Half an hour later, I shove the bastard thing into a preheated moderate bastard oven and run from the room, slamming the door behind me. I have fifteen to twenty minutes before I need to venture back. The key element I'll be looking for is a well-risen, slightly burnished quality.

I've never worked my poor old kitchen so hard. We've always had a cordial acquaintanceship, but nothing intimate. Between last night's cobbling together of starter, main course, side dishes and nibbles – most of which now require a good dusting to disperse the flour – and this, my first home-baked cake, I think we'll be seeing less of each other in the next few weeks. I came on too strong, too soon. We need an adjustment period.

Candles, soft music, wine: I could almost be scene-setting for seduction. Remember what manner of creature I'm dealing with. Jennifer glides along the shiny surface of things like a first-class ice skater. In this alone, she is truly elegant. Hers is a world of angles and outlines; she negotiates the visible, the labelled, the digital construct. What matters to Jennifer is how life appears. She has no time or inclination for the knotted mess of meaning bubbling inside, or underneath. Of vital importance, then, that my flat meets with approval, each time I manage to suck her in.

Everything's ready, especially me.

'God, I've had the most incredible day,' she's saying, hanging up her coat. 'I've brought some nice French wine to celebrate.'

'Lovely. What's happened?' I direct her into the living room.

I can see it; see her radar sweeping the room. She smiles and settles on the sofa.

'I met up with Gerry, and he's promised me an exclusive interview. Isn't it wonderful? That'll show the competition. Did you hear about Philip?'

'No. What?'

'Well. Oh, this is great, you'll love this.' She has the sort of expression one normally sees on people regarding a good, juicy steak.

'Hang on,' I say. 'Let me get us a drink.'

'Oh. I thought we could have the wine with dinner.'

'Yeah, we will, but we should definitely start in on some vodka. To celebrate.'

'Okay, great.'

I go to the kitchen, grab the vodka and some glasses and return.

'So? What's happened to Philip?' I ask, passing her a more than healthy measure.

'It's just so funny,' she giggles, in between slurps.

I surmise that she's already had more than a couple of drinks before getting here, with Gerry, probably. Gerry the Actor.

'Tell me,' I implore, with a conviction that could outstrip anything Gerry's done on the screen.

'He's getting married!'

'Married?' I am genuinely shocked. Married?

'To that awful Marion. And do you know why?'

'He loves her?' I offer up, weakly.

'Well, maybe he does and maybe he doesn't. But I heard' – her voice lowers to a whisper – 'that he's gone and got her pregnant. Isn't it just too fantastic?'

Jennifer's bitchiness seems to have increased with her size. I force myself to laugh.

'No way! Oh my God, that's brilliant,' I exclaim. Jennifer, your days are numbered.

She heaves herself off the sofa and clinks her glass against mine. I smile, and refill it.

'I hope you're hungry, Jen.'

I'm wading through plates and crumbs with my masterpiece of a cake. Mountains of food have been consumed here, and after the vodka and wine, we imbibed most of a bottle of brandy. My legs feel like water and my stomach like concrete. I notice that the sun is starting to rise.

'Here it is, then. I hope you like it, it's—'

I stop. I would freeze, if I wasn't so unsteady on my feet. She's passed out. Jennifer has passed out before she's tried my cake. And now the cake is sliding off its plate and on to the carpet.

I sink down beside it and raise my fist, bearing it down through walnuts and raisins, salt and cinnamon, whipped cream and wasted achievement. I'm crying, I'm wailing, I'm wiping my face with smeared, sticky hands.

'You bitch. You fucking bitch,' I spit, turning to look at her, no longer caring what she thinks, or what she says.

She remains unconscious, unstirred. I mean less than nothing to her.

I crawl towards her and shake her by the shoulders. She doesn't wake. Her head lolls against the back of the sofa, mouth open, teeth rotten. Her nose twitches once, and then she starts to snore. She hasn't even had the good grace to have a cardiac arrest. Jennifer, drunk and bloated, asleep on my sofa. I prod her in the belly. She shifts slightly. That's all.

I can't stop crying. I'm a snivelling, dripping mess of cake and anguish. I half-heartedly sink my fingers into her thigh and squeeze. She continues to snore.

Tomorrow, she'll wake up, feeling like death and drag herself home. I imagine her taking a hot bath and curling up in bed. I won't get the chance to feed her again for weeks. If only she'd eaten the cake. I'd pinned so much on it: it was something to keep me going till the next time. My private reward.

I slide back to the floor and reach for Jennifer's unfinished drink. I can barely get it down me.

I've gathered up the ruins of dessert and deposited them on to the sofa. I'm holding Jennifer's sleeping head steady with one hand and scraping up balls of cake mixture with the other. I'm dropping them into her mouth, then raising her head, hoping she'll swallow. I'm forcing her jaw shut, then massaging her cheeks. I prize open her mouth and peer inside. As the sun hits the two of us, my fingers are pushing past teeth and pressing soggy cake bits down into her throat.

✝

More Than Skin Deep

Becky Bradford

The first time we met, all those years ago in the Tivoli Ballroom, when Lou strolled over and began admiring the tattoo of a seahorse on my shoulder, I thought him ugly and a little short. And far too full of himself. In those days I could have had my pick, you see. I was what was known as a 'looker' with my curves, my almond eyes and my shining brunette curls. But he wore me down with his big ideas and relentless charm and before I knew it there I was, sat in his black leatherette chair, concentrating my attention on the rips in the upholstery in an attempt to ignore the pain, whilst he tattooed a love heart with his name emblazoned on it upon my arm.

It was a whirlwind romance and we were married within weeks. We spent a weekend in Bournemouth for our honeymoon, then moved into a tiny flat above the shop. Money was tight, but we didn't mind. I was working in the hairdressing salon; Lou was next door doing tattoos. On Saturdays we'd go dancing, or to see a film. In the summer we'd take day trips to Brighton.

There is a photo of the two of us, arm in arm on the Palace Pier. We'd been on the beach all afternoon, sunbathing, paddling and drinking from a pair of hip flasks. We were leaning over the railings, throwing the remains of our fish supper down to the screeching seagulls that swooped and circled below, taking bets on which gull would catch what, when Lou stopped a passer-by and asked if he could take our picture. What struck me the last time I looked at it is how happy we looked – and how fleetingly that happiness lasted.

The wind is ruffling my hair and my eyes are crinkled against the glare of the evening sun. I'm wearing a halter-neck sundress that is lifting in the breeze, showing the tats on my thighs, arms and shoulders. Lou is in his shirtsleeves. We are both sunburnt; both a little drunk. We are showing off for the camera. Lou has his arms flung around me and is squeezing me towards him. Our faces wear a pair of ridiculous grins.

That was in the days when Lou used to call me his masterpiece. And what a piece of work I was – before the ravages of time began to take their toll. There is hardly a part of me that has not been inked, that hasn't felt the burning drag of the needle. Only my face, the palms of my hands and the soles of my feet are bare. The rest is covered in an intricate web of tattoos: 365 at the last count, one for every day of the year – though where one begins and another ends isn't always easy to decide.

Ribbons of seashells daisy chain about my neck; blood-red roses whorl around my nipples; a pair of mermaids circle Venus as she rises from a scallop shell on my belly; a galleon sails across the oceans of my back; Chinese dragons breathe curls of fire from each of my shoulders; the signs of the zodiac crowd my buttocks; my calves are laced with lilies, orchids and exotic flowers; peacocks, parrots and birds of paradise roost in the boughs of my thighs; Jesus offers the world his bleeding heart from my left arm; the virgin Mary looks beseechingly from my right; flames lick my ankles; a snake coils around my wrist; and on the back of each of my hands an eye cries a solitary tear. Yes, my flesh tells a story. If you know how to read the hieroglyphs etched upon it, it tells of love, betrayal and a broken heart.

Nowadays the lines of the older tattoos are blurred, their colours fading. These were made when we'd just met, when Lou was fresh out of the navy and had only just set up his first studio. These love hearts, bluebirds and anchors are clearly the work of a novice and lack the refinement, the imagination and the deftness of touch for which he would later become renowned. I was his muse, you see; my flesh the canvas on which he painted. It was the place he made his mistakes, and honed his craft. I gave him my body and my life. I even sacrificed my aching desire to have a baby – all for him. How my eyes used to linger hungrily over the fat-cheeked contents of buggies and prams. There were times when the sight of a newborn baby would have me in tears.

But Lou was adamant. Twice I found out I was pregnant and twice he made me get rid of it. He even insisted on watching me take the pill, not knowing that I'd hold it under my tongue and spit it out when he wasn't looking. When I got pregnant a third time I planned to run away and bring it up alone, but he beat me so badly I miscarried. After that I just gave up. I couldn't bear to try again. All that heartbreak, just because Lou baulked at the thought of the fruit of his labours stretching and contorting as my belly plumped and my breasts swelled. The tragedy is that in the end gravity took effect regardless. As I grew older and the elasticity of my skin diminished, the mermaids' faces began to wrinkle, their bellies sagged. Now the flowers are wilting and the ship's sails are beginning to droop, whilst – like me – Venus is slowly withering into a crone.

Looking at my ageing, barren body, I've asked myself why I didn't leave him. After all, the waters we sailed on were turbulent almost from the start. Lou was always jealous, convinced that I was screwing around. It's such a cliché, but it's true. In the early days there was mostly just a lot of shouting, but as the months rolled on the rows became more and more severe. So why did I stay? I still can't explain, but when somebody calls you a useless piece of shit for long enough, something shifts deep inside and you start to believe them.

His influence over me was so strong that gradually, one by one, I abandoned or was abandoned by all of my friends. He even stopped me from working. He didn't want anyone thinking he couldn't support his own wife. So I was trapped at home, with nothing to do all day but clean and cook, and just daytime TV for company. Was it any surprise I started drinking? I was bored out of my mind.

I'd never had much family, only a mum I didn't get on with and a step-sister I never heard from. My dad was long gone, dead or drunk in a ditch somewhere, I couldn't tell you which. So, as our lives veered further and further off course, I found myself marooned, with nowhere to go and no one to turn to for help. Lou was all I had left. And of course, he was always so apologetic afterwards. We fell into that age-old pattern: violence followed by remorse, followed by periods of calm that could almost be mistaken for happiness, then violence again. Our marriage was no more than a shipwreck, with me desperately clinging on to the wreckage.

Now, looking back on it, I think perhaps he needed to control me because his own life was in such chaos. Lou had always liked a flutter. The bookies was just two doors down from the tattoo parlour and so, when things were quiet, he would drift down there and put a few quid on a horse. Or at weekends he might try his luck at the dogs. But then he got into late night poker sessions with some of the boys. That wasn't too bad, until he moved up a league and started playing serious games for serious money. Sometimes he'd win and then he'd roll in at dawn with a wad of notes, stinking of stale booze and fags. But more often he wouldn't, and then he'd take out his frustrations on me. He never let me know how much he lost. I'd open the door to be pushed aside by bailiffs or loan sharks, who would then promptly exit with the television, the stereo and half the furniture. One time he had to sell the car, another the house. The bastards even took my wedding ring.

It went on for years. He'd stop for a while, but soon enough he'd always slip back into his old ways. The violence, the gambling and the drinking all went hand in hand. 'What the fuck are you looking at me like that for?' he'd snarl as he lurched in the door. And that would be that.

It was during the honeymoon period, when we were still newly married, that Lou convinced me to have my whole body tattooed. He was obsessed by tattooing and with the idea of covering me in his own artwork. I was his girl, he said, and he wanted to let the world know. Strangely, for a tattoo artist, he hated the thought of needles – on his own skin that is – and so his body was completely bare. I guess that was another reason why he wanted me to have so many – to make up for his lack. And though being covered in tattoos isn't quite the novelty it was, well, it opened a lot of doors and meant that we got to travel around the world to tattooing conventions, galas and the like. I can't remember how many times I've had my picture taken. I even got to be an extra in films.

Tattoos are great for covering bruises, but Lou wasn't a fool. He made sure never to hit me when we had any kind of show or exhibition coming up. Over the years the publicity brought in plenty of trade. Soon the studio was booming and Lou had to employ a couple more tattoo artists, which meant moving to bigger premises.

My mum never approved though. She thought tats were common. Eventually she stopped talking to me altogether. Said she couldn't bear to look at me 'ruined' like that. But I loved them. Loved the attention if truth were told. They made me feel different, made me stand out from the crowd. Most of all I loved knowing that Lou was focusing all of his attention on me. It was just like when I was a kid, on those rare occasions when Dad was just drunk enough – but not yet too drunk – and he'd lift me onto his knee and sing. A psychiatrist suggested that I was seeking a replacement for my father. That's why I put up with everything I did. And who knows, maybe he's right? When Lou was tattooing me, well then I was his special girl, just like I had been with Dad. And I guess that in a primal way it meant that I was bearing his mark, and so would always be his. When you think about it, it was the ultimate act of possession. It even helped me turn a blind eye to his indiscretions. I convinced myself they meant nothing; just the odd brief tryst, no more. To be honest, I always wondered how he managed it. I mean, he's no Marlon Brando. But he did have a kind of magnetism I guess. And he looked after himself with trips to the gym, body waxes and sun-ray lamps. His vanity made me laugh. Not to his face of course. And then there was his reputation. He is one of the best tattooists in the country – and they say success is an aphrodisiac. Tattoo fetishists can be an odd lot after all.

Then Lynda came along and everything changed. We were meant to be attending a three-day tattooing conference in Blackpool, but I'd come down with a bad dose of the flu and had to stay at home. I was sat watching *Corrie* with a box of Kleenex and a takeaway pizza when Lou rang to say he was leaving me. Just like that, no warning or nothing. Said he'd met someone else and that he'd be along to pick up his stuff. A few days later I came back from the shops to find Lou's car parked outside, piled high with boxes, whilst him and this young thing were in the kitchen busily rooting through our CD collection. For a moment I was so stunned I just stood there and watched. What he saw in her was obvious – half his age, with pert breasts and a peach of a bottom – but what she saw in him I couldn't fathom.

When Lou saw the anger on my face he tried to make light of it, saying, 'Come on, sweetheart, don't make a scene.' That was when I flipped. 'I'll give you a fucking scene!' I screamed, picking up a vase and hurling it at him, just missing his head by inches. Next was a coffee mug, followed by a set of dirty plates. 'You fucking bitch!' cried Lynda as a candle holder crashed behind her ear. That really did it for me. Calling me a bitch in my own home. Whatever came to hand I launched at them in a wild fury. Ducking, hands held protectively over their heads, they fled for the door as a farewell volley of crashing crockery and glass fell around them like rain.

But my moment of glory was brief. They rented a house practically on my doorstep, which meant I ran the risk of bumping into them every time I went out. You'd think I would have been glad to see him go, but all I felt was humiliation. I'd been told what to do for so long I was barely able to think for myself. To make matters worse, it seemed each time I saw Lynda she was flaunting another tattoo. She'd walk straight by me, head erect and a bold look on that hard little face of hers, her gravity-defying breasts standing to attention. It took all my restraint to stop myself from punching her.

I was saved the struggle when a repossession order for the house arrived. Once again Lou had defaulted on the repayments and it seemed I had no choice but to move out. With nowhere else to go I took a chance and rang my old friend Sylvie. We hadn't spoken in years, but to my relief she invited me to stay at hers until I sorted myself out. Everything was fine until we got horribly drunk one evening and she admitted having had an affair with Lou when we were still mates. We had a blazing row and the next morning I packed my bags and left. I spent the whole of that day yo-yoing between the dole and emergency housing offices, my poor head pumping, my body in a sweat. I felt like such a fool. Lou had only ever given me housekeeping, so I had no savings of my own. After being pushed from pillar to post they told me I wasn't a priority and sent me out to a grotty B & B.

It was desperate. All the residents had to be out by ten each morning, so I found myself with little choice but to spend my time roaming the streets. Soon I started hanging out with a group of winos. I'd drink with them all day, then stagger back to my room at night to pass out. It was such a pathetic excuse for an existence that I suppose a breakdown was inevitable. I got so depressed that I attempted an overdose, but I couldn't even get that right. So I ended up in a psychiatric unit, where they made me do jigsaws and pumped me full of pills. Since then I've been beachcombing, sifting through the broken debris of my life, living in a halfway house full of other flotsam and jetsam like me.

Things were finally improving. I was going to AA meetings and was completely dry. I was also doing a day a week at college, brushing up on my hairdressing skills, and had finally decided to start divorce proceedings so I could make a fresh start. I was still on medication, but was beginning to look towards the future for the first time in years.

And then it happened. I was wandering through WHSmith, flicking through the glossies, when I saw Lynda looking straight at me. The little bitch wasn't there in person, just her photo on the front cover of *Needle and Ink*. Shaking, I whipped the magazine off the shelf and feverishly started leafing through it until I found what I was looking for. There, on a double-page spread, the pair of them were pictured under the title 'Covered Love'. Lou had his bare arms around Lynda, who was leaning into his chest. In the time since I'd last seen her she'd changed a lot. She had bright pink hair extensions and her head was shaved at the sides. A series of small photo inserts revealed that she had a pair of spectacular fire-breathing dragons tattooed on either side of her skull. She and Lou both wore matching leather waistcoats – which would have amused me if I wasn't so shaken – and her arms and neck were covered in tattoos. In fact from the look of it, her whole body was covered in them. Some of them looked like exact copies of mine. Underneath one of the photos it read, 'Lou calls Lynda his masterpiece'.

His masterpiece! Seeing how thoroughly she had taken my place, I started trembling; tears punched an exit from my eyes. But it got worse. There, at the bottom of the page, was another photo showing a close-up of Lynda's belly. It was swollen and round, in the last stages of pregnancy. And on the skin itself was an intricate tattoo of a foetus curled up in the womb. Lou had surpassed himself. It was beautiful. A real work of art.

Without even thinking I slipped the magazine under my coat, dashed past the security guard and out of the doors, heading straight to the nearest pub. As I sat knocking back one whisky after another I stared at the photos, fixated. I felt like an old piece of gristle, chewed up and spat out. All I could think about was how much he had hurt me, and how badly I needed to hurt him back.

By the time I found myself staggering up their street with a petrol canister and a box of matches in my hand, I was so drunk I could barely stand. Luckily the road was completely dead and there was no one about to see me as I lurched up the drive, opened the side gate and stumbled around the back. To my amazement, the kitchen door was unlocked. As quietly as I could, which wasn't very, in my inebriated state, I opened it and tiptoed into the darkness of the house.

There I was, swaying in the hall, ready to pour the contents of the canister onto the carpet, when I was stopped by a noise upstairs. Pausing for a moment I listened as, gently at first, then louder and louder, a baby gave out a tiny wail. Its plaintive cries were so heart-wrenching that they jerked me back into reality and I froze. A door opened upstairs and the sound of padding footsteps crossed the hall right above my head, then I heard a voice that must have been Lynda's attempting to soothe the crying child.

In those brief seconds I suddenly saw myself for what I had become – a madwoman so hell-bent on revenge she had nearly murdered a newborn child. Horrified, I turned on my heels and bolted, slamming the front door behind me. Halfway up the street I turned and caught sight of the house with all its lights blazing, and Lou in his dressing gown silhouetted against the door.

A few weeks passed and I was back at my AA meetings, still in shock after what I had done. And I was raging. My every waking moment was consumed with thoughts of Lou and a burning desire for retribution. And then, just when I was losing hope, Mica drifted into the shelter in need of a bed. I don't know what it was she said exactly, but after we got talking the seed of an idea started germinating in my head.

Mica was Brazilian. She had come to England with her boyfriend to study English, but when they broke up she had decided to outstay her visa and pick up any work she could. She wanted to be a dancer she said, but the nearest she had come was working in a strip club. Somewhere along the line she had got herself a habit and ended up on the game. But when a friend of hers was discovered dumped on a piece of waste ground bound in duct tape, she had decided it was time to get out. Now she was trying to get clean, and looking for a job so she could save enough money to get home. A grand was all she needed. 'I think I might be able to help you there,' I said.

Borrowing the money from Sylvie was easy enough as she had only just sold the hairdressing salon and still felt guilty as hell. I told her it was for solicitor's fees and that I would return it when the divorce came through. The rest went like clockwork. Dressed in a micro-mini and knee-high boots, Mica sashayed into the tattoo parlour. She flirted with Lou, batting those heavy-lashed eyes at him as he worked on a tiny seahorse on her smooth brown stomach. When she asked him out for a drink he only took a moment to think about it. And when, later that night, she nuzzled into his ear and said did he want to come back to her place, he said yes immediately. The only danger point had been when Lynda rang during the taxi ride home. In the background Mica could hear a baby crying, but as she deftly unzipped his fly and rammed her hot tongue in his free ear, Lou mumbled something about working late and hung up.

No sooner had they got to the flat than Mica slipped off to the kitchen and poured them both a drink, making certain to give Lou the one she had doctored earlier. Then she put on some music and, encouraging Lou to drink like a man in her sensuous Latino voice, began to dance, gyrating her hips slowly as she stripped for him, expertly pulling off her clothes piece by piece, biding her time whilst he slipped into unconsciousness.

When he was out cold I emerged from my hiding place and together we pulled off his clothes and heaved his heavy body through the hall and into the bedroom, carefully gagging and blindfolding him and handcuffing his wrists and ankles to the bedstead. Then we sat drinking coffee, waiting for Lou to come round. Mica, worried that she might kill him with an overdose, made me wait until he was nearly conscious before showing me how to administer the injections. She was a good teacher and I quickly learnt how to cook up the heroin, then bind his arm and slide the needle into the bulging vein, pushing the stopper down until the drugs swam intoxicatingly in his blood. Once I was certain I knew what I was doing, I handed Mica her plane ticket and some money and we made our goodbyes. Then I got to work.

I started just below the clavicle, and moving left to right continued on, line after line, down his torso until I reached his abdomen. Then I turned him onto his back and continued with my tale. Luckily all that waxing finally came in useful as there was no awkward body hair to shave off, but even with my new tattooing machine the job takes time, for I am still a beginner, and I have a lot to say. Every piece of him is inked – or very nearly. I am now on his right thigh and rapidly running out of space.

When he starts complaining, or becomes agitated, I give him another shot. And what a docile little junkie he has become. He no longer recoils from the needle, but offers his arm up willingly, looking at me with a need I hardly recognise. But I don't think he has any real idea what's going on. I try to get him to eat, but he will only take melted ice cream or yoghurt, sometimes soup. I have finally got the baby I craved. I clean him when he soils himself, putting fresh towels to catch the mess, but the smack has seized his bowels of late and he drinks so little there is less and less for me to do.

As the pounds fall off him it is getting harder to write on his loosening flesh, but I am nearly done. I have marked him, laid my claim upon his body, like he did with mine. These words are a stain that no scrubbing can remove. As the needle punctures his skin, I imagine the ink seeping through his epidermis and into his bloodstream, oozing along the network of veins and arteries to his heart, feeding and informing every muscle, every tendon, every individual cell, permeating every inch of flesh, saturating him to the core.

This has been an exercise in catharsis and with each word I have written on Lou's body, I have moved a step closer to wiping my own slate clean. Now *his* flesh tells *my* story, when I look at my own tattoos I find that their meaning has changed. Fading and a little wrinkled they may be, but like the tarnished surface of an old oil painting, their beauty has increased, not diminished with age. And just as a picture can tell a different story depending on where you view it from, my tattoos no longer speak to me of betrayal or of a broken heart, but of the power of survival and the strength to endure.

After so long gathering dust, I'm finally ready to leave the shadows behind. When Lou comes round he will wake to a rising tide of nausea, alone and in a strange and deserted flat. And I will be gone. I have a ticket out of here and quite a tidy sum to help me on my way – money that I cleared from his bank and credit cards whilst he's been out cold. The way I look at it is this: if our relationship was a balance sheet, then Lou is heavily in the red. Now it's time for him to pay back his debts.

I'm even thinking of using the money to set myself up as a tattoo artist – once I settle down. I was always good at art, and now I've quit the drink I've found I've got a very steady hand. Most importantly, I've learnt to love myself again, tattoos and all. And why not? I'm in the company of royalty: Catherine the Great, George V, King Frederick IX of Denmark, Kaiser Wilhelm II, King Alexander of Yugoslavia, Czar Nicholas of Russia, all adorned themselves in this way. Winston Churchill too. It is even rumoured that Queen Victoria had a tiny tattoo on an undisclosed 'intimate' part of her body – though whether this is true or not we shall never know. Tattoos are part of who I am and I will take them to my grave, just as Lou will take mine to his.

✝

Hell is Where the Heart is

Mitzi Szereto

Is it possible to want someone so badly, love someone so strongly, so overwhelmingly, you'd be willing to sell your soul to the devil to have him?

Sure, it's the stuff of literature, opera, film – that old pact with the devil scenario, works every time. It's easy. Just say hey, I really want this and I'll do anything to get it, then suddenly there's the smell of fire and brimstone, and *POOF.* Guess who? Yeah, some hygienically-challenged manifestation with horns, tail, and a pitch-fork, with eyes so red he could've been the last one staggering out of the local boozer the night before. There he is, grinning at you like that queer old uncle you used to run a mile from as a kid, and he's pushing this greasy piece of parchment at you, along with an old-fashioned quill pen – the kind people used to dip into ink jars. No ink jars here though. Nope. It's sign-in-blood time. That's the only way to be sure the terms of *this* contract will never be broken.

With me so far? Good.

Anyway, there I was in my flat, crying my heart and soul out – emphasis on soul here – over this bloke from Romford (it just gets better and better, dunnit?), sobbing and wailing like the best professional mourner money could buy when an unpleasant odour reached my nostrils. And no, it wasn't the week-long accumulation of rubbish that, in my misery, I couldn't be arsed to take downstairs to the bin. When I looked up from the darkness

105

of my palms, I figured I was hallucinating. After all, my eyes were nearly swollen shut from grief, plus I'd been drinking every form of alcohol I could find in my cupboards, stopping just short of the bottle of nail varnish remover which, although technically acetone, smells strong enough to do some serious damage. I must admit that bleachy stuff I use to clean the toilet with was beginning to tempt me as well. Ah, but I digress . . .

'Oi! Oi!'

The voice was sandpaper against my eardrums. I shook my head and blinked, but rather than fading, the vision got clearer. And, honey, it wasn't good! No one had a key to my flat except the landlord, and despite the amount of alcohol I'd been consuming, this character didn't look one bit like diminutive Mr Singh with his nut-brown skin and sing-songy accent and penchant for employing various relatives to do repairs rather than paying a qualified repairman or technician to do them. I'm surprised I haven't dropped dead from carbon monoxide poisoning after his brother-in-law fixed the boiler last time. Everyone told me I should've sued, but Mr Singh hasn't raised my rent in the whole two years I've lived here. Oh, there I go, digressing again. Sorry. Anyway, this horned and tailed vision was one hell of an ugly bastard, I'll grant you that.

'Why the long face, sweetheart? Book sales down?' Then he began to nod. 'Oh, I know. A bloke. Tell me I'm wrong.'

I offered him a scowl. 'Well, if you already know, why are you asking?' Not surprisingly, I wasn't in the mood for small talk.

'Just making sure. No need to lose your temper, doll face.'

'So who are you anyway?'

'Don't you know?'

'I have my suspicions, but humour me.'

He grinned. Well, I've seen some dodgy teeth in my day, but the ones displaying themselves in his manky maw were downright terrifying. Hello? Ever hear of a toothbrush? He offered me a courtly bow. 'I am Lucifer. Beelzebub. Mephistopheles. The Prince of Darkness. Satan. Or the Devil, for short.' He gave me a saucy wink. 'But you can call me Alf.'

The King of the Underworld and his name's Alf? Had I drunk that nail varnish remover after all? 'Well, you're not quite what I expected, Alf.'

'No? So what'd you expect, sweetheart?'

'Well, definitely not some geezer who sounds like he runs a market stall in Petticoat Lane.'

'So maybe I do a bit of moonlighting. Stop by sometime. I got some Rolex watches. Pick one out for your bloke.' He paused. 'Oh, yeah. He's done a runner, ain't he?'

I flinched. Like I needed reminding?

Alf shook his head sadly. 'The lads in this country, they don't grow up. They need mandatory conscription here. Put the spoiled little shits in the army, that'll make men of 'em.'

'Yeah.'

'A *real* army, like what they got in Israel. Not like this pussy army they got over here.'

I found myself warming to Alf. 'I couldn't agree more.'

That elicited a huge guffaw, and I found myself being overpowered by breath that could only have come straight out of Hell. 'So what happened, gorgeous?' He sat down on the armrest of my chair, his charred-flesh smell making me nauseated and light-headed. 'Tell ol' Alfie here all about it.'

I know it's crazy, but he sounded as if he really cared, really gave a shit, and that set me off. My voice shook with tears when I answered. 'I don't know what happened. One minute we were carrying on like two people madly in love, the next minute he's finishing with me, telling me he doesn't return my feelings and it's better if we stop now.'

'You're kidding.'

'I wish I were.'

He snorted. 'What an arsehole.'

'Yeah.'

'A real wanker.'

'Yeah.'

'A right tosser.'

'Yeah.'

Alf went quiet for a moment, appearing to be deep in thought, his fire-blackened fingers drumming a beat against the chair arm. 'So nothing happened to set off this sudden turnabout?'

'Nope. Not a thing.'

'You didn't by chance make him think you wanted to marry him?'

'No. Of course not!'

'Move in with him then? You birds tend to get all nesty when you meet a bloke.'

I laughed sourly. 'Well, not *this* bird.'

'Then what's the problem?'

'Hell if I know. It's like he just shut his feelings off. It's weird.'

'He a mama's boy?'

'I'm not sure. I mean, I don't think so.'

'Bet he is.' Alf commenced to chew on a blackened fingernail, as if seeking inspiration. 'Think maybe he's gay?'

'No, he's not gay!'

'Did he walk funny? You know, like this...' Alf rose from the chair arm and minced about the room, his right hand dangling in a limp-wrist pose. If we hadn't been discussing the painful demise of my relationship I might've pissed myself laughing.

'Listen, the only thing funny about his walk is that he sometimes has this little tough guy strut that he does. I don't think he even realises he's doing it. Guess it's an Essex thing left over from his youth. He used to be a bit rough, apparently.'

'Sure you don't mean a bit gay?'

'No. I promise you.'

I found myself being treated to another of Alf's dodgy grins. 'You sure? I mean, you never know these days. No evidence of him having his back door used?'

'Look, he's a very blokey sort of bloke...'

'No matter. Them's the ones that're more likely to...shall we say, succumb?'

I admit this got me thinking. 'Well, he did sort of like it when I used my finger to tickle his—'

'Oi! TMI!'

'Huh?'

'Too much information, sweetheart.'

'Sorry. But you did ask.'

'Yeah, so I did. Okay, so he ain't a bum boy. Then he was into you sexually? No wilting willies right at the moment of—'

'No! Well, not usually anyway.'

'Was he too small then? Blokes can be a bit weird about penis size.'

'Umm, well...'

'Ah-ha! That's it then! Small willy syndrome.'

'Actually, that didn't really cause too much of a problem.'

'Hmmm. You sure about that?'

'Can we change the subject, please?'

'Right, so this bloke ain't gay, and his small willy didn't put you off neither?'

'Correct.'

'Sounds like we got fear of commitment here then. Classic case. See it all the time, specially in these younger blokes. How old's he again?'

'Twenty-five.'

'Hmmm. Young, but not THAT young.'

'Well, he's gonna look like crap by the time he hits thirty, trust me. He's already showing signs of wear and tear. I'm sure he'll be bald in a couple of years.'

'Yeah, best stick with the younger ones, then trade 'em in when they go rank. They ain't all tied to mummy's apron strings, you know. I was just at a wedding last weekend, bloke was only twenty-one. Happy as can be too.'

'You go to weddings?'

'Sure. Specially if I have something to do with 'em.' Alf gave me another wink. 'Course I scrub up a bit first.'

'How do you mean, if you have something to do with them?'

'Well, see, the bridegroom was in need of my services. Bit of trouble with his woman and all. She just needed to see the light.'

'You saying she didn't want to marry him?'

'Oh, she wanted to marry him all right. She just didn't know it yet.'

'How could she not know it?'

'She thought she was in love with someone else. Anyway, nothing to do with you, is it?'

'No. I guess if my bloke had been in love with someone else, I might be able to understand all this – not that it would've made things any easier; I'd still be torn apart. But he's not. Well, unless someone can be in love with lager and fags and hangovers, which seem to be all he's interested in.'

'A lager man?'

'Yeah. Carling.'

'Say no more! We talking yob here?'

'No. He's not a yob.'

'Where's he from again?'

'Romford.'

'So he's a chav!'

'Not a chav either.'

'Bet he is. Bet he likes the bling.'

'Well, he does wear a gold chain around his neck. But it's got a crucifix on it.'

'A crucifix? That's disgustin'.'

Now it was my turn to grin. This Alf was quite a character.

'Glad to see you're cheering up a bit, sweetheart.' Alf resumed his position on the arm of my chair, forcing me to breathe through my mouth.

'Yeah. You're taking my mind off suicide. Well, for five minutes anyway.'

'Oi! None of that talk! So what's this bloke's name?'

'Well, I used to call him Blue Eyes. That was my special name for him. But lately I've been calling him Weasel. I think it suits him.'

Alf snorted. Something wet landed on my arm. I didn't want to look to see what it was. 'Where'd you two meet?'

'I hate to even tell you. On the personals.'

'You mean like them ads in the newspaper kind of things?'

'Actually, online. We met online.'

'So who messaged who first?'

'He messaged me. But I didn't reply. I'd seen his profile from before and to be honest, it was so lame I kept skipping over it. I'm sure he lied about his height on that thing. Plus he had this tacky photo of him without a shirt... he looked like a real plonker. I was already chatting to someone else anyway, but then something happened and a few weeks later I decided to reply to him. That was it really. We seemed to click and made a date to spend a day together in London.'

'Love at first sight then?'

'No, I can't say that it was. I felt ambivalent about him, he wasn't at all the sort of bloke I'd go for. He was very different from what I'd always been attracted to and to be perfectly honest, he was a bit of a dweeb. But there *was* something there, and I thought it only fair to give him a chance, especially seeing how keen he was on me.' Now it was my turn to snort. 'And look where it got me?'

'Maybe it's easier for him to have pretend relationships online than real ones. Ever think of that?'

'Yeah, my mum said the same thing. She says he's probably a nerd, and that online is safer for him. And you know what? He's still there too. He's on at least four sites that I know of – free ones since he's too cheap to pay – and he's always logging on. I'm surprised he hasn't been sacked, for the amount of company time he uses for this crap. He claims he doesn't want to meet anyone, doesn't want a relationship. So what the fuck's he doing still playing on the personals?'

'That ain't right.'

'No, it sure ain't.'

'Is he a hunk? A handsome stud? A babe magnet?'

I couldn't help but laugh. 'Let's put it this way, he wouldn't stop traffic. In fact, he's actually kind of nerdy looking. I mean, he's beautiful to me. But then, I'm in love and deluded.'

'He ever wine and dine you? Buy you gifts? Make you feel appreciated?'

I laughed bitterly. 'I was lucky to get a cup of tea out of him when I stayed over at his place. The last time I was there he had a brand-new high-definition television in the lounge, yet the following morning I had to practically beg for a piece of toast. One time he even accused me of breaking his toilet. I mean, he'd used it first!'

'That ain't good.'

'No.'

'So he never got you nothing – no tiny trinket of his affection? Flowers? Chocolates? Nothing to show he was thinking about you, missing you?'

'Nope. Never. And you know what? I always got him gifts whenever I went somewhere. Just little things, a stick of Blackpool rock, a jar of honey from Greece. I'd even bought his favourite shower gel for the next time he was coming to stay with me. Only he never came back. I still have the shower gel. And I still have his rubbish Carling taking up room in my cupboard and fridge.'

'Was he just thoughtless or cheap?'

'Both, really. To be honest, yeah, he was cheap. I mean, he always seemed to have money to go boozing with his mates or go off on stag dos, paying for hotels and flights to some arse-end country like Estonia, but when it came to me he was skint. Guess I should've known; on our first date when we were looking for somewhere to eat he said he'd be fine if we just went to McDonalds.'

'What a knob-head!'

'I wonder if he broke it off because he didn't want to pay the rail fare to come up and spend a weekend with me. Though I would've gone to him whenever he wanted if it was a question of funds; I'd have spent my last penny on him. I'd have gone without food.'

'Looks like you been going without food already, sweetheart.'

'I know. I've not been eating.'

'What's this Weasel geezer do for a living? He a barrow boy or something?'

'Why would you think that?'

'Just doesn't sound like a real class act, this bloke of yours.' Alf shook his head again, his eyes raking over me in what could only be described as lecherous admiration. 'The man's a fool.'

'Tell me about it.'

'He ever tell you he loved you?'

The L-word. How many times I'd wanted to tell him how I felt, but I was afraid to. Though he knew anyway. It was obvious. 'Well, not in those exact words, no. But he did tell me that I gave him a reason to live. And yeah, he was sober when he said it.'

'Fucking hell! That's a strong statement.'

'Tell me about it.'

Alf sighed. 'I can say you'll find better, but we all know what a load of bollocks that is.'

I began to cry again. If the Devil himself was saying this to me, then it looked pretty hopeless. A moment later I felt a tissue being pressed into my hand. I thanked him, wiping my streaming eyes and nose.

'So what do you want, gorgeous? Tell ol' Alf here what you want.'

'I want him back. I just want him back.'

'You love the Weasel.'

'Yes. More than anything in the world. More than life itself. I'd give away years of my life if I could have him back.'

I should've known. You don't make a statement like that to the Devil. Christ, what in hell was I thinking? Though, to be honest, I meant it. I really truly did.

I wake to the sound of church bells coming through the open window. The sound has a comforting familiarity, a significance I'm not entirely sure of, since my brain is still dulled with sleep. Though one thing I do know: I'm not at home, not in my own bed. There are no churches near where I live.

There's another sound, a bit jarring, gravelly, very close to me. I roll over, finding my progress impeded by a warm body. It's snoring.

Oh, God. He's lying beside me. The man who tore out my heart, who made me want to die rather than face another day without him. His chest hairs glow golden in the sunlight peeking through the edge of the curtains, and I nuzzle my face into the moist heat of his armpit, drinking in the scent of him, savouring him, desiring nothing more than to spend the rest of my days exactly where I am now, in the crook of his arm. I'd been dreaming. That crazy thing with the Devil, with Alf, none of it was real. I mean, how could it be?

With one final snore, he stirs, wakes, then turns to face me. His blue eyes light up at seeing me there. They are like jewels. I've never seen a blue like this, so brilliant, so beautiful. I never tire of looking into his eyes. 'Good morning, Princess. You look lovely,' he says. He leans into my face and we kiss, long and wet, our tongues seeking out each other in a hungry dance. We take turns sucking each other's tongue. We can spend hours in this way, and have. God how I love kissing him. I've never loved kissing anyone like this, ever. I've never kissed a man in the morning or wanted to, but with him it's different. Not even the remnants of stale fag smoke bother me. I love the taste of his mouth; I drink his saliva like a starving woman. He is sunlight to me, the thing that gives me life; without him I know I will die.

It is like before, as if we've never been apart, as if he never ended it. I raise my leg and rest it on his hip, opening myself to him. Our eyes lock as he slips inside me, so gently, so lovingly, moving in slow motion, always so careful never to hurt me. He touches me deeper than anyone ever has; it's almost spiritual. I begin to cry.

'Babes, what's wrong?'

'Nothing,' I sniff. 'Nothing at all. Everything is right. Everything is perfect. I've never been so happy in my life.' It sounds like a cliché, but it's true.

He smiles his cheeky little smile. All is right with the world.

The next weekend I'm home. Alone. He can't see me, some family thing with his cousins on the Friday night, then a stag do on the Saturday. He promises to text me on Sunday.

He doesn't.

The later it gets, the more concerned I get. I try to do some writing, but nothing comes out of my brain. The blank Word document on the computer screen tortures me, displaying the horrible images playing inside my head. Maybe he drank so much he passed out. Maybe there was a car crash. Maybe there was a stripper, a hooker, and his mates egged him on into doing something he wouldn't normally do. I hate these goddamned stag dos. I wish he wouldn't go to them, but it seems like everyone he knows is getting married. He's always telling me to relax, that I have nothing to worry about. But still I worry. I love him, how can I not worry? I can't bear to think of any harm coming to him. Nor can I bear to think of him looking at or touching another woman, or her touching him. The thought of it eats away at me like acid.

Unable to stand it any longer, I text him Sunday night.

He finally texts back two hours later reporting that he's hung over.

The weekend coming up he can't see me. His mate (the stag do one) is getting married on Saturday and he's to be an usher. I wonder why he didn't think to invite me as his date, but I don't ask. I am afraid to ask. Besides, the guest list was probably prepared ages ago – from way before we met. I console myself with this supposed fact, though I ask him teasingly if he has a hot date for the wedding. He tells me he's going alone. Alone. Guess it wouldn't even occur to him to take me.

I decide to spend the weekend getting some work done. I've barely written a word since this whole thing started. I realise that I need to feel more secure about our relationship. He's not intentionally neglecting me. Just bad timing, as he says. Social and family obligations, things he committed to ages ago. I need to relax. Chill.

On Sunday morning I ring his mobile, reaching a generic voice. I leave a breezy message saying that I hope the wedding was fun and blah blah blah, and do give me a ring later as I expect you're probably too hung over right now. Once again I sit at the computer in the pretence of doing some writing, but all I'm really doing is waiting for him to call. By nightfall I'm in a panic. Did he fall over drunk somewhere? Is he lying unconscious in a gutter in his rented formalwear? Or worse, did he meet someone at the wedding or at the reception afterward? Did he go home with her? Did she go home with him? I spend a sleepless night, fretting.

Come Monday morning I'm near hysterics, and as usual the first thing I do is check my email. Well, there it is, one of his *Good Morning, Princess. How are you today?* emails. Is he just thick or what?

I mention that I tried ringing him on the weekend and he says oh yeah, he forgot his phone at work on Friday. He often does that.

Pillock.

★

We chat by email during the week. It's all arranged; he's coming up to spend the weekend with me. However, since there's an office party on the Friday night and he expects to be sick and hung over the following day, he has no idea what train he'll be getting, though he imagines it'll be sometime in the evening. I suggest that maybe he should refrain from drinking too much, since it sounds as if the entire Saturday will be wasted when we could be spending it together. He agrees, but says the booze is free, so how can he resist?

I spend Friday evening and half of Saturday getting things ready: cleaning the flat, changing the bed, cooking so he'll have something to eat when he arrives. He's never that bothered about food, but he sure as hell eats like a horse whenever he's here, and I'm a crap cook too. I then turn my attention to myself, beautifying everything I can possibly beautify: shaving, plucking, trimming, waxing. I make sure I am perfection incarnate.

I have butterflies in my stomach all day as I wait to hear from him.

I get a text late Saturday afternoon. He's too sick and hung over from last night's office do to come up.

I toss the roast chicken, mashed potatoes, and buttered carrots into the bin. The mocha almond fudge Häagen-Dazs I chuck out the window, punctuating the action with a can of Carling. Good thing no one was walking past outside.

He tells me he can't see me the next weekend; it's a mate's birthday and he can't let him down (though he never seems to have a problem letting ME down). He also informs me there's another stag do coming up right after that. Great. So it's to be another three weeks before we see each other? He's sorry, just bad timing, all these things happening at once. He'll make it up to me.

Okay, I take affirmative action. I make plans of my own. The weekend of what should be the stag do I arrange to visit my mates in Blackpool. So there. Let him wonder what *I'm* up to for a change. Blackpool. Hotbed of sin. Den of iniquity. Favoured holiday destination of yobs. Chavs. Council scum. Those who can't afford Ibiza or Tenerife.

Are we having fun or what?

I'm in fucking agony. I miss him. It's Sunday evening. In the lounge my mates have a music channel on the TV and it's showing a Nickelback video and Chad the lead singer's watching as someone's being taken into an ambulance and I just want to die and I have to excuse myself to run upstairs to my room so my mates don't see how upset I am. We always play that song, whether I'm at his or he's at mine. I actually burned a CD for him and it has that fucking song on it so it follows us everywhere. Whenever I hear it I can feel his arms around me, feel his lips on mine, see his beautiful blue eyes as they smile into mine. I want to text him, tell him how much I miss him. But I don't. I feel like I can't, as if it would be wrong for me to do so. Isn't that crazy – not to be able to tell the bloke you love that you miss him?

I decide to stay in Blackpool one more night, going home on Monday instead of this evening. Let him wonder where I am, if I've gotten home yet. I'm sure to find a worried email from him sent on Monday morning. He usually emails me as soon as he gets into work. I can pretty much count on one of his *Good morning, Princess. How are you today* emails in my inbox come Monday morning, in his trademark blue text. I live for those emails.

I arrive home late Monday afternoon. First thing I do is go online. No email. Well, I'll be damned if I'm going to email him.

Tuesday morning I check my email first thing, before I even brush my teeth. And there it is, at long last. I expect to find his words full of concern: was I all right, why didn't I let him know I'd gotten home safely. I read the blue words again and again, searching for some hidden meaning, some worry disguised as levity, some sense that I've been missed. 'Good morning, Princess. Good weekend?'

Good weekend?

What a fucking letdown.

I let it sit till afternoon, then reply that it was nice seeing my mates, but that I'd really missed him. I ask how the stag do went, hoping he'll give me some reassurance that it was an innocuous event, just lads out drinking at the pub, nothing I need to worry about.

Well, it turns out that this past weekend wasn't the stag do weekend at all, it's *next* weekend, so he was home for the entire time, just chilling out. Which means, there was no reason why we couldn't have seen each other. I didn't need to go to Blackpool after all.

Sadly, the upcoming weekend is a no go because of the stag do. He promises to text me on Sunday when he gets back from Bristol, which is where they're all headed. Come Sunday night, still no text.

Monday morning I get an email from him asking if everything's okay and why didn't I reply to his text. *What* text? I never got any text. He swears he sent one and says he thought I was trying to prove a point. I insist I never received any text. Well, he's either lying to me, or else he was so drunk he sent the text to someone else. Of course I don't say this. I am calm, relaxed, chilled. Hell, any more chilled and I'll be in the fucking freezer.

Finally, at long last, we are together. We meet at his local near work, an old Bohemian literary haunt. I like the place; it's got character, a good vibe. I think he likes it because the lager's cheap and he can walk there from the office. He claims to be a regular and they know him there, yet none of the bar staff appears to recognise him (I mean, it's not like the Queen Vic where Peggy Mitchell greets everyone by name) and he has to repeat his order every time for 'The Man in the Box', which is what he calls the lager he drinks when he's not drinking Carling – it's got a picture of some dodgy-looking Alpine guy on it.

As we're making our way to the other end of the pub to find

a seat, he's suddenly waylaid by four of his workmates by the bar. The young men stare at me like hungry wolves, not missing a thing. 'Hey, thought you were supposed to be with your girlfriend tonight?' one of them quips, his eyes not moving an inch off me.

The teasing is apparently lost on my beloved, who looks ready to punch the speaker's lights out. I am then besieged with questions; clearly this quartet want to know all about me, and not a detail of my appearance is overlooked. A moment later I'm virtually dragged off, without even learning their names.

Later that night my altar is being worshipped at with more vigour than ever before. If his tongue could have thrust any deeper it would've popped out of the top of my head.

Funny how attentive men can be when they think someone else is sniffing around their territory.

During yet another weekend alone, Alf pops round to see how I'm doing. It's Sunday morning and I'm sitting at the kitchen table eating some healthy cereal that crunches in my teeth like bits of rock. The PC hums in the corner; as usual a blank Word document fills the screen. 'You don't look so good, sweetheart,' he quips. 'Ain't it working out with Weasel?'

Okay, this might sound stupid, but I actually believed I'd imagined this whole thing with Alf. Clearly not. Alf was real. His charred smell testified to that.

'I don't know. It just seems like we're going down the same road again. He never has time for me, it's always mates mates mates. I'm fucking sick of mates!' I am nearly shouting. I've been keeping it in for so long that I feel like exploding and suddenly I'm banging my fists on the table, upsetting the bowl of cereal. Chill. Relax. Let boys be boys. He's young, his mates are important to him. Fuck that shit. Aren't I important to him?

I didn't speak the words aloud, but Alf evidently heard them. 'I'm sure you're important to him, but maybe he just needs to grow up a bit.'

'Grow up? Everyone in his peer group's either married, getting married, engaged, or in a solid relationship. And he can't even manage to see me one weekend a month? Jesus Christ!'

Alf grimaces. 'Please don't mention that name! I hate that geezer!'

'Sorry.'

'Sounds like you got a real winner on your hands.'

'Yeah. You'd think he doesn't care about me at all from the way he carries on.'

'You sure he does care?'

'Do you know he pledged his complete fidelity to me? I didn't solicit it. He offered it, and did so more than once, I might add. He said he is only for me, and no one else will ever touch him. He doesn't want anyone but me, and yes, he's sure of us. So what in hell is that about?'

'He's either very serious about you and doesn't know how to go about having a relationship or he's dicking you around.'

'Well, you're the Devil. You know everything. Which is it then?'

'Can't answer that, sweetheart. Even this one's got me stumped.'

Great. I fall for a bloke so screwed up that even the King of the Underworld can't figure him out? This is not good.

'It sure ain't,' he answers, though I hadn't spoken.

'You know, he did something really weird the last time I was staying with him.'

'What's that, sweetheart?'

'Well, it was the next morning. We'd been making love most of the night, hardly even slept either of us. Anyway, the shirt he'd worn the night before, he'd left it draped over the back of a chair and somehow or other it'd fallen to the floor. Without really thinking about what I was doing, I picked it up and put it back on the chair. And—'

'Yeah? Go on.'

'Well, he went over to the chair and knocked the shirt right back onto the floor. I was stunned. I mean, what was he trying to tell me here?'

Alf scowled. 'You sure you wanna be with this bloke? He sounds like a fucking psycho. He on drugs or something? Sounds like he's stuck too much charlie up his hooter.'

I threw up my hands. 'It doesn't make sense. I mean, he made love to me the night before with such tenderness, such feeling. Then it's like he wants to erase me from his sight.'

'Sounds like we got a dual personality here.'

'Yeah, that's exactly what it's like! It's as if he hates me for loving him. In fact, the more emotion I show, the crueller and nastier he gets. I mean, I give him my love and he shits all over it.'

'Could be you got too close and it scared him.'

'You think?'

'Did he mention anything about previous relationships? I mean, has he ever HAD one?'

A familiar sick feeling comes over me as I remember for the umpteenth time a thoughtless remark he made to me on our second date. 'He told me he'd once dated a stripper.'

'A stripper?' Alf wrinkles his charred nose. 'That's just skanky.'

'Yeah. And the imagery – I can't tell you how much it's tormented me. You know, he said he could never bring himself to go see her dance, but he didn't mind that she spent all her money on him taking him out.'

'Sounds like your Weasel has the makings of a pimp.'

'Maybe I should've walked out on him then.'

'Maybe you should've. I think this Weasel needs to be taught a lesson.'

'I feel so helpless. I'm trying so hard to be cool, I don't want to come on all hennish. I'm not like that. I'm not trying to railroad him into something. I just want to be with him. That's all.'

'Maybe you need to start seeing other blokes.'

I laugh without humour, remembering my attempt to distract

myself from heartache, to do what is called MOVING ON – which had taken the form of a cute young bloke from Hertford-shire who liked me to straddle his face so he could lick me.

Alf grinned wickedly, as if he could see into my mind. 'Maybe you should've videoed it. Bet your Weasel would've sat up and taken notice. I got wood just thinking of it!'

I flushed.

'Move on, sweetheart. Best advice I can offer.'

'But I tried that already. All it did was make things worse. It made me realise how much I wanted him back. It's like he's a part of me. Do you know, he told me we were like Siamese twins?'

'Charming.'

'Someone once said that you never truly realise how greatly you love until it's gone. I feel as if I'm living that quote.'

'And Bertrand Russell once said "To fear love is to fear life, and those who fear life are already three parts dead." So maybe your Weasel's dead. Maybe what you think's there ain't really there at all. Maybe he's just a hollow shell.'

Great. A Devil who can quote Bertrand Russell. I sure find them, don't I? 'No, I can't believe that. I know what we had – *have* – how we've bonded. I've never had that with anyone. Ever.' I begin to cry again.

Alf's not listening, nor does he offer any tissues. 'Maybe you need to try again, play the field.'

'No. I don't want to see other blokes.'

'Could get him to appreciate you more, make an effort. Could wake him up a bit. I mean, you're a gorgeous bird. Intelligent. Sexy too. Any man would be glad to have you.'

'But I want THIS man!'

'I'm just suggesting is all. I mean, you signed a contract with me. And I don't want people saying I don't keep my end of the bargain.'

Shit.

'The deal was you'd get him back. Technically you got him

back. I got no control over the specifics of the situation.'

'But I'm right back where I started. Nothing's changed. The same thing's happening that led him to break it off with me in the first place. He's just not making any effort. It's like he wants to, but he doesn't know how. It's like it's too much bother.'

'Not my lookout, sweetheart.'

'But—'

'He dumped you. I sorted it so you been un-dumped. Far's I'm concerned, my job's done.'

'What if it happens again? What if he realises he can't do this and he ends it again? I won't survive it. I won't.'

'Oh, you'll survive it. We got us a deal, remember?'

All that week I think about Alf's advice. I know his primary interest is in claiming my soul, but I do believe he's trying to help. He does seem to have some integrity, despite being the Devil.

The weekend coming up is a certainty; it's marked on both our calendars. I plan to use it to find out exactly where I stand.

Only I never get my chance, as the rug's pulled out from under me. *Again*. It arrives in the form of an email. This time the text isn't in blue. And there are no rows of electronic kisses either.

I know what it says without having to read it.

There's no going back on bargains struck with the Devil, no refunds or exchanges, no *oh I changed my mind*s. I tried asking Alf if he could take your soul instead of mine, but he said you don't have one. I fear he's right.

I'm resigned to my fate and I welcome it. Now I just want Alf to take me down to Hell with him, and the sooner the better. Not that I'll notice a change – I've been living in Hell already, thanks to you. I wish I could take you with me. It's what you deserve, better than. But maybe my writing this will be your Hell. You did say you wanted to be my muse. Now you are. This is my parting gift to you – that you shall live forever on these pages, that everyone will read this and know what a nasty piece of work you are, that the smiling happy laughing boy is a fraud, an illusion, someone who's empty inside. I did warn you this might happen. We even joked about it, remember? The first time when we were making love and I said I would pour everything out in words since I couldn't say them to you and you smiled your cheeky little smile and said fine, write it all down as long as you don't end up in my revenge story, then the last time we were together when you were acting all hard-arsed and removed and I said that maybe I *would* write you into my revenge story after all and you gave a little half laugh but I could see you wondered if I might actually do it. Well, I have.

Bet you'll never forget your Princess now, will you, Blue Eyes?

†

The One

Georgiana Nelsen

The nightmares always start the same, the fall down the dark tunnel, the blackness, the purple inside eye staring, shifting back and forth, nervous, suspicious. It is my own eye. I know it from the mirror even though my eyes are green, not purple. It spins around backwards, and I can see the tunnel, like what I think a coal pit emptied of everything of value would be, there behind my brain. It shouts echoing ugly words, words I remember from my marriage, which it must actually be writing, as even in my sleep I know eyes don't shout. All I can hear is breathing, sucking me in deeper and deeper into the black.

I wake then. This time the breathing is not just mine, but comes from the huge mass under the sheet next to me. I have to shake my head to remember where I am, who I am. The motion rocks the purple eye, sends it crashing to the sides of the pit, bruising it and distorting the image. A beam of streetlamp yellow, splitting the drapes like heavy thighs, shines on his face. I cannot remember his name.

The room is hot, though I shiver with cold. There is moisture all around, a fetid dampness. Sweat pools in all the bends of his body, which are bent across my own, and the scent of last night's sex blends into my pores. The stench radiates from the man beside me, but clings to my skin.

I try to place him. He was at the meeting I think, not just

another barfly caught in my two glasses of wine need-to-fuck web. I remember he is a lawyer: educated, smart, cynical. He is not handsome, though his eyes have a gentle inquiry about them beneath thick brows, and I see the lashes that grace them are long, curled like a Maybelline television ad. His nose is straight, almost delicate, and would be perfect on a man a third his size. I remember his hair as rich-mink luxurious, remember twisting the soft curls around my fingers, but in the amber glow, nothing shines but the damp sheen on his face. His hair clumps, matted wool on a sheep in need of shearing. I curl my fingers into my hands at the memory of mindless pawing.

I remember he told me about his wife, home with their children, getting fatter every year. A great cook, he said as he rubbed his hands across the beach ball of his belly, just no fun anymore.

The black pit is spinning. Nausea rises, a tornado reversed in my chest. It evaporates, leaving confused gooseflesh as my only defence from the cold surfacing from deep within me. I need to move.

I disentangle myself from his limbs, and drop from the bed. He snuffles, then snores. The room is cheap, one bed, and the entire bathroom is contained behind a single hollow door. The light is on in there, and I slip into the green fluorescent glow, my eyes sticky with proteins and puffed from the night's libations. The reflection in the mirror is not kind; my hair is bumped and I look my age or more. I am not used to that. I am used to being the young one, the one still vibrant, still pretty. I am used to being the first sip of the finest gin Martini. Instead, I am the last call of the house whisky.

His wallet is on the counter there; I pick it up and read the licence. His name is Adam. Perfect. Adam the attorney. I remember I'd told him my name was Eve. I flip the wallet to the photographs. Two children and a pretty blonde stare at me, as though I am to blame. My husband carried one like it in his own wallet. Only the mirror reminds me I was not enough either. Now I am no one's pretty blonde.

I turn away and twist the shower knob to 'on', and swallow the need to vomit. The nausea thickens the debate inside, between consciousness and dark rage.

The water is hot, and my need to wash is desperate. I step into the spray and let the needles pierce first my face and eyelids, and then turn and offer the back of my neck to the heat. I remember Adam kissing me there, using his tongue in a way that fascinated me even as it made me want to wipe it away. He was offended when I told him I didn't like to be wet like that. I tried to pretend. I know I did. I know that men need to think they are the best, the sexiest, the most virile. I give them that. At least I try, but suddenly I am unprepared to follow through, an actress on stage with no costume, no props, no prompters. I have forgotten my lines. I just want out.

The room clouds with steam and every breath I take is still that combination of stale musk and spoiled garlic that lingers, pooled in my sinuses. I scrub hard, but I can't get rid of it. Each breath brings back the memory of what I have done, with the full force of shame. It is all part of the nightmare, this taking, waking and loss. I wonder if I will ever breathe fresh air again.

I start to reach outside the shower, for another cloth. Soap alone is not enough. I realise then that he has joined me in the bathroom. I realise it not when he pulls the curtain aside to bathe with his lover, but when I hear his explosive release of waste on the other side. The sound paralyses me. I don't want to hear this man, this animal, this human. I want him to disappear now, the way I know I will disappear as soon as I can find my clothes. But instead he laughs, a deep laugh that bears his weight, and I am trapped, frozen in the headlights that laugh carries with it. He flushes, and the heat of the water intensifies.

Enough. I have had enough.

I step from the shower spray and he smiles. He pulls me to

him and his lips are on my throat, his hands squeezing my wet breast. I don't think, but close my eyes to the glaring light. The purple eye takes over then and through it I see the sharp file in my cosmetic case on the counter. I know what to do; now I know my lines. I lift the cool steel, feel it warm in my palm and then I traverse the dark tunnel, finally leaving rage and confusion. I find control.

His mouth is latched onto my nipple when I locate the notch between his vertebrae that leads to paralysis. The blade is true; it stops him cold. He has time only to clutch at the shower curtain before his body stops working under his will. It takes all I have to remove the blade, but I have to. The rage is strong within me, and I pull hard, the snap of the tissue I've severed clicks as the sharp file strums against it. The blade is free. He falls forward, but not before I plunge the blade once more into the pulse of his throat where the blood flows warm, and smells copper sweet.

The red against the white porcelain tub is beautiful. It mixes with the hot water, and I soap him, cleansing the stench and the wound, letting him harden. Phrases run through my head: a clean kill, hot water hell.

When I am finished, there is nothing left of our time together but the tangled sheets and empty glasses by the bed. More considerate in death than life, he has given me a way to move him, by pulling the shower curtain from its grommets as he descended. I wrap him in the curtain and wedge the laundry cart left outside the door beneath him. He slides into the cart with more ease even than he'd slid into me hours before.

The halls are empty, the parking lot dark and his compact mass makes it easy to dump him into the trunk of my car. I lock it, return the cart to the hall, and even remember to tip the maid.

Back at home, I drag him slowly to my special room, my trophy room. Until I have him there, I almost wish I had chosen smaller game. I am tired and he is heavy; the adrenalin high of performance waning, the thrill of the hunt gone. I am ready to mellow, but the wine was cheap and a sulphur headache coats my brain.

I wander the room, rubbing my temples, and take some time with my lovers to relax. Each one stares at me, precious in his devotion. I am the only woman in the world for them, despite their past, despite the rings that encircle their fingers. I am the one.

When I reach Adam, I smooth the mink hair back into place, close his curling lashes over the small glassy eyes. He no longer smells of stale sex; instead he wears the sweet perfume of fresh death. It took two hooks and a pulley to hang him in the slot with 'lawyer' etched on its shining brass plate. The breadth of his shoulders was just too wide, his weight slung too low to balance. The purple eye inside my head joins the green ones he smiled into, and together we wander the length of him, unashamed. I compare him to the accountant, hung next to him, and replace shame with pride. The accountant was much smaller, younger, not so smart. On the other side is a silver fox whose impotence robbed him of his own last hurrah, my bargain with the eye, that they should feel their maleness one more night. I glance down again at Adam, and wonder if I would have chosen him for my collection at all, if he had behaved.

He shouldn't have laughed.

There aren't many spaces left in my trophy room. Before I close the door, I look back again and touch my fingers to my lips. I send them each a silent, soft kiss. The hundred brass plates capture the early glow of dawn coming in from the transom window; they glint, sharp knives in the dark. I close green eyes and know. There is light at the end of the tunnel.

†

Echo

Rosie Jackson

You'll find this hard to believe, looking at me now, but I used to be a feminist. I did. I was as strident as a bullfrog. I banged on about this right and that wrong, declined to walk through a door a man had opened for me, reclaimed the streets at midnight. I talked all the time; no one could get a word in edgeways. But that was before the fatal blow: the ambush that has weakened so many female hearts. I fell in love. I mean, really fell, as from the summit of Centre Point. How could I not? I met the one: the man of my dreams. At last I could tick every box on my checklist: he was clever, witty, solvent, sexy, not a British can't-be-arsed but an American high-achiever with beauty to die for. Even more incredibly, he was available and inviting me to live with him. We'd only known each other a few weeks, but it was one of those Dick Whittington turn-around moments: if I hesitated a second, some other woman would be in bed with him and I would lose everything. I didn't even pause.

His flat was in Primrose Hill, split-level, on the first and second floors, with a huge skyscape over London. Downstairs there was an open lounge and narrow galley kitchen, with one double bedroom, en-suite and a spiral staircase which led to the upper floor, where he had his office. From the skylight here you could see the Post Office Tower, the Millennium Wheel, St Paul's and Big Ben. It was reckless, I admit, surrendering the lease on my own flat and getting rid of most of my own possessions, but what's love about, if not surrender? My two suitcases and a box of books had to be squeezed into a corner of the bedroom, but I didn't care. I was in love for the first time in my life. It was one of those once-in-a-lifetime experiences: pure magic. I absolutely adored him. Even when his back was turned – which I have to confess was most of the time, he worked such long hours – I would admire the broad shoulders, the thick dark hair curling over his collar. He'd be at his computer before I awoke, and I'd step lightly up the wrought-iron staircase bearing a tray of his favourite coffee, Blue Mountain, freshly ground, clearing a space for the cup amongst his papers and planting a kiss on the nape of his neck.

I don't want to be misleading here: I was not at all dismayed by my new role. On the contrary, I revelled in it. Being a feminist hadn't worked, after all. It hadn't brought me the love. I found it a delightful novelty now, putting another person first, just relaxing and being feminine. I transformed the flat. I bought colourful Gabbeh rugs, hung new pictures, found Italian ceramics for the kitchen. I transformed myself. I toned and depilated my body, bought new lingerie, wore softer, more diaphanous garments. Within the space of weeks I'd changed from harpy to nymph.

Not that he had much time to notice these frivolities. He was a consultant, an entrepreneur, and the upstairs office was the hub of a worldwide web.

'I've just landed a deal in Hong Kong,' he said.

'Hong Kong?'

'They think the proposal's superb.'

'Superb,' I offered, before slipping quietly down to the galley to wash the previous night's dishes.

Those first weeks, everything went extremely well. He worked all day and half the night, bashing away at his computer and logging on and off conference calls, while I stayed quiet and beautiful and floated up and down the spiral staircase. Mostly, he would be so engrossed, he didn't even notice when I was there, standing behind his swivel leather chair, watching him. He would stare into the monitor as intently as if it were a mirror and he were seeking himself in its glassy depths. Before the files came up, the screen would be blue, like a pool, and he would crane forward, closer and closer, as though about to dive into it.

'This is the best document I've ever produced,' he said, rattling away at the keyboard. 'It'll knock their socks off, it's so damn good.'

'Good.'

'I'm on such a winning streak, I won't stop for supper now. I'm on too much of a roll.'

'Roll on,' I agreed.

I knew this was the way to convince someone you were listening, acting as a kind of ghostly echo. I'd been in therapy once, trying to work out why I was still single and whenever I paused, the therapist repeated back to me my final words, which was all the reassurance I needed to set me off again. So I wasn't too worried about the one-way process now. I was confident that with enough love he would turn round to face me, would want to see who I was, want to listen to me and show me a similar amount of devotion. That's how therapy works, after all. When you've been given enough attention, you become a normal human being. You remember you're not the only person in the world.

The single hiccup was when I almost forgot my metamorphosis and was tempted to lapse back into my former outspoken self. It was when the war was impending and we had a rare exchange on politics.

'You Brits are being altogether too harsh on Bush,' he complained.

'Harsh? On Bush?' I wondered.

'Going into Iraq. You never know what Saddam Hussein has up his sleeve.'

'Up his sleeve?' I asked.

'Weapons of mass destruction,' he explained.

'Weapons of mass destruction?' My voice rose in disbelief. 'Up his sleeve?'

But I bit my tongue. I wasn't going to argue. I'd done my share of disagreeing with men and it only drove them away. I wasn't going to lose this one, no sir. I kept my comments to a minimum, mumbled my supportive chorus, and continued to siphon wine, drinks, and snacks throughout the day.

So the months went by. His work prospered as if a beneficent spell had been cast over it, and the computer continued to mirror back his glory. If I became a little heavy-hearted at the lack of dialogue in the flat, I reasoned it away by looking forward to the luxurious holiday he promised we would take next summer, the new clothes he encouraged me to buy, the unprecedented lack of material worries. But a certain depression refused to be pushed aside as I came to realise I was not the only living thing he was ignoring. So preoccupied was he with his multi-national corporations and massive business deals, nature had ceased to exist for him. It was as though the seasons themselves had vanished, wiped out by the delete key on his computer. Neither a fall of snow nor an azure sky nor midnight stars nor soft white cumulus brushing the roof of the city held any charm for him. One day replaced another as mechanically as the digital calendar in the bottom corner of his computer screen. He was so busy, nights were as taken up as days and days were cursed for not stretching further. Even when the darkness started visibly shrinking and winter gave birth to spring, there was no change in his effective hibernation.

I grew desperate to graft some passion for life onto him. I would walk to Camden Market and bring back profligate bunches of flowers: string-tied clusters of snowdrops, shy violets, streaked tulips, mournful anemones, vibrant primroses, rampant cowslips, deep blue iris.

He only noticed when he reached out for what he thought was fresh coffee and almost put a little posy in his mouth.

'Flowers!' he exclaimed in dismay.

'Flowers,' I repeated.

He paused only a second before announcing, 'Tokyo's tendering a new contract for next month. Top rate.'

'Top rate,' I tried to enthuse, but my voice was limp.

'I could do with a slug of whisky,' he said. 'This is an uphill slog.'

'Uphill slug,' I confirmed.

He didn't notice I'd confused my words. He was rushing through sites on the screen, one dissolving into another like ripples in water and all the time they were expanding outwards: Australia, Indonesia, Japan. It was after that initial verbal slip, almost as a game at first, that I started to experiment with my responses, deliberately letting them falter.

'I got the deal, honey,' he grinned. 'You'll be so proud of me. The world's my oyster.'

'Oysters in honey,' I fumbled. 'Deal the pride. Get the me.'

When he showed no obvious reaction, I became more daring, rebellious.

'Something's not right here. I need to get back to my previous vein.'

'Vain,' I pointed out.

'I'm running out of time here, babe. Maybe you could put together my invoices?'

'Maybe you could put my voice in.'

There was never any sign of him noticing, not consciously. But little by little, as my words became increasingly jumbled, the more his confidence began to decline. Little errors at first, like hairline cracks in plaster: sending a document to the wrong company, mistaking time differences round the globe, missing critical deadlines. He hated being seen to make mistakes. The mouse would crash down on the desk and he would explode in rage. It was like living with touch-paper.

'Don't they know the time in the UK for Chrissake? We're not ahead, we're eight hours behind.'

'Behind ours.'

'If I'm not careful I'm going to lose this fucking contract.'

'If you're not careful, you're going to lose this contract fucking.'

He'd been impeccable when I arrived. He couldn't put a finger wrong. Now, only a few months later, he was forgetting his own access codes, his password, his alibis.

'Damn it!' he swore, smashing his hand into the keyboard. 'They want too much. They're asking too many bloody questions.'

'Too much want,' I nodded as I came over from the top of the stairs. 'Blood asks questions.'

'Enter your verification code,' he snarled. 'To confirm your password, enter the make of your first car. Fuck it, how should I remember that? Peugeot? Acura?'

'Accurate,' I said, going over to try to help.

'First bloody car. I don't remember. I have no damn idea.'

'Remember me first,' I said mildly. 'Damn your idea.'

That day, I'd found in the market an especially beautiful tall white narcissus. I'd placed it in a slender glass vase and was leaning over him to stand it by the side of the keyboard. A spring fragrance lingered in the air, I'd brought it in with me, but he paid no heed. He was sitting so close to the monitor, smashing the mouse around, I half expected him to make a hole in the screen and fall into it. When I rested a hand on his shoulder to try to calm him down, he shrugged it off.

'Don't cling,' he said. 'If you go down, I'll come on later. I need to sort this out.'

'Out of sorts,' I sighed, but retired to the bedroom anyway. I lay on the bed, staring at my two battered suitcases, pondering all the lies I'd come to believe about love. I must have dozed off, for when I awoke it was night and outside a full lemon moon hung like a Chinese lantern over the park. Everything was eerily quiet: no clatter of the keyboard, no smashing of the mouse, none of the vehement expletives I'd grown used to recently. Wary of his anger if I interrupted him, I trod gingerly up to the office.

He lay there, my American beauty, in the ripe yellow moon-light, his body slumped over the keyboard. The narrow glass vase had been knocked over and the perfect white narcissus rested in a pool of water close to his head. Above him, the computer screen was still flashing: 'Enter your ID, enter your ID'.

But he couldn't, could he? I wasn't behind him any more. And without me, his true love, his echo, helping him know who he was, how could his heart keep on beating?

†

Remember Me

Dee Silman

At first it was hard. There was so much distraction and I was just a tiny speck – a mote of dust – and I couldn't make you see me.

That first night, I watched you leaning across to fill her glass from the ruby bottle, pausing just long enough to whisper something in her ear, before filling your own glass and bringing it to your lips.

Colours had become more vivid to me.

When you wiped the wine from the corners of your mouth it left bloody streaks on the back of your hand. They glittered in the candlelight like fresh razor wounds. Her hair was pure gold as she twisted it coyly between her fingers.

At one point, you seemed to look straight at me and I noticed that your eyes were azure blue, their surface so clear, so calm, I could almost see myself reflected.

For that moment, I was afraid. Afraid you might see me, afraid you might not. But I needn't have worried. You just turned nonchalantly back to her. You were wrapped up in your own private universe: yours and hers. I didn't exist for you.

I was often afraid in those early days. Not in a heart-stopping, blood-pounding kind of way. It was more of a cold stupor. I didn't know where I was, who I was. I didn't know how I'd got there.

That night, I followed you in the taxi, found out where you lived. The dawn sky was so vast above your rooftop. I watched the

141

early morning breeze lift your curtain out of the opened window: an angel spreading its wings.

After that, I followed you to bars across the city. I shared the bottles of wine and the intimate conversations. I became entangled in your glances of love, your blossoming love affair.

I couldn't feel the touch of your hand and I couldn't smell her expensive perfume but I dashed with you to the waiting taxis, giddy with the whole speed and purpose of the thing.

I began to find out a little more about you. How you liked your wine red and your coffee black. What you liked on your toast in the morning – yes, even that.

Sometimes, just as the evening was getting interesting, something would pull me away as if I were being sucked out in a vacuum. I would find myself somewhere else completely – perhaps sitting on the grass outside, or pressed underneath one of those long, hard benches in the park. It only took a moment. Distracted, perhaps, by a crystal of spilt sugar on the table by your hand. Or by suddenly finding that the flowers on her dress reminded me of some garden I had once walked in.

I never went far. And I could always find you again if I concentrated hard enough. But it taught me quickly that I had to have focus if I was to stay with you. And I did want to stay with you. I had decided that.

You seemed so confident in your city suit. The young entrepreneur, in charge of any situation. I followed you to work one day, but the whole atmosphere of calculated flattery and plotting hurt my head. It was a first-class lounge for survival of the fittest. I had no place there and I felt myself fading away as soon as I stepped through the door.

I much preferred our evenings. By then, your tie was slightly askew, your hair ruffled – it was a studied casualness that I saw you perfecting in the mirror. I enjoyed watching you get drunk. It loosened your tongue, made you more human.

Strangely, it brought us closer together. We were not so different after all.

Often, I wanted to tell you that. I tried whispering it in your ear. But you couldn't, wouldn't listen. I stared at you across the table, imploring you to see me. But you never took your eyes from her face.

I became brazen, following you everywhere. Each time you got up from your seat, I got up too. Each doorway you entered, I walked in right behind you. I was your darker shadow, too negative, too irrelevant, to notice. Once, you even walked right through me.

Which was when I decided I'd had enough. Because something like that had happened between us before.

I'm trying to remember the first time I discovered I could make things move. I think it was in your bedroom. You were standing in front of the mirror, putting on your shirt. She was in the bathroom, running a bath. I was standing slightly to your left, glaring at our reflection, willing you to see me. But of course you wouldn't. My anger flared up. Until then, I had not really questioned what I was doing. I was on some kind of power kick, enjoying the fact that I could spy on the intimate details of your life. But, suddenly, in that moment, it began to dawn on me that actually I was just as impotent as I had ever been. Maybe more. My presence made no difference to you. Nothing I did could affect you. I might as well not exist.

I swung out with my arm, trying to hit you somewhere, anywhere, trying to feel that satisfying contact of skin against skin. But, of course, my arm just floated right through you. You didn't even flinch, just kept on buttoning your shirt. Kept studying your face above it. Until, that is, the sound of the china shattering on the floor brought even her from the bathroom. I had made contact with something, after all.

'Are you all right?' she asked.

You looked at her, shocked. 'It just fell off the table.'

She helped you pick up the pieces.

When you both left, I was still standing in the same spot, trying to take in what had happened.

I let you go out alone, that night.

And stayed in, making plans.

Don't be fooled into thinking there is justice in the next world. Nothing is mended or made good. No one comes along to pick up the pieces. As always, we're on our own.

And there's no end to it, no forgetting: just a continuation of what went before.

What a killing joke, that is.

I had never been a success. I had never been a fighter. There was no escape. For that, I wanted revenge.

I soon perfected the art of making inanimate objects move. I found that if I concentrated hard enough I could cause a minuscule readjustment in an object's positioning. I could pull it out of time, then push it back, in a slightly altered state. At first, the movements were barely perceptible. I might manage to shift a spoon so that it slid against the side of a cup. Or I could roll a cork half an inch across the table. But the more I did it, the better I got. Until I was lifting objects completely free of the surface against which they rested for a period of three or four seconds or more. Then letting them drop haphazardly to the floor.

To begin with, you put it all down to stress at work. You had never been a nervous sort. And you had never had troubles of this kind before. Each time she came in to find you white and shaken, you mumbled your apologies.

I don't know what's come over me, you said. *It must have been me that knocked it. I'm getting clumsy, that's all. My mind's on other things.*

But she could tell you weren't yourself. You were becoming different. Together, you were becoming different.

Have a drink, she would say. *Relax.*

And for a while, you would.

But then, in a fit of spite, I would wait until her back was turned and knock over your glass. Or send the bottle crashing to the floor. And you would leap up in a rage again. Your face contorted. Out of control.

It must have been awful to be at the mercy of something you couldn't fight.

It must have been awful to see yourself losing her, and not to be able to stop it.

Awful. Really.

It was when you started to bring the books home that she left. *Poltergeist Phenomena; The Paranormal Explained.*

She accused you of externalising your problem. She said you should face up to what was really bothering you – that what you were doing was crying out for attention like a child.

You swore at her then. And that was more or less it. Except that you did take her advice. You did go and see someone.

I was with you that day, did you know that? (Because you were beginning to sense my presence, too. I had seen your frightened, backward glances).

I paced the room as you talked, smiling at some of your more elaborate descriptions of my handiwork.

Your doctor made a few notes. Nodded occasionally. Then, towards the end of the session, asked: 'Is there anything you feel particularly guilty about? This kind of activity can be caused by transference of some repressed emotion...Have you done anything of which you feel ashamed?'

Finally, I thought. *We're getting somewhere.*

Go on, I whispered, leaning close to your ear. *Think.*

But you just shook your head. 'Nothing,' you said. 'There's nothing.'

I remember I was suddenly disgusted with you.

IDIOT, I shouted, so loud I thought the windows would break. But all that happened was your jacket slid off the back of your chair. And your doctor quietly made more notes.

It's amazing how fast a person starts to deteriorate when they feel that all their former certainties are gone. Ask me, I should know. Just as you reach for a handhold to pull yourself back up, it disappears and you are left clawing for empty space.

And when you're right back at the bottom, in a heap, there's always someone waiting there to kick you. Just in case you thought it couldn't get any worse. Because you don't even know that for sure. No comfort, you see. None at all.

I was with you in the night when you lay awake in a cold sweat, trying to unravel the darkness in front of your eyes. I sat at the end of your bed, willing you to make out my shadowy figure. To finally find your clue.

I was your loyal companion to every dread night.

I still am.

Is it my imagination, or am I becoming a little clearer? Do you stare in my direction for longer, screw up your eyes with the effort of trying to decipher me, strain your ears to hear what I would whisper above the clamour of your heartbeat?

Listen. Do you want to know what you have done? Do you?

It is no more, no less than anyone.

You didn't cheat on me, beat me, emotionally bully me... though other men have done that. You didn't steal from me, trick me, rape me, or even murder me.

You didn't even know me.

But that night, the night we met, I sat at a bar in my red dress, drinking whisky until it stained the whites of my eyes. The weight of the world had crashed in. It sat on my shoulders like a huge, black crow. And I couldn't shake it off.

You came and stood next to me to order your drinks and I saw you recoil slightly. Was it the stench of whisky on my breath? Or something about me that spelt failure?

As you reached for your drinks, you knocked my glass into my lap. I shot out of my seat, trying to stop the liquid seeping through the thin material of my dress. The glass went crashing to the floor, turning the heads of the people standing around us.

'Clumsy bastard,' some man said.

You looked around, slightly panicked. The bar had fallen quiet.

'Do you have something?' I asked. 'A tissue or...' I eyed the hanky in your jacket pocket.

You pulled it out and pushed it across the bar towards me.

'At least buy her another drink,' the same man called.

I saw a muscle begin to twitch in your jaw.

You turned to me. 'What do you want?'

'Whisky.' My voice trembled.

You looked at me as if you wanted to crush me beneath your foot.

The hum of conversation resumed as people began to lose interest in us. I stared at your profile as you waited for the bartender to pour my drink. You were young, much younger than me. A boy, really.

What did I want? Just a little respect. Just someone who would listen.

A tear slid out of the corner of my eye. It reached my mouth and I licked it away. Hot, salty.

You began to drum your fingers on the bar, your eyes following the bartender's every move. I noticed how incredibly long your eyelashes were. Pretty, like a girl's.

You must have felt me staring at you then because suddenly you turned to meet my gaze.

The tears poured down my face. I couldn't stop them. I watched your lip curl with disgust.

'Here.' You slid a ten pound note across the bar towards me. 'For the drink.'

'But... what about the change?' I pleaded.

I heard you mutter something under your breath. Some swear word.

'Keep it.'

Then you turned sharply away, sending the hastily placed note fluttering to the floor.

I struggled off the stool and crawled on my hands and knees, feeling for the money amongst the spilt beer and cigarette butts. I had every intention of giving it back to you.

But in that moment, having picked up your drinks from the bar, you turned to walk away, grinding your heel onto my outstretched hand.

You didn't even notice. I cried out, but you just kept on walking.

And from my position on the floor I saw you saunter to your table and sit down in front of a girl.

I heard you laughing together. Saw her tossing back her head of long, golden hair. Watched you leaning in, sharing some joke.

I took the tablets in the toilet. That's where they found me. I knew exactly how many to take. I'd carried them with me for a long time. My insurance, I called them. The insurance of the weak.

But the insurers never paid up.

Otherwise why would I still be here now? Back here with you?

I really thought they would take me to some other place.

There's not a lot for me to do. My mind tends to run on one track. Sit here. Wait with you. Be patient. Eventually, you'll remember.

I'm not really sure how I'll feel when you do.

Vindicated, somehow? The tables turned? I don't really want to follow that train of thought.

You see, this whole thing isn't even personal. You just happened to be the last kick waiting for me at the bottom.

And you were the first person I recognised when I leapt into the night. You were just leaving the bar, hand on the glass door. So I followed you home, something familiar.

Like a mote of dust, a tiny speck, falling back to earth and settling on the first recognisable shape it finds.

So I found you.

✝

Love and Death in Renaissance Italy

Clare Colvin

The statue dominates the great hall of the palazzo. Duke Vespasiano Gonzaga of Sabbioneta is mounted on a black stallion. Its gilded trappings match the gold ribands on his ebony armour. The wood carver has given him hyacinth curls and a trim beard. He has a stern face and protuberant eyes.

'They say the story about him murdering his first wife is a myth, but I would rather believe that he did it. He looks like a psychopath,' said Lucretia.

'What was the story?' asked Max.

Lucretia was looking in the guidebook. 'It's not in here because the tourist office prefers his more respectable image as the builder of an ideal city. But as I remember it, from that old library book on Renaissance princes, he suspected his wife was unfaithful and he killed her lover. Then he locked her up in a room with the corpse. Every day he would enter the room with a chalice of poison, and say just one word, *Beva!* then leave and lock the door behind him. It was a very hot summer. On the fifth day she drank the poison.'

'I'm surprised she lasted that long.'

'So many murdered wives and lovers.' Lucretia moved closer to the statue. The flaring nostrils of the horse were directly above her, its eyes rimmed with white. 'Do you remember that castello, where was it? The lover had been visiting by swinging down on a rope from the tower above her window. When the husband caught them in the act, he ordered the servants to despatch the lover, and reserved for himself the killing of his wife. The chamber had a distinctly creepy atmosphere.'

'I wouldn't know, as there was no way for me to reach it.'

'And the palazzo near Florence where the husband rigged up some sort of rope device that literally snared his wife and strangled her?' Lucretia stretched out a hand as if to touch the Duke's armoured foot resting against a stirrup.

'I wasn't there, either.'

'Always the husbands. No one ever hears about the wife's revenge,' said Lucretia, smiling up at the Duke's wooden face. 'Time is the best revenge of all, isn't it? What's the difference of a few years between two deaths, centuries later?'

'Can we get out of here? I've had enough for the day.'

'Of course, darling. I'll get the attendant to help with the wheelchair.'

'He can help me as far as the car. I don't want you pushing me over the cobbles again. You nearly crippled me last time.'

Lucretia is never sure when he's joking. 'I'm sorry, darling,' she said. 'I know – I drive like a maniac.'

You can tell that Max and his wheelchair are not at one. Look at him, a big man, the broad shoulders and large hands demand a more impressive chariot. At home he has a motorised buggy and he hates the dependence on others of these primitive human-propelled chairs. He's impatient with the attendant, who is no more adept than Lucretia at steering him over the uneven ground towards the car against which the chauffeur is leaning, examining his nails, apparently unaware of his employer's approach.

Max has the sandy hair of someone prone to sunburn. His reddened skin is evidence of his aversion to sun lotions and hats. Lucretia has given up trying to protect him from the sun. It's not worth the darting look of hatred. A powerful man, furious at his half-useless body. Max shouts at the chauffeur who gracefully unfurls from the side of the car, smiling one of those eager Italian smiles that mean nothing at all. What does the chauffeur see? A cross red-faced *inglese* in a wheelchair that he himself would be pushing were he more attentive to the signor's needs. And the signora, serene as usual, in a black linen shift with a bandana under her panama. The chauffeur is sensitive to the latest style of the fashionistas, of which a bandana under a panama is one. He notices her slim legs and the feet that turn out, duck-like. It's the walk of a dancer.

The difference five years makes to a life. Imagine Max walking, or striding, rather, along the Strand towards Simpson's for one of those lunches where business is discussed over a dead cow. Bullock, said Max, let's be accurate at least. And overcooked cabbage, said Lucretia. That was in the second year of their marriage, when the light he had shone on her in the early days began to diffuse and she realised areas of his life were becoming shadowy for her.

As the chauffeur, galvanised into action at last, helps to arrange Max's inert sandaled feet in the car's front passenger seat, an image from the past comes into Lucretia's mind of Max bending over her as she slid into the front seat of his silver Porsche – Max had always owned luxurious toys.

'Does it really hurt?' he had asked, his hand cradling a foot that was smaller than his hand.

'It's agony. The block inside the shoes gets soaked with blood.'

'All for our delight,' and he kissed the arch of her foot.

'Excuse me! We do it for ourselves. We have to dance. It's part of us.'

That was the part that Max never saw, the sweaty striving at the barre in baggy leotards, the consumption of sliced white bread soaked in honey in rehearsal breaks to re-fuel the body, the intimate smells of your dancing partner, that you noticed no more than your own. What he had seen and fallen in love with was

Lucretia on stage, her arms undulating like ribbons in the breeze, her face tender with love as she appealed to her prince not to reject her for his rich fiancée. Max had felt an overwhelming tenderness that began in his heart and rushed to his loins. At the first-night party he was introduced to her, and holding her infinitely supple hand, said, 'Such a slim little thing.' As she widened her eyes in scorn, he quickly rescued himself, 'And such power. I could hardly believe it...' After a few minutes of flattery, she had forgiven him and accepted when he had asked her out to dinner.

How much was love, and how much pride of possession? Lucretia asked herself just a year after their marriage when she felt the need to decide between children and dancing. For the next five years anyway, until she had danced all those great roles, and then after that, well, we would see. Max's pride in his ballerina wife masked whatever other emotions may have been coursing through him concerning the need for a son and heir. He introduced her at parties as *la prima assoluta*, and she would smile with demure complacency. Not that there were many parties, for she was often working in the evening, or tired out from rehearsals during the day. 'You have to realise', she said, 'it's not a job that ends at 5 p.m.'

'Nor does mine,' said Max.

There's so much you don't know about someone with whom you live. As Lucretia settles into the back seat of the car, comparing the back of her husband's head, sandy hair streaked with sweat, with the chauffeur's polished sleekness falling in tendrils over his shirt collar, she casts back in her mind to the moment that she realised. It's the statue of the Gonzaga duke that's set her off on this track. Jealousy can do terrible things. She remembers the pain in her chest, so acute that she had bent over, retching, as if someone had punched her. And then a profound feeling of loss. She hadn't realised in her absorption with the dancing, how necessary it was to know that Max was there, even if not physically present.

'I wanted to warn you, before it was too late,' said the so-called friend, whom she wouldn't have believed if she hadn't already been subliminally aware of Max's infidelity. Those odd phone calls that would suddenly end when he heard her coming down the stairs. The wrong numbers. There may have been other women, but the one about whom it was perhaps too late was someone from his office, a blonde, large-breasted girl, nubile though with a mind like a calculator – the sort he should have married in the first place.

Jealousy can make you do terrible things. Even now she doesn't like to think of the way she behaved, the screaming rows, the dangerous questions, 'So you don't love me anymore? So you want a divorce?' It was as if she was programmed to push him to the edge, as if her mother was insidiously playing out her own life through her daughter. The rows that Lucretia had listened to as a child, that had driven her father from her life, were returning to haunt her.

Finally there was the night she was driving Max home from a dinner party. He had handed her the keys of the Porsche, saying, 'I'm not sure who is the worse driver, me drunk, or you sober, but I don't want to lose my licence.'

The evening had been an ordeal for the eyes watching her, the people who realised their marriage was foundering. She said to Max, 'At least you might have defended me against the man who was accusing me of being anorexic.'

A lifetime ago, Max had been her rock, and it was on this rock she was now wrecking herself. She said, the words coming out of her mouth, uncontrolled by her rational mind, 'But of course, you wouldn't be interested. Now that you don't love me any more.'

The headlamps lit the road like theatre spotlights, illuminating the long grass on the verges. Out of range of the beams, the black shadows of the trees made a frame against the backcloth of a sky lit by the waning moon. The steering wheel of the Porsche seemed alive under her hands. It was a living beast, a sleek, silvery panther gathering speed.

She heard Max's voice beside her, cold and matter-of-fact. 'Well, there's not much to love any more, is there? You're not the person I married.'

'Whose fault is that?' And the darkened landscape blurred into a watery abstract through her tears. She pushed her foot down on the accelerator.

'Slow down, for fuck's sake!' shouted Max, but all her anger was directed down into her foot, the foot that had bled so that Giselle could display the hurt of rejection, could tear round the stage, her hair loose, tracing wild patterns with the sword. She swung from the road onto a slipway, and then, with Max shouting beside her, on to the M25, gathering speed, scattering cars from the fast lane.

'Where are the police when you need them?' Max cried, and covered his eyes with his hands.

'*Scusate, mi dispiace,*' says the chauffeur. He has nearly gone into the back of a lorry, having had his attention distracted by a blonde speeding by in a sports car.

'*Piu lentamente per favore!*' exclaims Max. He flinches as Lucretia's calming hand rests on his shoulder. There are moments when he can't bear to be touched, which is hard on him as he relies so much on other people's hands. She leans back against the seat and smiles at him but Max shifts his eyes from the driving mirror and instead she catches the chauffeur's neutral dark gaze.

They are approaching Mantua from the south, from where the city seems to float serenely on the lake at the end of the causeway. The red walls of the Castello di San Giorgio, the bell tower of the cathedral, and the great watchtower are silhouetted against the sky. Lucretia says to the back of Max's head, 'This evening let's eat at one of the outdoor restaurants on the Piazza delle Erbe. Much nicer in this weather than the hotel.'

'As long as you book somewhere beforehand. I don't want to be shuffled from one place to another, and make sure they've got enough space for the bloody wheelchair.'

'Don't worry, darling, I'll get it sorted,' says Lucretia and, that having been settled, gazes out at the green and pink of the lotuses on the shining mirror of the lake.

After the accident, people were hugely sympathetic to Lucretia. It wasn't just that she had given up her career in order always to be there to care for him, it was the fact, known to a number of them, that Max had been unfaithful, even, it was whispered, to the point of leaving her. It was so good of her to be staunchly there, on hand with the carers to get him up in the morning and to bed at night, to organise the move from a house to a ground floor apartment designed for the handicapped, so good when the accident would never have happened but for his affair.

The circumstances were explained away. Of course, Max was staying at the hotel in Cannes for a conference involving his colleagues, so it was quite natural that she, the young woman, should be there. And what more natural than to have a swim at midnight after a hard day's work, and to dive into the water with his usual ferocious energy, cutting through the silky coolness, trailing bubbles, the wash slapping against the sides of the pool, and then the accident, his head thudding against the azure-washed concrete of the base. The pool was designed for splashing around in rather than for Olympic dives, but Max had been displaying his swimming prowess. He was lucky, said the doctors, not to be totally paralysed, and for a while there were intense physiotherapy sessions to regain the use of his limbs, but while the chest and arms grew stronger, the legs remained wasted and useless. And what a surprise! The young woman to whom he had been showing off deserted him. One day she was there at his hospital bed, timing her visit not to coincide with that of his wife, the next she was on a plane to America and a new life.

'I suppose it was to be expected, now that I'm a cripple,' said Max.

'It was never more than a passing fling,' said Lucretia, assigning the passion that had torn him apart and ruined his life to a mere dalliance. 'I'm with you, my darling, and I'll never desert you.'

He sighed and looked at her with infinite weariness. 'No, you won't, will you?' he said.

Max is more difficult on some days than others. At times it seems he is testing Lucretia. She catches a glance of real hatred as she adjusts his shirt collar. He hates to be driven by her, for that night of the demon drive along the M25 is imprinted on his mind. It was then, that night, he had decided to leave her and he had resolved to make the final break on his return from Cannes. Lucretia must know this, he is sure, but like a true performer has chosen a different role to that of rejected wife. She is now the self-sacrificing, infinitely loving nurse and companion, her dying swan arms undulating around his helpless body. She knows where her duty lies. She knows, too, that he is hers for life. The restless energy stilled, the libido depressed by the reaction of the world – there are no significant glances at a man in a wheelchair. Lucretia concerns herself with him, admired by the world, and secure in the knowledge that he won't run away.

Today, while Max is resting in the afternoon, she walks through the city to the Palazzo Te, the summer palace of the Gonzaga dukes. The sun is less strong and she has abandoned the panama, shaking out her newly-washed hair to dry in the warm air. She buys a ticket at the entrance hall and begins her journey into the bizarre imagination of Giulio Romano whose frescoes decorate the walls. Her guidebook says the artist and the Duke of Mantua were in sympathy, both of them in love with the sensuous and the pagan. On the ceiling above her a charioteer is whipping his horses to a frenzy. The viewpoint is from below, so the bare buttocks of the man are exposed as his short tunic flares up, as rounded as the ample rumps of the horses.

In the mid-afternoon she has the place to herself. There are no attendants and few visitors. She's able to wander from room to room, absorbing the calm emptiness of the palace and the energetic frescoes on the wall. There's a motif that runs through the rooms, a little stone lizard gripping the cornice with prehensile toes. And now she has reached the hall of Psyche, and there's a scene of a wedding banquet that is a jamboree of unbridled drunkenness and lust. A Pan figure with testicles hanging down between his hairy thighs is leering, tongue protruding through his teeth, at a naked maiden handling a bunch of grapes. At the other side of the table, with its embroidered cloth and dishes of fruit, an elderly satyr has collapsed, clutching a flask of wine. His belly overhangs his diminished penis that nevertheless emits a stream of semen. In the background someone is doing something unspeakable to a goat.

Lucretia is glad that she's alone and can gaze as long as she likes at the erotica. The mythical wedding between Cupid and Psyche is, says her guidebook, a celebration of Duke Federico's love for his mistress. Psyche, naked at the centre of the fresco, is a portrait of the mistress. She has blonde hair, a turned-up nose and slightly protruding teeth. Just like young women of today, those blondes whose teeth are always on view through their parted lips. Like the one who fled to America.

What is happening in the less obtrusive plaques next to the cornices is also quite fruity. There's a triton, his member rampant, about to penetrate a sea nymph. She imagines one of Giulio's assistants on a ladder, paintbrush in hand, outlining the penis with deep concentration, and the master standing below, calling out, '*Ancora piu grande!*' She laughs aloud and then, sensing an indefinable change in the room, turns to find herself no longer alone but looking straight at the chauffeur. He smiles at her. '*E bello, vero?*'

She had not heard him come in and she is suddenly thrown off balance. It's too complicated to explain in Italian the image in her mind of the master's assistant and the paintbrush, so she just says, '*Si, e bello.*'

'Bumpity, bumpity, bump!' sings Lucretia as the wheelchair hits the cobblestones. It's the evening hour, and the *passagiata* is at its height. The young Mantuans are performing their courting dance, boys straddled across their motorbikes, symbols of phallic power. Girls sauntering in twos and threes, in short skirts studded with rhinestones or tight jeans cut low to reveal a concave stomach. Stiletto sandals clicking on the stone, low-cut blouses revealing still developing breasts, sequinned shoulder bags swinging against their narrow hips.

'For God's sake, why are we going over this bloody assault course?' shouts Max.

'Because, darling, youth has taken over the streets. I can't steer my way through this crowd of *ragazzi e ragazze* celebrating the joy of their hormones.'

'I don't see why not – if only to show them what life may bring.'

Lucretia smiles at a contretemps going on between a boy on a motorbike and a couple of girls who are alternately upbraiding him, and turning their bodies to display them to best advantage.

'Italian girls always look as if they're on the pull,' she says. 'Now here we are, at the Piazza delle Erbe, and there's a nice waiter to take over.'

'Why isn't the chauffeur helping us – that's what he's paid to do.'

'Paolo's taken the evening off,' says Lucretia.

'Probably pulling some little tart. You should have a firmer hand with him.'

'Don't you love the bottles of olive oil on the table, like golden globes?' says Lucretia, as the waiter manoeuvres the wheelchair into place.

Eating with Max is easier now that he's regained the use of his arms. Those first months after the accident, she used to tell people, were the worse. Sitting beside him, coaxing food into his mouth, wiping off the surplus with a napkin. But what she didn't tell anyone was the satisfaction of his dependence that warmed her whole being. Now, as he awkwardly cuts the Parma ham on his plate, she refrains from intervening. He hates to be helped.

She picks up one of the figs, its purple skin stretched over the crimson interior that's revealed as she splits it apart. 'A lesson in figs,' Paolo had said, 'it's Mantua's special fruit. Do you not see it in the frescoes?'

'No, where is it?' she had asked, but he only laughed, the sound echoing round the hall of the giants, like a rumble of falling stone. She saw the Titans crushed under the pillars that Jupiter had brought down with his thunderbolts, their faces twisted with rage and pain. And then he took her hand, '*Andiamo*,' and she followed without question, a strange feeling, as if entering another dimension, suffusing her. The atmosphere seemed more dense as their footsteps reverberated around the great chamber.

'You see the first Duke, Federico?' he said, and she looked at the portrait of a dark-eyed man staring directly at her, a ringed hand resting on a lapdog. His mouth under the growth of moustache and beard was curiously feminine and the eyes had a calculating awareness.

'You know the opera *Rigoletto*?' Paolo sang the first lines from the Duke of Mantua's aria in a pleasant tenor voice.

'*La donna e mobile, vero?*' He smiled at her, white teeth between parted lips.

'No,' said Lucretia, 'the Duke was fickle. *He* should have died.'

'Instead, it was the lady. Come, *vieni*, we see the secret garden of the Duke.'

'This veal is tough,' says Max. 'They should have beaten it more.'

'Have some of my *fegato alla veneziana*, darling, it's quite delicious. Melts in the mouth.'

Lucretia shivers almost perceptibly as in her mind Paolo's tongue meets hers, his hand caresses her breast, and her body melts into burning liquid. She feels a blush come to her face and a tingling between her thighs. To distract herself from the sexual desire that has seized her, she says the first thing that comes into her head.

'Did you know our chauffeur is a budding opera singer?'

She can't think what possessed her. Of course, Max now wants to know when she learnt this. Somewhere in his brain she can sense a curling thread of suspicion, like smoke on dry timbers. She says, 'I saw him at the Palazzo Te. He was singing in the Hall of the Giants – as one does – testing out the echo. It reverberates, round and round. I complimented him on his voice, and he said he was studying to be a singer. Chauffeuring is something he does to earn money.'

'Complimented...' Max emphasises each consonant. He has homed in precisely on a false word, one that she wouldn't normally have used. 'So what sort of voice does he have?'

'A tenor, I think. He was singing the Duke of Mantua's aria.'

'Was he good?'

'Quite... but not the next Pavarotti, I would say. Why don't you ask him to sing and find out for yourself?' Lucretia smiles at Max, and then concentrates on the menu. 'What about something alcoholic to end with – limoncello with biscotti?'

The odd thing about the *passagiata* is how quickly it ends. One moment the street is thronged with burgeoning youth, the next it's deserted. They've all gone home for Mama's ragu. Theirs is the only restaurant on the piazza that still has customers, just themselves and an elderly man who is sitting contemplatively over a grappa. The waiter has retired to the interior with a couple of friends and seems happy for his customers to remain there indefinitely, having brought two brimming goblets of limoncello and a bowl of hard almond biscuits.

Lucretia sucks on a biscuit she has dipped into the liqueur, and gazes up at the tower of the palazzo del Podesta silhouetted against the darkening sky. A few stars are glimmering in the grey half-light. The limoncello is slipping down her throat in a viscous glow. She thinks about different meanings that attach themselves to the same word. The life of an invalid – an invalid life. Is her life invalid, despite all the care she takes of her invalid? Thoughts like this could drive you mad. The limoncello is warming her interior and images of the afternoon send shocks of sensation along her skin. The sensitivity of his hands in the shaded garden behind the secluded loggia, the fading frescoes on the wall of nymphs bathing in a pool. A lizard sliding along the stone arch of the grotto near her head. His eyes, a calculating awareness in them that she'd seen somewhere before, quite recently. It was very quiet. There was no one around.

The elderly man has paid his bill and gone, so now they're the only people sitting out on the piazza. There's the sound of a bicycle bell in the vicinity, and laughter from the restaurant's interior where the waiter is entertaining his friends. Cries of *Ciao!* as one of them leaves and brisk footsteps as he crosses the piazza. She recognises the walk before he turns his head. They stare at each other for one endless moment. It's as if there's a thread between them, she's only aware of his eyes looking at her. Then he moves on, he had hardly paused really, and she hears the footsteps quicken, the echo as he passes through the dark archway by the palazzo.

She glances at Max and realises he has understood the significance of the wordless interchange. He says, 'He seems to get everywhere, doesn't he?'

Lucretia blushes and remains silent. It would be shabby to try to divert the subject, and perhaps it's best to face it. She has nothing to say to Max and he has nothing to say to her. She waits for the outpouring of hatred, but instead she hears a rasping noise. For a second, she thinks Max is having a heart attack before realising the sound that she's never heard before is Max crying – sobs heaving up from his chest to be suppressed in his throat.

'Don't leave me,' he says, 'I need you.' And he covers his eyes with his hand as if ashamed of what he has said.

She reaches out and takes his hand, wet with tears, holding it to her lips. She sees his eyes, gazing helplessly at her, red-rimmed and slightly bulging.

'Of course I won't leave you. Why should I want to do that?'

She is aware of many answers to that question, but she is aware most of all of a feeling of warmth surging through her. Max needs me. The sentence rings through her head like a triumphant chord. For the first time, he has been jealous of her. And he needs her. She strokes his hand and says, 'Why would I leave?'

It's night, and a pale moon has risen over Mantua. The waiter is approaching with the bill and a bottle of limoncello. He presents the bill to Max and, seeing Lucretia's empty glass, pours more liqueur into it. She protests half-heartedly, but he says, in a voice thick with admiration, 'Is good, yes? *Beva, signora.*'

What is the chauffeur thinking about, as he saunters along below the high walls that turn the street into a canyon, lit intermittently by lamps that catch his shadow as he passes, to throw it huge and dark against the stone? Is the Duke's aria still running through his head? Is he feeling a sense of satisfaction at having put one over the red-faced *inglese* who has been driving him mad with his orders? Paolo is not thinking much, but he feels a number of pleasant sensations coursing through him, the uppermost being the most recent – the delicious *fegato alla veneziana* and the zabaglione his friend the waiter had ordered for him. Further back, the signora is another pleasant sensation. He's not pondering whether they will make out again. *Forse che si, forse che no*, according to the cryptic motto carved on the labyrinth ceiling of the ducal palace.

Thoughts run through his mind of *Rigoletto* as he passes the house reputed to be that of the court jester. Ah, the two-edged sword of the vendetta. He walks to the edge of the lake, aware of his well-being, the life coursing through his body, the beauty of the water shining in the moonlight, the hooting of an owl, the splash of fish rising. *Che bella vista!*

He has always liked looking at beautiful things, beautiful people, which is why one day a few years from now, he'll be looking at the glittering ink-coloured sea as he drives his car too fast along the Amalfi coast, instead of watching out for the next bend. His reactions will not be as quick as they were. But that, *ragazzi e ragazze*, is what life does to you. Things never turn out as planned.

†

Be Very Afraid

Vicki Hendricks

We were doing ear candles when the cable guy arrived – five women, aflame, in the living room. It was almost 6 p.m., time for a third or fourth blender of frozen margaritas. Enya played low in the background, the blackout drapes were pulled against the searing Florida sun, and frangipani potpourri perfumed the air. I had completely forgotten about the cable appointment, and having already waited a month for their visit, I wasn't about to send this guy away.

'Tom', according to his name patch, was a dark, long-haired thirty-something in a backward cap and strategically-holed, low-slung jeans. Judging by the bold fit of the pants, 'Tom' was short for Tomcat. He had something large in there, for sure, and a smooth square jaw that made up for a seeming lack of personality. 'Cable', was the one word he said at the door. I recognised Tom's type in an instant, and I didn't like him. My major in college had been business administration, but I'd gotten a contractor's licence and worked in construction for fifteen years. Being in charge of men, I was sick of tilting my downcast face, batting innocent lashes, and purring 'pretty please' daily, in order to meet a concrete inspection deadline or get the mess cleaned up after an installation of a popcorn ceiling. As a woman I'd learned, even in the twenty-first century, authority and reason got you nowhere with these guys – most guys really. After a fifty-hour work week, I didn't need Tom to remind me on the weekend.

Irritation swirled in my margarita-soaked head as I directed him across the smoky room to the hall. By necessity we wound through the midst of my four mid-forties friends, expensively coiffed, bejewelled, and toned by personal trainers, reclining on their sides on the sectional sofa and loveseat, flaming paper cones in their left ears. The movement of Tom's eyebrows conveyed his amusement, as he strolled loosely, exuding the feeling that he could make his way into any pair of those tight designer jeans he so desired. He was unaware that his tool belt caught momentarily in Beth's hair as he passed her, and she reached quickly, untangling it, but not without losing a few strands and glaring upwards at him.

Tom noticed nothing. He was cocky, like most of them – men – as if, regardless of the gap in both education and economics that must have been obvious between him and us, we were laid out for his casual pleasure. Pure male confidence, a trait to envy, yet despise.

Tom stopped short in front of me when we came to the hall, and looked back into the room, saying in a low, amazed tone, '*Mira que las mujeres comen mierda*,' as if there were other Latinos in the room to agree. Just as I hadn't guessed he was Tomas, he must have had no idea that we understood some Spanish. Like me, I doubted that any of my friends could have translated the expression, but the words 'women eat shit' certainly stirred some feelings. Clearly he thought we were gold-diggers and bonbon-eaters! Men never wasted their time, of course.

Eyebrows elevated and mouths dropped open across the room, although nobody could move without danger of starting a fire. Tomas's glance ran from one woman to another, sizing them up, until I stepped closer, blocking his view and directing him to the left down the hall. Yes, I should have escorted him outside and called in a complaint to the office, but again, thinking how long it would take to get another appointment, I just wanted to get it over with. I ushered him towards the back room, disgusted with myself for allowing this moment to spoil the ambiance of the afternoon.

This was Girls' Weekend. We all had boyfriends or husbands, one each most of the time, and several nearly-grown children among us, but once a year we cleared our calendars to make plans for gourmet restaurants, chick flicks, and shopping on the beach. I was hosting, since Allen was away on a business trip/golf combination and our son stayed at his dorm.

Getting together was always a feat – and a needed time of stress recovery. Carol's job was busiest on weekends, so this was a special exception. She had devoted her life to social work, but given up in hopelessness ten years earlier and bought a make-your-own pancake restaurant that had been about to go under, developing it into a thriving tourist attraction, with gift shop, tour boat, and kayak rental. It was in a state park and un-air-conditioned, with a built-in griddle in each table, so her time off came during September, when the heat and humidity were still vicious, and kids being back in school kept the crowds down. Earlier, she'd given us all the giggles with her description of the tourists, after a two-hour wait, finally getting their tables in the rustic and renowned establishment nearly to pass out in the heat – a tattoo-covered biker had – and then encounter 'irritable staff with drips of sweat running off the ends of their noses'. We all knew Carol was in there at six every morning with her staff, baking homemade bread, mixing batter, and cutting fruit, even though she didn't mention the sweat on her own nose. For months one spring, when wildfires engulfed the county in smoke, and the only customers were a few off-duty firemen, she had paid her full staff, rather than lay them off to save money. She hadn't left social work far behind. I was proud to call Carol my friend, and the others were as admirable in other ways.

I shook my head as I led Tom into the exercise room with the flat TV. I waited as he unhooked the cable box and got out his tools. With his sneering attitude I wasn't sure I wanted to leave him the run of the bedroom area. He had no idea what we were all about. None of us had enjoyed easy lives, and we were all proud of our accomplishments – like Beth. As a veterinarian, she often worked weekends also, doing volunteer spaying and neutering at the Humane Society. And Dorothy was an emergency room nurse. After recovering from a violent rape several years earlier, she had given up her job as an investment broker and gone back to school. She wasn't the only one among us to have been raped. I'd had an experience in my twenties, although I never mentioned it to the group. I assumed others had incidents also, that they didn't talk about, even to closest friends. To be a woman out in the world carried risk. Of course, staying at home was no guarantee either. Katie was a survivor of sexual abuse when she was a teen. She never let it hold her back, however, and was devoted to her job as a high school English teacher, always struggling to make a difference for the foreign students and lower economic groups.

Tomcat was taking forever, apparently in search of the right tool to unscrew the box. I was antsy to get back to my friends. This celebration had been months in the planning, and all of us were in need of the venting and relaxation only possible with close friends. The five of us had connected over ten years earlier, through an adventure travel group, and since then taken trips together to Greece, Guatemala, Finland, Namibia, and Peru. We were of like minds, kindred spirits, always up for something exciting. Playing with fire was a cheap thrill, and it was wise to candle in groups, since the smoke detector had to be dismantled.

I had parked my cone, burning with a tall flame, in a glass vase on the coffee table. I needed to get back to it. I decided to leave Tom on his own. Being a prick didn't make him a thief.

We finished our left ears and lit our rights, about twenty minutes elapsing by completion. Carol started mixing the last blender of margaritas before dinner, while I went to check Tom's progress, hoping he'd solved the mystery as to why the high def wasn't coming in.

He was sitting on the mauve carpet facing a rock video, bars of black still across the screen. His tool belt and hat were in a pile by the cable box, and his hair flowed loose down his back. He didn't hear me on the plush carpet. He was busy with something in his lap.

I walked to his side. 'How's it going?' I said.

He jerked and fumbled, and I was staring down at the huge cock that he was trying to stuff into his jeans.

'Oh...'

Just then, Beth came down the hall and walked into the room. 'Judy, we're thinking we would open a bottle of red...'

Her face shifted from shock, to aversion, to wonder. 'Whoa,' she whispered. If she was talking to herself, it was ineffective, because she dropped to her knees in front of Tom, as if for a closer look. Breath hissed on intake through her pursed lips, just like the preceding evening when her plate arrived bearing a twelve-ounce *filet au poivre*, garlic mashed potatoes, and asparagus with a boat of Hollandaise on the side.

Through instinct or the wafting of pheromones, the rest of the group assembled, Dorothy, Katie, and Carol pressing in for a look, sipping their drinks. Rather than dwindling at so much vampirish attention, Tom's erection gained resilience and he quit trying to do anything with it. His jaw hung slack as he looked at each of us. Then a slight smile showed gleaming white teeth. The cell phone on his belt began to play a hip-hop tune. He reached for it and turned it off, then sat back, his legs straight out in front, seeming to enjoy his position as the centre of attention.

Beth was always the most forward of the group. She had toyed with a variety of boyfriends since her divorce a few years earlier and admitted picking up one from a gas station and another at Home Depot. Neither relationship had turned out well, and she'd shown up for Girls' Weekend the year before with her arm in a sling and a space in her lower jaw awaiting a bridge. We'd all felt her pain. I understood the blue-collar attraction, as much as I despised it. I marvelled at these men who ate in huge bites and could muscle off a lug nut or wield a sledgehammer, the kind who are completely comfortable driving a semi or sitting naked in your kitchen, but they could easily become the enemy.

I was with Beth in spirit when she leaned forward and yanked at Tom's jeans, exposing the pale skin of his slim thighs, but I had no idea how far it would go.

My memory gets spotty from here on, blurred with the fever of events, but I remember Beth's hands grappling at his organs while Katie, Carol, and Dorothy drifted to his sides, their eyes riveted to the hand job in progress. It was mostly unexplainable, although tequila played a role. The room was charged with power. Sadistic lust, or maybe revenge, sprang from our guts, born of disappointments over the years, aspirations we'd been robbed of by men and their universe. Our souls were bruised by male-inflicted pain, either wilfully dealt or unsuspectingly.

Stifled feelings merged into a lightning bolt. We craved Tom's primitive boldness and strength, the image of the male we had spread our cunts and hearts for over and over, with unfair results.

Katie squatted near his thighs, took his head in her hands and pressed his mouth with a hard kiss that drew blood. Carol knelt on one side, forcing his arm behind his back, and Dorothy pinned the other. Beth worked his cock hard with her dry hand, and I held down his legs when he started to squirm.

His shirt came off, with a little help, then his shoes and socks. His jeans were pulled from under him and tossed across the room. No underwear. The sight of his firm ass, hairless and white, and the tender testicles dangling like bait, set us off with the ferocity of piranhas, nipping at his ears and neck, pinching everything we could reach. He used his elbows and knees to fight back, but there were too many of us, and we held him tight till he wore out. Somebody turned up the hard rock on MTV, and Katie muffled his whining with her palm, then stuffed a sock into his mouth.

'Come to Mama!' Beth bellowed, and we helped her push him flat on his back and held him, while she slipped off her Capris and string bikini and climbed on top, riding him hard, banging his hips into the floor, her vaginal lips hot pink and slick when she rose, sweat dripping from the small of her back down the crack of her ass. We were all caught up in an act we had never imagined. At some point, Beth crawled off to the side, panting. Tears streamed down her cheeks, but her eyes were wild, the blue turned violet.

His cock stayed hard. The size of it enraged me, the sheer audacity, the undeserved power, and Beth's seeming defeat. As if reacting to my rage, Dorothy went down on him with a grin of flashing teeth, jerking her head like a lion ripping meat off its prey. It flashed in my mind that this was one blow job without a hand forcing her head until she gagged. We'd all been there, done that.

When she sat up, the shaft of his penis was scratched in many places and cut in two crescent teeth marks. The organ shrivelled into innocence as we watched, cuts welling blood. Dorothy stared as if dazed. Blood ran thickly down his inner thigh onto the carpet. Someone screamed. Tom writhed with supernatural strength. Katie's hand came off his mouth, and he pushed the sock out with his tongue and wailed, whipping his torso from side to side, despite hands on his arms, pelvis, and legs. His shrieking was needles to the eardrums. I grabbed a yoga mat from behind me and dropped it over his face, leaning my full body weight into it, my elbows on either side of his head. The silence was a relief. His body jerked and rolled harmlessly beneath me with the others holding his arms and legs. Finally, he went limp.

'He's dead,' someone whispered.

It took a few seconds to sink in. This was murder, a human life destroyed; without reason, but not by accident. It was sick and horrible, and even if we could somehow keep from getting caught, the secret would become the focus of our lives.

The vision of a mother's grief replaced my anger. I sat back.

All hands let off. We fell away from him, into a wide circle. Tom coughed, popped up, threw the yoga mat across the room, and grabbed hold of his bleeding penis, to coddle it and shield it.

Nobody moved. We waited as he found his jeans and fumbled into them. Blood spots bloomed at his groin as he zipped. His eyes roamed from one of us to the other with the expression of a captive animal, unsure whether to bolt or creep slowly away.

He left shirtless, swiftly, carrying his shoes. Still nobody moved. Sweat cooled on my back and chills crawled up my neck. The incident would become public for its unusualness. Lawsuits, break-ups, and job loss were in our futures, possibly even arrests.

We sat as if frozen in the dusky room, our shoulders rounded, the shadows of evening deepening. It could have been a dream, except for a dark, gelatinous stain on the carpet and the forgotten tool belt near the wall. It was a nightmare. Gone were the days when he would have been too ashamed to admit being the victim of women. We would face our consequences like men.

✝

Hurting Hugh

Madeline de Chambrey

January 1
I'm going to hurt Hugh.

January 21
I'm stuck in a place of hate. Yet I'm reasonable enough to know that hurting Hugh is out of the question, because it would be wrong, right?

I spent the middle of the first decade of the new millennium meeting, loving and losing Hugh. Now I'm at a loss as to what to do.

It didn't take long to realise that I wasn't crazy enough to kill him, so I decided to kill myself instead. No doubt I subconsciously hoped I'd work myself up into enough of a frenzy to take Hugh down on my way out. A neat little murder/suicide.

I booked a week off work over the Christmas holidays. That'd be enough time to do one or both, since maybe once I'd gotten crazy enough to kill him I wouldn't want to kill myself. I'd be sorry if I didn't have any holiday time left come summer.

I wrote the notes, but that's it. I didn't really want to hurt myself or even call attention to myself. I just wanted to hurt Hugh, and I couldn't do that.

The way I see it, even if I could commit a murder, the only way I *would* is in a passion, know what I mean? Unpremeditated.

I watch TV; I know how smart those forensics guys are, how thoroughly the police investigate. I understand DNA and epithelials. I wouldn't get away with a *planned* murder, never mind an act of passion! They'd find me and lock me up. Since death is too good for Hugh and I'm too good for jail, that would hardly count as revenge.

I've tried to get better. I connected with my inner child. She tantrumed, furious. I sat in a still place and meditated – I saw the white light of my hate emanating from my body like an aura. My third eye is red with rage. I persevered, delving deep within, only to discover that the skin of hate I wear is stretched over bones that ache with it and organs that swell with it; my blood is thick with it, my heart beats to the rhythm of it. Hate, Hugh, Hate, Hugh, Hate, Hugh . . .

I decided to drink myself to death. It was tough but I did my best. I started with the hard stuff. It tasted vile and gave me head-aches. When I managed to choke down more than two glasses of wine I promptly fell asleep. Liqueurs had me bouncing off the walls from the sugar, happy as a girl, only to find myself in a state of near paralysis the next day.

So I decided to stop trying to drink myself to death and just get drunk enough to be charged with impaired driving. Surely that would get me the help I probably needed but was too proud to ask for.

I picked rye. That's what my dad drinks. I bought a twenty-six ouncer, not because it would take that much to get me high but because I thought it would look better to the arresting officer that way. More serious than a mickey, but still less expensive than that bottle with a handle like a jug.

Once I made it to my (brand new) Lexus in an inebriated state, I was scared to turn the ignition. I put the bottle beside me in the bag from the store. I'd had a couple of belts, though I'd up-chucked one so I suppose it doesn't count. This was before I stumbled to my car, of course. I'd hoped to be spotted by a neighbour and arrested just for having the key in the ignition but I was alone in the lot. It just seemed so stupid. Why would *anyone* be so dumb as to drink and drive? Unless...

Unless she plans to career around Ottawa until she spots her ex and runs him down!

My fingers flew to the key. The engine roared to life. Two thousand pounds of steel at my command. Say it loud, girl. 'I'm gonna hurt you, Hugh!'

I backed out, gunning the gas, cranking the wheel too hard and crushing the right headlight of my brand-new bright red Lexus against the rear pole of my parking spot.

My head snapped back against the seat, like a splash of cold water in my face. In minutes the car was parked in its spot; the bottle was in the garbage and I was on my way up to my apartment to sleep it off.

That was last night. This morning I woke up with a pounding headache; the rhythm of revenge is bashing my brains from the inside out. I swear my skull is dented. I'm out of ideas. My problem is that I'm *ethical*. (Hugh was an ethics professor.)

Once I've had a couple of cups of coffee I'll explain what happened. I'll start at the beginning. Perhaps journaling will be my healing path. All I want to do is reignite the tiny blue pilot light of my soul, that little flicker of hope that never ever entirely died until I met Hugh.

February 1
Obviously it's taken a couple of weeks for me to get back to this. I work (computer analyst, stats, Govt of Canada) and see family and friends so I'm kept busy putting on a brave face for the world. I'm sleeping less, now, and not drinking at all. I thought I'd look at the unfortunate and expensive 'accident' with my Lexus as an opportunity. I'm going to have it painted cerulean blue when I have the bodywork done, and that isn't a colour that's easy to find, so that's kept me busy, too. Also, although I don't mind

rehashing my past, I'm reluctant to write it all down.

Maybe that's because once it's captured on paper I won't have to delve so deep into my psyche to make sure I get every bit of it. There's a perverse enjoyment to that. I imagine it's the way a bulimic feels when she just lets go and digs into a carton of ice cream. She wants it all. Of course she gets to throw it all up again. Maybe I can compare writing it down to throwing it up. Spewing Hugh. Now, *that* makes perfect sense.

I guess I should say that before I failed miserably at DUI but after the non-suicide attempt, I tried to force myself into a full-blown nervous breakdown. I'd started seeing an eager young female psychologist who was my unwitting assistant, but it failed to take. I'm from strong stock, prairie people. We don't fall apart over anything so silly as a failed romance.

Even so, I stood on the street corner for the longest time, willing my synapses to snap. It didn't work. Now I'm stuck with the silly psychologist and no nervous breakdown. Oh yes, I'm also (patiently) waiting my turn to meet some spiritual adviser who's done wonders, apparently, for a ditzy friend of mine. All this in the interest of full disclosure.

I met Hugh through an online dating site, at the start of the new year. There's no shame in online hook-ups, not any more. I was between dating experiences, by which I mean I'd just finished doing the speed dating thing and the singles dinner and dance scene. Before that I did the meeting guys socially or at work thing.

Hugh and I 'connected' right from the start. While I absolutely believe that it's what's inside that counts, I know myself well enough to know that my man must be taller than me. I'm five ten. I've tried short men; not to be mean but, if that were all I wanted, a Pokemon would do just fine. No, he must be taller than me and no more than twenty pounds overweight. Again, this is from experience. I exercise and keep fit and while I know I can't expect much from a man, I do expect him to have enough pride to stay healthy.

Also, he must be employed and living on his own. Oh yeah, of course he must be single but let's face it, 'single' in the dating service lingo means 'available today'.

Hugh met my criteria and I guess I met his too, so he sent me a private message, calling me 'Milady' and himself 'Sir Ethicksprof'. The medieval times thing was hokey but I was in the mood for something more than, 'What're your measurements?' so I went along, playing the fair lady to his chivalrous knight while not for an instant suggesting I was a real damsel in distress.

Once I got his real name I googled him while we were still private-messaging online. He really was an ethics professor! Right here at Charterhouse University!

I was impressed. I like a guy with a mind, since most of them have shit for brains. Besides, professors make decent money. I typed, 'tenure?' He typed back 'track'. Just as well, that probably meant he really was thirty-three to my twenty-nine.

'Meet me?' he typed.

'Why not?' I replied.

February 13

This 'journaling' is proving therapeutic. Of course I go to work every day, but I always have. I'm not new to relationships, or the inevitable end of them. The only time I took off work was the week when I was going to hurt Hugh/have a nervous breakdown/get arrested for drunk driving/kill myself (in no particular order). I'm more rational now. I've even tended to a few overdue chores. Like picking up my dry cleaning and trying to get my car booked for repairs and that paint job. I smashed in the right front pretty bad. I'm having a hard time finding cerulean blue but I'm definitely going to wait for it. A love of aesthetics, sometimes, is the only thing that keeps me going.

Some things are so damn beautiful you have to be happy just to see them. Like Northern Lights. Or a train crossing in the rain, with the bright beam of the engine lighting up the rain like a spotlight, and the red lights of the crossing bars flashing and the blaring whistle of the train competing with the clanging of the crossing bells. It's surreal. How about picnicking on a glacier? Much too good to miss, and something I haven't done yet.

Before I get into meeting Hugh, let me just say that I think it's particularly detestable to be something that suggests intelligence, like an ethics professor, and be a real bastard. I'd already tried dumb guys, reasoning that it's better if a guy is too stupid to be nice than too smart to be nice, and that hadn't worked out. I was back to looking for a smart one who might be nice.

When I arrived, the guy at the bar that I hoped would be Hugh *was* Hugh. Phew! So I guess my heart leapt a little, right away. We'd seen photos of each other online but you can't expect to meet in the flesh what you saw in an online pic. An extraordinary number of guys think if they can just get you in person you might be so taken with their personalities (i.e. pity them) that you'll throw them a (mercy) fuck. I'd had my last mercy fuck in the previous millennium, thanks very much.

He grinned when he saw me, so I guessed he liked what he saw, too. Yeah. It sucks so bad when you meet and instantly know it's going nowhere. I usually try to let the guy off easy with twenty minutes conversation before extricating myself. Of course, when it's the other way around the guy can be brutal. One said, 'Lose ten pounds and call me.' This was right after Thanksgiving. I always lose ten pounds in the spring. That guy vamoosed without ordering a drink and left me to pay for mine. Swine.

Hugh had a guileless smile and again, though I'm no fool, it worked. Deep dimples, big blue eyes set wide apart – these are universally attractive traits. If anything, he was too cute to be handsome.

I was all dolled up in a casual way so it wouldn't look like I'd put a lot of thought into my outfit, which was new. I'd chosen my lipstick, mascara and blush out of my forty pounds of natural-look makeup.

I'm attractive (grey eyes, fair skin, sucky-face lips) and, since the 'Lose Ten Pounds Guy', slim no matter what the season. I'd learned that a woman has to keep in shape at all times. It's a jungle out there and I'm Mrs Livingstone, I presume. I wore contacts to hide the fact that my eyesight isn't perfect, and a push-up bra to emphasize my modest assets.

Hugh was cute, as I said, and maybe ten or so pounds heavy. He was in jeans, but I expected that. We made small talk and he was good at it, better than me. (I used to be shy until I realised that shy girls attract psychos.)

First we'd discussed meeting for coffee but we'd finally settled on one drink after work. After all the homeless guys I'd encountered, 'after work' was appealing.

We'd already talked on the phone, so his husky voice was no surprise. I'd asked where his family lived, then googled his folks while we talked. They were small town, and, since he said he'd gone to Upper Canada College, probably wealthy. All small town people end up in the newspaper at one time or another. I found a couple of pics, one taken at an exhibit of taxidermy in a mall and a second from when his mom hosted the euchre finals after the town hall was damaged by lightning.

It's not like I believed that decent parents begat decent sons. It's just that the opposite, a guy with a distant mom, is often a woman-hater. I couldn't tell if the lady smiling amidst the animals loved her son or not but she had a pleasant face. She *seemed* nice.

The main reason I'd asked about his parentage was because one of my homeless boyfriends had been born of mentally challenged parents. His mentally-challenged brother had a mentally-challenged girlfriend, who had a couple of kids who were, at the very least, delayed. They were on the mentally-challenged spectrum.

I ended up letting that poor schmuck sleep on my couch a couple of times. There were a few occasions when he just couldn't face going home, and after just one dinner over there I understood why.

It's not that I necessarily want to have children; I've barely considered it. Maybe my brooding instinct will kick in and maybe it won't. But I'd like to be open to the possibility and with that guy, only an idiot would consider bearing his offspring.

Suffice to say that I was cheered by the photos of Hugh's parents smiling out from the online pages of the *Dinkytown News*, or whatever. They looked normal.

I liked that introductory drink at the bar. We'd set the customary thirty minutes maximum rule but an hour passed while we nursed our drinks and talked.

Lucky for me, I'd made sure to have plans that evening so we really did have to cut it short. Even though I knew better than to let it happen, a great guy could still talk me into dinner if I didn't have plans so I always made sure to. I met my friends for a movie and I got to drift back and forth, from the frothy fable on the screen to the one that wafted through my mind.

I was long past mentally marrying my dates. Nothing good comes of that. I just hoped for something fun and sexy to happen. I hoped for an adventure that would be terrific, but not so terrific as to leave me devastated when it ended, which at the beginning of my relationships I was still able to perceive as likely. I start out expecting it to end but as we move along, from first meeting to first date and first kiss, I forget about the ending part and embark on the adventure. I still don't see what's so terribly wrong about that, so *misguided*, but I accept that it is.

Our first date was simple. Thai food at a little place in the Market (no allergies or alcoholism for either of us, and a shared love of coriander), followed by a walk by the Rideau Canal at sunset. We had to scurry because it was cold, but the sky was clear and there were lots of stars up above and a few skaters, like animated Christmas decorations, whirling on the blue and white ice of the canal below.

We snuggled on a wooden bench, equidistant between a streetlight and the street. The first kiss made me swoon. The ol' mojo kicked into gear. There's nothing more hopeful than desire, is there? It seems so little to ask, that two people might create joy together. But ultimately it's a wasted wish.

I loved sex. At almost thirty I knew what worked for me and how to get it and I sure knew how to give it back. I was willing to experiment, sanely and consensually, of course. That night, I just wanted to fall into kissing Hugh and see where it went. But I couldn't afford such sloppiness.

You can't let him think you're a slut and you can't let him think you're leading him on and you can't let him think you're a prude. It all has to do with timing and an awareness of the peculiarities of the man you're with. Information that you just don't have by the end of the first date.

Still, it was so terrific we kissed until our butts were frozen and it wasn't dusk any more, it was night. He tugged off a leather glove with his teeth and slipped his hand inside my many layers of clothing and cupped my breast. I rubbed his hard-on through his pants. He seemed satisfied with his handful and I was perfectly content with mine. Now I knew he could get it up and that he had decent-sized equipment. That was enough information for one evening so, reluctantly, I admit, I insisted it was time to go. At the door to my building we kissed some more. We could see our breath rising like steam from two kettles on the boil. It was so great I hated to leave him there, alone, but I did. I *always* try to do the thing I will least regret if it turns out later to have been a mistake. Know what I mean?

Before bed, I indulged in a little creamy milk chocolate and a lot of dreamy anticipation. I was really eager to go to the next level. I didn't care about the eventual ending, any more. I just wanted the adventure.

Enough of that. Remembering how able I was to believe in the possibility of love, not so very long ago, makes me sad. Even remembering how, as recently as this time *last year*, I believed I could be transported by sex, that sex was an adventure and not a catastrophic event, makes me feel like someone who used to live somewhere else, like Narnia, but now just lives in Plainville with the other suckers.

By the way, I've decided to go back to my natural hair colour, brunette, so I'm seeing a stylist this afternoon. It's not that I think being more honest with the world will make me happier or healthier, because I think I've always been plenty honest. Maybe I played the game of love, but I never made anything up. There's no crime in trying not to be moody or needy or boring when you're with a man you like. Is there? It isn't wrong to put your best foot forward, as long as it's your own foot. That's what I think, or thought. Now I don't know what to think. Well, now I think it's all shit on a stick.

March 21

Only a week to go until I meet with the spiritual adviser! I hope to be able to drum up some passion for God.

After that first date we enjoyed each other's company a little longer and then we had sex. It was at my place and it was pretty good, though maybe not as good as I'd thought it might be. I chalked it up to first-time nervousness on both our parts. He praised me a lot, especially my 'talented tongue'. It didn't seem like he was trying to make a point, though, like, 'How many guys have you *been* with, anyway?' so I just shrugged and grinned.

I'm gorgeous when I'm freshly fucked (aren't we all?) and I'm usually pretty sure of myself in bed so I tend to get a lot of post-coital compliments. This was no exception. Since I'm shy at heart the process of returning to my skin, so to speak, after orgasm is a quiet time for me. That's the only reason I didn't respond in kind. Oh, I complimented him, to do otherwise would have been rude, but maybe I didn't say enough or something. Hey! I know! Maybe he was really a miserable lying woman-hating sicko with no self-esteem! Anyway after I said, 'You're a great fuck, too' or whatever, he said, 'Don't get used to it, babe.'

Now that's a buzz kill. Here I am basking in the afterglow and he calls me needy. When he saw how shocked I was he laughed and said, 'I'm an idiot.' (He thought it was funny to call himself stupid because he was a professor so, obviously, he wasn't stupid, although he never talked about his work. Sometimes I still can't believe the whole 'professor' thing wasn't a big lie, but it wasn't, so I guess it just goes to show that even Institutions of Learning can make big mistakes.) He kissed me and left pretty quickly, but not as quickly as my mind filed that little tidbit away under 'D for denial'. One doesn't dump a guy over one little buzz kill, does one?

I feel a huge hate-on surging up from the very area where my lust used to live. Since I'm not trying to have a nervous breakdown anymore, I'm going to take a few minutes to compose myself before I head over to my latest appointment at the salon. I like the new cut but the colour still isn't right. I'm thinking reddish highlights. It's great not to be a blonde anymore; I already feel smarter.

If I had time I might mention all the other things I've changed at the behest of my friends and my silly psychologist. They think I'm coming along well. I do too, except when I think of what Hugh did. Then I despair. Blonde or brunette, wavy or straight, who am I kidding? Love is dead. Magic is for children.

Oops, did I let slip the ultimate four-letter word, love? There's no way I'm going there today. I should get moving anyway. It's snowing outside and I still have only one headlight working, so I like to give myself plenty of time to get places. I don't see as well as I used to at night. Like Hugh, I seem to be suffering from poor night vision. He was so vain he didn't wear glasses at all; he just travelled by taxi. I'm wearing glasses now. Contacts are for women who want to make contact. I don't.

March 30
This time last year Hugh and I were in love. How did that

happen? You can be sure, in this case, that it wasn't me who said it first because I never do. This is not a guideline for me; it's a rule. Whatever happens because 'love' has been introduced to the equation can never be pinned on me. I don't even care, frankly, if the declaration 'I love you' is ever made. Maybe because my reaction to it is so strong it's scary – it's visceral. My gut relaxes. He loves me! My throat opens. I can breath deeper. My smile widens. I loved being in love. Who doesn't?

With Hugh, I couldn't have been more in the moment if I'd known that it was the last time I'd love. I couldn't have been less judgemental if I'd been warned that it was my last chance. I was the best I've ever been, but it just wasn't good enough.

He used his air miles to fly my dad to town over Easter, which was genuinely sweet of him. We took a road trip into small-town Ontario and I met those friendly-looking folks in the newspaper pictures, and they really were friendly. He was cute and funny, but I've said that already. I know, Ted Bundy is cute. Is he funny though?

Intelligence and a sense of humour mean absolutely nothing. I see that now. Good looks, of course, I've known for a long time only mean he's probably arrogant and used to getting what he wants from women. A man who says he's a truthful man is usually a big fat liar. I get that now, too. I get all of it, now. That's why the little blue pilot light of hope is gone. But then I remember the glacier picnic, the train in the rain. I don't have to be able to trust and love in order to live; I just won't be a complete woman any more. But I'll be alive and I'll be much, much safer.

I'm seeing the silly psychologist this afternoon, for what is going to be our last session. If she could prescribe drugs I might be tempted to stick around, but all she does is say, 'I know what you mean,' and then relate tales from her own life. Please. Anyway, with my new *look* masquerading as my new *outlook*, I've convinced her I'm fine. Which I am. I'm fine.

April 10

Today I started a belly dancing class with my friend Tina. Afterwards we had a drink and agreed that the class will be even more fun once we get big scarves with jingly coins attached. I think I'll go for bright blue, the same colour my car is going to be, someday. The guys at the shop talked me into taking the Lexus in for repairs even though my custom colour hasn't come in. I promised I would but then I totally forgot. I think that kind of carelessness might be a good sign. It made me feel normal to have forgotten something.

It was late when I started driving home, but I took the longer route, okay the *Canal route*, anyway. Why be coy? It's not like I'm trying to impress anyone here. The thing is, if I take the route along the Rideau Canal, I can just see, from the road, the bench where Hugh and I sat and warmed our hands on each other's private parts. Tonight, new foliage cast strange shadows on the lamp-lit walkway. Spring is here. I've made it through my first winter without him. How life does march on! A little gang of guys straggled out of the bush. I sped away.

Holding my tears in until I'd parked the car took all my strength. In the elevator I chanted, 'You can do it,' to keep from screaming. I made it inside the apartment just as the force of my roiling, pent-up pain drove me to my knees. There's no hope, no hope. That's my real mantra. I shall never recover. I'm the one thing a woman can never afford to be – bitter.

I made it to my bed, past the French doors that lead to my balcony, over which I could leap to my death, which isn't something I'm considering, any more. What if, though, I stood on that balcony and cried out, 'What are we going to do?' How long would it be before another woman's plaintive wail joined mine, and then another, and another, until we howled like a pack of dying she-wolves, 'What are we going to dooooOOooooo?' Except they won't join in; they can't afford to be tarred with my bitter black brush.

They'll continue throwing happy little wedding showers for each other, toasting a bride whose groom is, at the very moment she celebrates her upcoming nuptials with giggles and gifts of lacy lingerie, banging a whore.

We keep the secret because only the luckiest of us, now, will ever be in the enviable position of that betrayed bride. Most of us will be used and discarded a thousand times more and never make it down the aisle. We didn't know, when we didn't marry our high school sweethearts, that we were condemning ourselves to lives of desperation. We didn't know we'd stepped up to the post, not only with the other women in our class but with every woman on the planet. In this race, only fillies and thoroughbreds win. I hate you, Hugh, I hate your reeking guts.

I think I hate my spiritual adviser's reeking guts, too. I think she's a dyke in guru's clothing, looking to score. I don't think I'm going to see her again. I've no passion for God. God is dead. My passion is for vengeance.

I really think I'm dying. Hugh has dealt me a mortal blow.

May 9

So, Moira, you would be saying if my name was Moira, what did he do to break your heart with such finality that your pilot light went out and you are as oft as not to be found in the foetal position on the floor? This cute ethics professor, this Hugh of whom you speak—

Hugh? Well, Hugh and I had progressed from, 'Don't get used to it,' to 'Love you, hon,' which had its own kind of, albeit faintly embarrassing, charm. I swear there were times when I felt like *he* was crowding *me*, but I dealt with it like a grown-up by getting together with my girlfriends or putting in extra hours at work.

Once we got our rhythms in sync, the sex was always stupendous. I'd long since come to terms with the fact that, though a man might live for great sex, it's not enough to keep him. Go figure. But with Hugh, I really felt like we were on a roll.

Sometimes it was passionate and sometimes it was romantic and a few times it was mind-blowing and a few times it was kinky. The make-up sex was good but not our best, which is a positive sign, I figured. I mean, you don't want to be arguing just so you can have good sex. You want that animal magnetism that's essential to a relationship if it's going to last for any length of time. Whatever emotion it is, whether irritation or insecurity or adoration or lust, it's imperative that it can be vanquished with a good, solid toss in the hay. Afterwards you *must* be able to meet each other's eyes with pride in the quality of your lovemaking. Hugh and I had that, right to the end. Sometimes that's what hurts the most.

He turned out to be a pretty effusive guy once he got going. He was always saying stuff like, 'My students wonder what's come over me,' and, 'You bring a sparkle to my eyes,' which I can now see were compliments to me that somehow managed to put him in the spotlight. But his eyes really did sparkle. He'd lost the extra weight by this time and I could well imagine his students, especially the female ones, wondering what had come over him.

Okay so what happened, Gertrude? How'd you let this one get away, Getaway Gertie? PMS? Did you froth at the mouth right in front of him? Maybe you started whining for a baby? Is that it? Or did he catch you spitting out his semen? Did he see the look of disgust on your face when you first saw the skid mark on your white cotton sheet that proudly proclaims, 'A *man* was here?' Maybe you complained about his snoring, or took offence at his humour? Was your protest strident when he said, 'Hey, babe, I figure now that we're an item I'm halfway to a *ménage à trois*'?

Au contraire! I laughed. I thought that was funny. I still do! I didn't *do* anything, I swear. Maybe later I'll tell you what happened, but only if you *promise* not to see me as a victim.

May 30
Cerulean, the exact shade of blue I want my car painted, has

finally come into the repair shop. I've booked the Lexus in for repairs. I'm lucky to have gotten away with having only one headlight for so long, especially with all the night driving I do.

Now that spring has hit my spirit seems lighter. I've lost a few pounds. I'm one of the lucky ones, by which I mean that heartbreak doesn't ignite my appetite, it destroys it. I bet you, I bet Hugh, wouldn't recognise me as the same woman who mourned so raggedly only a few months ago.

(Of course, after spring comes summer and last summer was the best ever. Hugh and I shared a love of camping and swimming and sailing. Oh how we enjoyed the great outdoors!)

I'm getting out on my own more and staying out longer, though I still cruise by the Canal from time to time, straining to catch a glimpse of 'our bench'. Sometimes I see people sitting on it, or lingering nearby. That always gives me a sick thrill.

Here we go, girlfriend: I trace the beginning of the end back to my gentle insistence that Hugh get in shape. This was well into the third month of our relationship, and only after he'd complained that the meals I served weren't man-sized. He took up jogging.

As I've said, the results were gratifying. The thing was, he jogged at night. In truth, he never did sleep well at my place. I didn't see that as a sign of anything much, although now I see it as a sign of guilt. He said he preferred to be at home. His place was okay, a rental downtown, a little seedy but it could be construed as 'atmospheric'. Okay, so after we'd had sex, sometimes after lots of canoodling and sometimes right afterwards, Hugh would jog home. A sane woman can live with that. I saw it as a consequence of my request that he shape up. I slept better without the snoring, anyway. All was well, or so I thought. Until...

It was a Saturday afternoon in late November last year. Hugh came over. He clutched a little paper pharmacy bag. I assumed it contained condoms. (Even though, from time to time, he'd tried to take a ride bareback, so far I hadn't let it happen. My STD baseline, I hasten to add, was at zero when I met Hugh.) He looked stricken. I thought someone must've died, which was pretty close to the truth. The whole 'story of Hugh' had died. The guy before me was merely his closest living relation, come to tell me the bad news.

'Hon,' he said, 'I've given you crabs.'

If you've ever had crabs you know that the moment you're told is the moment you know it's true. There's no chance of denial. The memory of that sudden, fierce little itch you so innocently scratched seconds ago rears up in your mind, screeching the truth. Below, there is the unmistakable sensation of a thousand, nay a *million*, mini-crustacean legs skittering through the forest of your pubic hair.

'How?' Stupid, I know, but we'd agreed to be monogamous and use condoms. That was our sexual arrangement, made necessary not so much by a desperate need for commitment as by the constraints of present-day society. Right?

'Not the way you think.' My mind was a blank. That didn't compute. He handed me the bag. 'Everything you need is in here.'

'Thank you.'

'I wasn't with another woman. I swear.' (Like I should believe anything that comes out of his filthy mouth?) 'It's just that sometimes I jog by the canal and jerk off with the guys.'

'Is this supposed to make me feel better?' I laughed. Actually it was more like a bark.

'There's stuff you don't know about me . . .'

'That's become obvious, Perfesser.'

'Don't throw *that* in my face, okay?'

He was actually getting testy. What had he imagined, that I'd weep for joy when I discovered that he'd only been unfaithful to me with a gang of gay hooligans, circle jerking by the Rideau Canal?

'Hugh.' His name dropped from my lips. I started bawling. He did, too.

Once there was a time when the tears of men could move me. That time shuddered to an end during the few minutes that Hugh and I shared our pain. He kept saying he was sorry and I just kept saying his name, in a long drawn out moan of despair.

He left, promising to call.

I set to the task of delousing my home and myself.

He didn't call, of course. When I called him, days later, he sounded much better. By then I'd discovered that, like all horrible human behaviours that one wouldn't imagine in one's worst nightmares, this behaviour had a name. It seems Hugh had been on the 'down low'.

If the fact that it was a phenomenon was supposed to make me feel better, it failed. I felt like an ignoramus. My willing suspension of disbelief, my sense of magic and romance and possibility, all of it died. Hope expired. I shed my last skin as a woman and emerged hissing.

I kept my voice steady on the phone. I said I had a few questions. He said, 'Sure, fire away,' but *his* voice was already unsteady.

'How do you get crabs from a circle jerk?' I asked.

'Wow. Brutally frank there.'

I bit my tongue to keep all eight searing retorts that leapt to my lips from escaping. I waited in silence.

'You're making me talk about stuff I'd rather forget,' he finally said.

'Sssorry,' I was already beginning to hiss.

'Sometimes we'd grab each others' dicks and the last time I went, you know, when I was jogging, some guy wanted to give me a blow job. I think the crabs must've jumped out of his hair or off his hand. I didn't let him, though. Blow me.'

'Oh.'

'It's not like I'm gay,' he said. An Upper Canada College whine had begun to inflect his speech.

'Perish the thought.' I started laughing. It still didn't make sense but I couldn't stand listening to him. It didn't really matter, anyway, as long as crabs were the only things that had leapt from one cocksucker to another. 'Is there anything else I should know?'

'You should be grateful. I didn't cheat on you with a woman and, and . . .'

'And what?'

'And I was careful not to give you herpes.'

'You have herpes?' It sounded more like, 'You have herpeeeezzzzzzzzzzzzzz?'

'I told you about it, before we ever even kissed.'

'No you didn't.'

'Did so.'

'Did not.' (He didn't.)

'Yes I did.' Then he said it. The line that broke my heart. 'It's not my fault if *you weren't paying attention.*' (The italics are mine.)

'Oh, but I was,' I wanted to say. 'I was there for all of it, Hugh. Where were you?'

'Look, can I go now?' He was openly whining now. I guess he had things to do and all that, no more time to spend talking to the ol' ex.

'I hate you, Hugh.'

'Join the club.'

'You're a real prick.'

'Thank you.'

'Fuck you.'

'Fuck you, too.' He hung up then, but I was still on the line.

'I'm going to hurt you, Hugh,' I said to the dial tone.

June 7

I never saw Hugh again. Not until a few hours ago, that is.

I'd spent the evening with the graduates of my belly dancing class. We went to a Greek restaurant and wiggled and threw plates. It was fun.

Once again it was late, almost midnight, by the time I decided to head home. It's the weekend and I'm young and single so why the hell not? A guy was even hitting on me. He was young and cute so it was flattering at first, in a vaguely cougarish way, but after awhile he was sort of a pest. I advised him that, 'No one messes with my baseline,' but he kept on, so finally I said, 'I don't like men very much.' That shut him up! It was good for a laugh.

I almost didn't take the Canal route because it was so late. My car was already overdue at the garage, and now I'd lost the opportunity to drop it off at the lot and walk home. Even in Ottawa I didn't think I'd enjoy walking alone in the dark, especially on a rainy night like this.

It was the rain that sealed the deal. Any kind of weather, taken to the extreme, can be surreal but rain doesn't even have to be extreme to be so. It's incredibly destructive, in one way, and restorative, in another. It just depends on the degree.

So, even though I only had one headlight and it was almost midnight I drove home along the Canal route in the rain. Ever since I'd seen that group of guys come out of the bush, I'd been dead sure that if I drove by 'our' bench enough times, sooner or later I'd see Hugh among the satyrs emerging from a fresh frolic in the grass. If he'd been telling the truth, that is.

Then it happened. Just like that.

Rain poured down my windshield. I cruised, glancing out my window at the bushes from time to time, straining a little to see through the windshield the rest of the time. My one headlight was on.

A 'jogger' jumped right in front of my car. It was Hugh. It looked like he tried to step back but he slipped on wet grass and got nowhere. He put his hands up, a look of horror on his face.

I went to crank my steering wheel to the left but then I didn't. I cranked her to the right and took the bastard out. I hurt him, just like I always wanted to! He bounced off my bumper and up in the air in a little arc and then landed, thrump, across my windshield, his face plastered against the glass. My windshield wipers batted at his head. I hit the kerb and up he went again. Bye, Hugh! This time he didn't land on my car. Maybe he didn't land at all. Maybe I bounced Hugh all the way to hell.

Weird, eh? How it all came together? Almost as if I'd planned it? When all I did was plan to get well. Here's the thing. I have this sure sense that I might be better at the game of love, now that I've come up with a nice new rule all my own. Piss me off and you die!

I really hope I get away with it. I figure the odds are good. I don't even look like the same Dimwitted Dora who fell in love with Down Low Hugh. That's what flashed through my mind in that instant when I had to decide, left or right, right or wrong. But it was the rain that really tipped the balance. I knew he probably couldn't tell who was behind the wheel, not with his poor night vision and all that rain streaming down the windshield. Plus, I knew the rain would wash away the gore so I wouldn't have to get my hands dirty hurting Hugh.

Afterwards, I parked the car at the repair shop and walked home after all. I got soaked but no one saw me. There was this wonderful, light, empty space in the place where my hate for Hugh used to live. It's still there, like a soufflé replacing a pound cake, nothing I'd want to throw up. I'm thinking I might drive my freshly painted car all the way to Lake Louise and find a glacier to picnic on. Although if I want to do that I'd better move quick!

In just a few more months I'll have my baseline back, right smack dab at zero. Maybe that bastard Hugh didn't give me anything worse than a case of crabs, after all. I sure hope so.

†

Dolls, Revenge, Dolls Again

Chris Dunning

Tomlin was an evil toy, according to Mrs Wilson's class of infants. His eyes seemed to follow you everywhere and he was always grinning when they peeked through the window into the toy cupboard.

They had to call Jessica's mummy one day because she was crying so much. She'd gone to find Brussels the Bear; her hands got busy sorting though the jumble of soft animals until she felt Brussels' silky ear. She stood up and saw that Tomlin was right next to her head, grinning like he was about to bite.

Jessica said she'd never go near the cupboard again, in fact, she sat on the opposite side of the room to prove her point. Her mum and Mrs Wilson only rolled their eyes, but the children were very worried.

The toy cupboard was avoided. The kids started drawing more pictures because the crayons and felt tips never left the teacher's desk.

Jessica stared at a blue colouring pencil; the lead had fallen out of the centre. She pouted her bottom lip as she shaded the sky purple.

The next day during lunch Jessica and four others went into the toy cupboard and pulled Tomlin out of it. They held him with one hand each; some were too afraid to look at him. He was thrown across the room, his head thudded against the blackboard.

Feet battered him, stomped him and squashed his round head flat against the floor. He was put in the sink and green paint dripped onto his face. They did their best to colour over his eyes. One boy grew excited, '*I hate you, I hate you!*' he screamed. The rest told him to be quiet. Each child took a pair of scissors, they snipped at his arm but it just bent and sprung back. They stabbed him instead. Yellow stuffing rained like snow over their heads and lined the floor.

'We've got to clear this up.'

They gathered up the stuffing and threw it in the bin. Tomlin dropped in afterwards and was buried with sheets and sheets of newspaper.

As the children left, inside the cupboard Dolly was being held back by a crowd of toys. She was hysterical.

Dolly pushed the bin but it wouldn't budge, 'Come on, everyone. I can't move this on my own.'

A few toys lingered behind the cupboard door, some refused to move off their shelves. Dolly made a few more futile attempts to knock over the bin. 'Why aren't you helping?' There was an almighty sigh, then a sound of creaking wood. The rocking horse with the broken mouth threw himself forward and out of the cupboard. His legs were still attached to the castors which had been nailed to his feet when he was one day old. He lurched sideways with such force he nearly toppled. As he shuffled across the classroom Dolly was awestruck. She'd never seen him move.

'Mmmvvvvv,' the horse growled. Dolly stepped to one side. The horse rocked back and swung forward, ramming the bin with his mouthless wooden head. The bin dropped and spread sheets of newspaper across the floor. Dolly rushed in and started digging with her hands.

She pulled Tomlin out, the point of the scissors through his head dragging along the floor.

For the rest of the day Dolly hid Tomlin underneath a blanket in the toy cupboard. The teacher picked up the bin and shouted at the class for it being overturned. When the kids had left the school Dolly rested Tomlin's deflated body on the floor.

'Sweetie, I don't know if you can hear me, but I'm just going to take the scissors out. I'll be as gentle as I can.'

Tomlin didn't answer. Dolly linked her arm through the finger hole and eased the scissors away from him. Tomlin's arms jolted. He made a tiny squeal.

'It's okay, honey, it's okay.' The scissors clattered on the floor, then Dolly held him. 'It's okay, we've done the hard part.'

As she gently washed the paint off his eyes she remembered the first time they met.

The door of the cupboard opened, and a bag of toys were thrown in. Tomlin hit the shelf behind her and landed on her head.

'Excuse *me*,' Dolly said.

'Sorry, total accident,' Tomlin stood up and looked at her plastic legs. 'It was good luck landing on you though.'

'Hardly.' She climbed to the shelf above, and neatened her hair so it was back behind her shoulders.

The next day she debated what shoes to finish her outfit off with: pink or purple. Pink looked prettier, but purple wouldn't get as dirty if she was dropped on the floor.

'The pink looks SOOOO much better,' Tomlin was standing behind her. He chuckled.

'Someone's jealous they don't have any different clothes.'

Tomlin looked down at his tuxedo. 'Being sewn into this is all right – stops me from losing anything.'

Dolly remembered the ball gown she used to have.

'You know the funny thing about us?' He gestured to the room of toys.

'Not interested in anything you have to say.'

'The funny thing about us is we'd be human if we had one thing.'

Dolly glanced away from her shoes. 'What?'

'They make us look like them, give us clothes so that we're as beautiful and pedantic as they are, they build us little hospitals and fire stations. But they won't give us death. Can't or don't want to.'

Dolly was starting to see his perfect circular pupils as the water dissolved the thick paint. 'Can you hear me?'

'Yes...'

'Are you okay?'

'Can't feel anything.'

Dolly looked down at his flat body. 'I was thinking about re-stuffing you, but didn't want to put you through any more tonight.'

There was no response.

'Tomlin?' She touched his chest, 'Tomlin...'

'Sorry. I keep forgetting where I am.'

'You're in my arms.' She bent down and kissed his head.

'I sometimes wish that there was an end...'

Dolly could feel him shaking.

'...Forever scares me. I saw a rubbish tip once, it was full of headless Barbies trying to climb out.'

'It's okay. As long as you've got me I'll fix you.'

There was no response.

'Tomlin?'

He was silent. She got up and started looking for sewing needles.

The toy cupboard looked different. The rocking horse facing the opposite direction made it unfamiliar.

'Horse,' Dolly tapped him on the bum, 'thank you so much for your help earlier, but I need to ask another favour. Tomlin's stuffing is still in the bin. I didn't think about taking it out at the time. My brain was a total wreck.'

'Srrryyyy...' The horse's deep rasp echoed through the cupboard. 'Agggnnny.'

★

'Are you angry with me?' Tomlin climbed to the top shelf.

'Yes! You're so cruel. This is what I do: dress up and look pretty. You don't have to come and upset me.'

'Why did I upset you?'

'I hate thinking about things like that, there's nothing I can do about it, nothing I can change, I don't want to think about life later on.'

'It's not so bad for us, I've seen dolls made of china, locked inside glass cases.' Tomlin grabbed her hand. 'At least there's things we can do.'

Dolly tore up a pile of newspaper, she ripped it in half and built it up around her feet. She pushed handfuls of it inside Tomlin's chest. Thankfully he was still sleeping. After awhile he was as fat as he used to be although, to Dolly, he didn't feel as soft any more.

'Come on, live a bit.' Tomlin sat in a red car in front of Dolly. His legs were big enough to cover both the passenger and driver's seat.

'Don't crash.'

'I won't.'

'Don't. Crash.'

'I won't.'

She held out her hand. He took it and she climbed onto his knee.

They ducked as the car sped under the table. They cleared the doorway and their speed multiplied. The wind forced Dolly's head back; she wrapped her arms around Tomlin. He gripped her thigh and drove faster.

Red stitches now crossed Tomlin's chest. He made a crumpling noise as she dragged him back to the toy cupboard. 'I love you.' Dolly kissed him and slept.

Dreams, dreams, dreams... They'd lost every bit of their

glamour but she still dreamt about what she was made to do. Dolly put dinner on the table and waited for her husband to get home. She waited tentatively as he took the first bite. She cocked her head as he spoke about his day at work, and giggled at the part when the boss told him, 'One day you'll be doing my job, big guy.'

ARGGGHHHH GOD IT ITCHES SO MUCH, Tomlin's cry rang through her dream.

She woke up slowly. The dream faded out. Possible promotion. Keep up the good work. They'll talk on Monday. What's for dessert, hon?

Dolly looked around. Tomlin was gone. Red thread sat by a handful of newspaper. She opened the cupboard and ran. Piles of newspaper dotted the corridor. She heard Tomlin's agonised bawls come from the cellar. She dashed towards the stairs. The air became thicker the more steps she took. The glowing light astounded her. The door of the furnace was open. Tomlin's head rested on the coals. His eyes melted down his face.

'I can still save you,' she said, looking at his charred face. She could sew him a new body. She could do it.

'Please. Don't,' a voice came from the furnace. 'I love you.'

Dolly picked up the poker in both hands. She could barely carry it. She pushed his head down with the tip. His remains ignited. Dolly sat down, making sure every bit of him was gone.

Dolly lay underneath the bottom shelf. She heard Tomlin talking beside her but carried on looking at her little pink shoes; the radiators could sometimes sound like voices.

The next day Dolly sat on the middle shelf. She looked cheerful, pretty and inviting.

'Tea party!' Jessica shouted and started gathering guests. She smiled and stuffed Dolly under her arm.

Jessica sat everyone in place. Dolly slumped on her side and lay prone on the desk, hugging a pencil close to her chest.

'Oh, Dolly, sit properly, you're meant to be a lady,' Jessica giggled and picked her up, looking at her face to face. 'Now. If I put you down, are you going...'

Dolly shoved the pencil in her eye.

†

Wig

Tara Ison

The long black hairs on the white tile look like a child's wild scribbles, each strand a separate graphite scrawl. I think that I should sweep them up. Save them for something. Didn't women used to do that, save their hair combings? To make padded wiglets of their own hair, robust false curls? In high school we'd used those long black strands of her hair for dental floss after lunch. It was that strong. That healthy, that thick. She always had the prettier hair. A thick, glossy black, while I had to blow-dry and torture and gel for an angelic or Botticelli effect. I would've killed for her hair. I sat behind her in chemistry and made long tiny braids of it, like those bracelets of black elephant hair, like shiny jute. At the beach she'd coat her dark hair and skin with sunscreen, her melanin-rich, impervious skin, while pale blonde me slicked on the baby oil to get a glow going, heedless of burn or the later shredding I'd do. We took tennis lessons together, and I was the better player – I had to win no matter what, heaving, jolting off oily sweat with each lunge – but she enjoyed it more, was beautiful with it, queenlier, fat black ponytail swinging, moving serene as Greek or Egyptian royalty in the sun.

It should have been me.

'You don't have to do all that,' I hear her call after the toilet's second flush.

I should get her a glass of juice, maybe crackers, sometimes that helps. I'm desperate to do something for her.

'Shut up, please,' I yell back.

'I don't want you doing all that.'

'Remember my sixteenth birthday?' I yell. Me falling down in the cantina bathroom, her shoving fingers down my throat so I could vomit up the cheap, fruity tequila, her lifting my limp bangs from the bowl, her giving me cupped palmfuls of water, her wiping flecks from my mouth. I owe her. I rinse the basin again, wipe it with a fistful of tissue.

'Hey, it's what friends are for,' she calls. Weak.

'Exactly. I just wish your aim were better.'

I hear her try to laugh, and I marvel, again, at how she's bearing this. But the energy's got to give out soon.

The air in here is still rank, despite my double flushing and basin rinsing and healthy blast of pine. Despite the bathroom's cheery mess of little boys' bath toys, the husband's rosy *I love you* card masking-taped to the medicine cabinet. I examine my own healthy, guilty glow in the mirror. Twenty years' exposure, and my price is just a minor and epidermal leatheriness. My own hair is still a natural blonde, even at thirty-six. Just helped out a little. A few chemicals, and *voilà*, I'm still blonde as sixteen.

I evaluate my eyebrows; the one very dark brown hair beneath the right brow arch, the one that always grows in fast, is poking its way back. Her wild eyebrows will probably start slipping away now, too, bristly hair by hair by hair. I find some tweezers in the cabinet, pluck, and toss my tiny whisker in the sodden-tissue trash. I get down on my knees and pick up her thick long black hairs, hair by hair by hair, and bury them deep in the sodden-tissue trash so she doesn't have to see. She shouldn't have to face that, yet.

I look at my own fair face one last time in the mirror, next to the *I love you*. It really should have been me.

★

We go shopping for a wig. It's time, she'd said. I don't like scarves, I'm tired of scarves. They're too resigned. Come help me buy a wig.

I'm a little surprised by this; a wig seems, well, dishonest, and she's the most honest, artless person I know. No make-up or plucking. Those heavy black eyebrows, too thick and undefined. Not a woman to wax or bleach or shave anything, to moisturise or scent. Her husband impressed me on this. I'd watch him run an affectionate hand across her hirsute shin, playfully tweak her armpit's floss, lovingly tease her for the faint moustache dusk on her upper lip. She wound up winning a prince of a guy, sensitive, devoted, stroking, the kind who sticks it out. Maybe it's ironic, now that she's getting barer every day, the follicles giving up. Now that she's getting fairer, wispier, her skin going bruisable and fine. Soon she'll need to pencil in some brows if she wants them at all, but I imagine she won't even bother. I would've expected those straightforward scarves from her, maybe some baseball caps, honest and resigned. But she wants a wig, and of course I want her to have whatever she wants, whatever makes her feel better, and I want to be with her through all of it, it's what friends do, so we wait for a day her energy's up, and her husband is crazy busy at work and her boys are at school, and we go.

But we can't find the right one. We go from shop to shop to shop, from Hollywood to Pico Robertson to Encino, smiling at balding old ladies and transgendering people and other translucent-looking women in scarves. She's flagging but determined, and we learn a great deal about wigs. She immediately rejects synthetic hair for its artifice – I say nothing to what seems like a mild hypocrisy – and for its lesser durability, although an impassioned sales guy in an upscale West Hollywood boutique assures us a good quality synthetic can last two years with the right care. This moot, insensitive question of *durability* hangs in the air a moment, and I say nothing to that, either, but agree she should go for human. We learn there are four basic kinds of human hair – Chinese, Indian, Indonesian, and Caucasian – and we learn that Indian and Chinese hair, because of its strong nature and thick diameter, is able to undergo harsh chemical processes to make it smooth, shiny, and tangle-free Processed Hair, but that the most glorious hair, the only kind, really, we should be looking at, is Virgin European. We learn that wig companies send employees out to remote villages or monasteries or convents in Russia and Italy to contract for hair; the hair-growing people must agree to always keep their hair protected and safe from pollution and sun damage, to never blow dry or style. The wig people then return years later to harvest the crop with razors or close cutting at the scalp. This all makes me slightly queasy – it sounds too much like people stripped naked and yielding, handing something precious over to someone else with questionable or inhumane intent.

She finally finds one she likes, a bright auburn, pre-Raphaelite mass, kidney-length and decadent, with a hand-tied mono-filament top. I'm stunned by her choice. She takes off her scarf to try it on and the exposure of the holdout black hairs on her tender white scalp makes me look away in pain. The sales guy is talking passionately about ear tabs and cap size and maybe the need, soon, for special Comfy Grips to hold the wig in place against a smooth dome of bare skin. You know, some guys, he tells her, when it's time for a piece, they actually have snaps surgically implanted in their scalps to hold it in place, can you imagine? and I finally look. She's smiling, but I don't think it suits her at all, it's too outrageous and it doesn't work with her olive-going-yellow skin. But she's excited by it, turning to see all angles of her head, flipping the tendrilled ends behind her, and there's no point in being honest at a time like this – let a little denial grow, I think. The bravery'll have to crack, at some point. I tell her she looks beautiful, Go ahead, you look like a Russian Empress, a Queen, and, when the sales guy nods agreeably at that and she hesitates, looking all at once timid and drained, I say, Do it, be unabashed, be wild.

She smiles at that, then: 'I'm worried...' she says.

'Don't be,' the sales guy says. 'With that face, you can pull anything off.'

'What are you worried about?' I ask quietly, and the sales guy, sensing a new level of intimacy, squeezes my arm, nods, and discreetly moves away.

'You want some Compazine?' I offer.

'No, I'm okay, thanks.'

'So, what?'

'It's been a while,' she begins.

'Since?'

'You know. Since.' She pulls panels of long red hair down in front to cover her breasts, Godiva-like. I've noticed her breasts have been going limp. Everything about her is losing tone.

'*Since*,' she repeats.

'Oh.' I look away to examine a bottle of wig shampoo. 'Maybe that's just normal slackening off,' I suggest. 'Two kids, married eight years. It's nothing, it's totally normal.'

'I'm not talking slackening. I'm talking a real while. Like being cut off.'

'Maybe he's worried about hurting you,' I suggest.

'Maybe.'

'Maybe he feels guilty,' I say.

'Guilty for what?'

'Oh, I don't know.' I don't know what to say. 'For not being able to fix things.'

'Maybe.'

'Maybe he's got stuff going on, too,' I say. 'He's going through this, too. He needs taking care of, too.'

'You're right. You know, why don't you come over some night? We can just hang out, rent a movie or something. The three of us, like we used to. Before all this shit.'

'Sure.'

'And he's been working such crazy hours... I'm almost feeling like he doesn't want to be around me.'

'You're being ridiculous. He adores you.'

She tugs the wig further back on her forehead. 'Does this look natural? Or just whorey? Tell me the truth.'

'He loves you, you know. He couldn't care less.'

'But do you think he'll like this? Come on.'

'It's great. He'll love it. He loves everything about you.'

She nudges me her thanks, gets out her wallet, and I applaud her. She's paying and I'm smiling, stroking her new marrow-coloured curls, but all I can picture is some peasant or nun shorn of her hair, her naked baby bird head bent low over bills for oil or coal, counting the coins for a new church bell, a new milk cow, medicines for the orphans, loaves of black bread, all so my friend can entice her husband, cling to illusion, grip at fading hope.

But then I listen carefully to the sales guy's complicated directions about styling and cleaning and care, because I know that, although her husband is such a prince of a guy, this exhaustive task of tending will probably fall to me. It's what friends are for.

Do it, be unabashed, be wild.

I don't remember which of us said that. We all used to say it to each other, first, when they were dating and they'd include me, we'd hang out and get a meat-lovers' pizza, rent a movie plus two sequels at a time, get stoned and drunk on scratch margaritas and tell ourselves we hadn't yet outgrown a single impetuous thing. Then after, when they got married and they'd include me, we'd hang out and get a cheeseless veggie pizza, rent movies, get selectively stoned or drunk, then later, when they had kids, the first boy and then rapidly the second, and they'd include me, and we'd put the kids to bed and hang out, eat the kids' leftover canned ravioli off their plates, watch TV but not get stoned or drunk any more, because the kids might need something and we all needed to keep it real.

Then the weekend, six months or so ago, before *all this shit,* when she and her kids went off and away to her mom's for the weekend and one of us called the other one, I don't remember which, it seemed natural either way, *Let's hang out, get a pizza, rent a movie.* I probably was the one to call, yes, I was worried he'd be lonely all alone. And the getting stoned on a forgotten, leftover Ziploc bag in the freezer and drunk on vodka and kiddie apple juice just seemed to follow, seemed natural, too, although it had been a long while. And then cracking up, being too silly, the playful shove-touching we always did and then not so playful, and then groping and stroking as it all of a sudden went rash, and then just doing it, being unabashed, being wild. Waking up the next morning, in her sheets, one of her long healthy thick black hairs stuck to my right breast, like a reminder to floss. *It was nothing, Let's forget this happened, It doesn't mean anything, doesn't count. I love her, I love her, too,* batting clichés back and forth to each other and spraying the fetid air with pine. *We can't ever tell her, Not ever, I love her, I love her, too,* and both of us feeling so so sick with it.

I'll never tell her. She shouldn't have to face that, now. She deserves it all to be as pretty and clean as we can make it.

A while later, she changes her mind. It was trying too hard, she says, it gets in my way, falls into food, the toilet, the boys keep tugging at it. She's back in a scarf, she's shrugging, resigned. The wild red wig is carefully rewrapped and back in a box; she's donating it to a special group that gets wigs for poor women and kids.

'It just wasn't me,' she says. 'It just didn't work.'

'I thought you looked beautiful,' I tell her.

She bites her lip, looks out the car window.

'He didn't like it?'

She shrugs.

Maybe he's not the problem, maybe it's you, maybe you're the one who can't handle losing your looks, not him. I think this, but I don't say it, I loathe myself for the mere thought.

'So, right, we'll keep looking,' I say. 'It's a quest. We'll find the perfect wig.'

I picture some twelve-year-old girl with leukaemia wearing the donated wig. Some little girl who'll never get married or have kids, never get laid or kissed, who'll probably be buried in that mass of whorey, Virgin European hair.

'I appreciate your doing all this with me,' she says, quiet.

'My God,' I say. 'How many places did I drag you to to find that horrible pink dress?' Twelve stores. I was desperate to find the perfect dress for our Senior Prom, consistently unhappy with the look of my pasty arms, my negligible breasts, my pastel hair, my washed-out skin tone. She drove us around from place to place in her mother's gassy Toyota, the patience of a saint, encouraging me, all the while looking perfect in the first thrift shop dress she'd found, darkly glamorous next to her perfect boyfriend of the moment, me going with his irrelevant best buddy, by default, actually, she'd arranged it so we could all be together. We took a group photo, camera snapping at the exact second I looked at her burgundy satin and thought, *That would have worked on me, better on me, she should have offered to swap.*

In a Miracle Mile shop that markets to Orthodox Jews she finds a simple, chin-length brunette bob, sleek on her, actually, more sophisticated than her own old ponytail and bangs, and I'm shocked at the price – it's a chunk of money I'd expect her to put in her boys' college fund, not blow on vanity, on a lie of hair. But she raises her thin sketched-on eyebrows at it, too, shakes her head.

'Such a pretty girl,' the saleswoman says. 'What a shame.'

'Will you just go on?' I tell her. 'Write the cheque, you deserve it.'

She glances nervously at the saleswoman.

'Oh, well, you have insurance?' the saleswoman asks. 'You can get a prosthesis prescription, you know.'

'Too late for that,' my friend says. 'I already blew it.'

'Well, it's a lot, I know,' the saleswoman says. 'But it's like buying a car. You can buy a Chevy, or you can buy a Cadillac. It makes all the difference.'

My friend just gives her a wan, brief nod.

'Okay. That's fine, I'm going to let you two talk about it. Such a face... such a face deserves the best. Tell you what, dear, I'll take off twenty per cent if you want it, make it a sale price, all right? You let me know.' The saleswoman veers off towards a young bewigged housewife in a turtleneck and lisle stockings, carrying a bakery box.

'You look very elegant,' I tell her. 'Sleek.'

I can see the pulse in the sad, stark vein on her temple.

'Listen, why don't you let me chip in?' I say.

'Oh, please. No. Thank you.'

I can see the tremble to her sallow chin. 'Are you tired?' I ask. 'How about something to eat? Should we get you a snack?'

'I'm not hungry.'

'You want some juice?'

'Stop babying me,' she snaps.

'I'm sorry,' I say, taken aback. 'I'm trying to help.'

'No, I'm...' She takes my hand; hers is looking like an old lady's, waxy and clawlike. I wonder if she's toxic, if the chemicals can seep out of her pores to poison the atmosphere around her.

'I'm not used to the role reversal, you know?' she says.

'It's okay.'

'Thank you for being so patient with me.'

I take my hand away to fuss with a wig stand. It's a wire armature of an empty and featureless human head, like the model for a Cyborg.

'I'll just get this one,' she says, tired. 'It's fine. It's nothing. Really, it's fine.'

'Good,' I tell her. 'You're a Cadillac, you know,' and she smiles.

★

213

You're seeing someone, aren't you? she'd said to me those months ago. *You have that glow.*

Not really.

Come on, tell me the truth. My life is so boring.

So I made up a story, because she knew me too well, could probably smell it on me, a story to throw her off, *Yeah, some new guy, but it's complicated, we're keeping it just casual, nothing serious, nothing worth talking about. Don't you think I'd tell you if it were anything interesting, anything important?* I pointed out.

Damn, she said. *I'm dying at least for something sordid.*

It doesn't even rise to the level of sordid, I told her. *Sorry. It's nothing. It doesn't even count.*

So yes, it went on a while, a little thing that took surprising root. Shaving my legs and puffing my hair up wild every day and keeping a fresh sweep of make-up on, trying to get to, and stay, ready and perfect, in case he called to say he'd found us some time. He found it now and then, and I got good at patient. *Just until it's out of our systems*, we told each other, *It'll die a natural death and everything will go back to normal.* And *We'll never tell, never tell a thing, It isn't even anything. We'll spare her.* Until the mole took us all aback. Until that once-teasing wink of a birthmark on her brown thigh abruptly went lethal and foul. *This is it, We need to stop, now, We need to think of her, now, Stand by her, Be there for her. Let her have both of us, all of us.* Both of us avoiding each other, now, we can't even bear to be in the same room with each other. It's too intense. And bad timing, now, or maybe just ironic, that we're supposed to be the prince of a husband and the beloved best friend in the world, and be there in it together, happy smiles and keeping it all caring and real, for her.

Wig #3 is a Farrah-esque blonde romp.

'Does this look like I *know* it's retro?' she asks me. 'Or like I don't get the joke?'

She strikes a Farrah pose, head tilted back, a manic, toothy grin. We're back on Hollywood Boulevard, in a place where all the wig styles call movie stars to mind. There's also the 'Halloween Line': witches, vampires, Elvira, Rainbow Clown. Can I have you today? she'd asked on the phone. Can we have a quest day? Let's go out in search of. Be silly. Play. She's between cycles and has had a renewed burst of energy, a manic buzz. There's a glow from her skin, and I wonder if she's radioactive.

'I wonder if it comes with the red bathing suit,' I say. 'And the nipples.'

'*Those*, I really do need. Mine have snuck back inside somewhere. Like turtles.'

'What kind of nun did *this* come from?' I ask the sales person.

'Now, that one's a human-synthetic blend,' he tells us. 'Good value for the price. Look at the rich tonal dimensions of colour-play. You only get that with natural.' He fluffs the wig's feathered waves.

'So . . . it's a *natural* synthetic blonde?' I ask, and she laughs.

'No, you never get those highlights with synthetic. It's the human hairs that do it. Of course, they've been chemically processed to get that colour.'

'Chemically processed,' she repeats. 'Boy oh boy, can I relate.'

'But this hair is still cuticle hair. Still high-quality. Now, a blend like this should last you two or three years if you're lucky.'

'Listen,' she says, '*I'm* not going to last two or three years,' and we both laugh. Her days are numbered and look at her, laughing. I'm edgy with the counting down. I'm too aware of waiting for the egg timer to ding, for it all to be over and done with.

'Right. Excuse me.' The sales person leaves to help a dowager-humped woman with wisps, waving at him from across the store.

'What was wrong with the kosher one?' I ask.

'I don't know . . . it was too plain. Too serious.'

'Too severe?'

'Yeah. I want to play, a little. That one didn't make me feel . . . fetching.'

'You think he'll find this one fetching?'

'I don't know. He's always liked blondes.'

I put down a blonde Afro wig to look at her. 'He's told you that?'

'A million times.'

'That isn't very nice, to tell you.'

She shrugs. 'Doesn't bother me. It's honest. One of his best qualities. Honesty.'

'Really?'

'Sure. Don't you think so?'

'I think you can be an honest person without being honest about every single thing that comes up. Little things that don't do anything but hurt someone.'

'But that isn't hurtful.' She shrugs again. 'Just honest.'

'Sometimes being a little dishonest is the kind thing to do.'

'But I think that's what's held everything together for us. Especially through this shit. Knowing everything. Knowing everything's been said. Shared. I think ... it'll make it easier for me. And for him.'

'I suppose. So, well, okay, he likes blondes, huh? I didn't know that.'

'Always. Always had a thing for blondes.'

'Yeah, well. You won.'

'Won?'

'He chose you. I mean.'

'Right. He chose me ... but he didn't choose all of this.' She gazes in the mirror, shakes her head so Farrah's blonde swirls go mad as foam, then settle. 'Eighty-seven days and counting,' she tells me.

'Are you kidding?' I say. 'Is that all? It's been longer than that for me.'

'What about that guy from a few months ago?'

'Yeah, exactly, a few *months* ago. We broke it off. I mentioned that.'

'Oh, honey. I'm sorry.' She looks upset. 'You seemed hopeful about him.'

'No, I didn't. It wasn't anything. It was complicated.'

'Well, maybe down the road, you guys. Maybe it was just the timing, then—'

'It didn't count. I told you that.'

'I'm sorry.' The look of compassion on her face is a look I've seen before, a look that doesn't fit. It's the look when I'd score the point, I'd win, and she'd be the one to kindly, misplacedly ask if I was okay, how was my ankle doing, the blister on my thumb, did I need some water, did I want to take a break.

'Let's just forget it,' I say.

'I guess I've been pretty self-absorbed, huh?'

'That's okay. If I had any stuff worth telling you about, I'd just tell you. Your stuff is more important stuff.'

'Yeah. My eighty-seven days. And I've been feeling good. The last week or so. I've been doing so well. Don't I look good?'

'You look great. You look beautiful.' It's a lie, she doesn't, but I say it to make her feel good. 'All your colour's back. It's like you're all back.'

'Let's go get pedicures. Eat cheesecake. Play tennis. Let's find a river to skinny-dip in.'

How sad, that this is the extent of her imagination, that she can't see more. That she can't see she's on her last gasp. It *is* her last gasp, after all, I remind myself. It's just a matter of time now, after all. I unclench my fists. I tell myself to get back to patience. To pity.

'Whatever you want,' I say. 'But you need to make a decision, first.'

She glances around the store. 'Maybe the Veronica Lake. Or the Marilyn.'

'The Shirley Temple? The Dolly Parton?'

She looks at me, smiles, looks away. 'I've always wanted blonde hair, you know,' she says. 'I guess I've always had a thing for blondes, too.'

That fat black ponytail, swinging.

'All right, fine, just come out and ask him why. Ask him why you guys aren't doing it any more,' I say. 'Make him tell you.'

'Maybe.'

'If honesty is so great. Go on. Ask him to tell you the truth. See what he says.'

'Yeah . . . Okay, here's honest.' She faces me. 'I'm going to be honest with you.'

'Oh, please don't.'

'Really. I want to know everything between us has been said.'

'Are you sure?'

'I've always envied you.'

'Me? Why?'

'I've always hated you, just a little. For your hair.' She flips a lock of the Farrah at me. 'Really. The attention you always got.'

'That was you. You always got the attention.'

'The blondes have more fun thing. The fairy princess thing. Guys and blondes.'

'You're deluded. You're the one guys have always gone for.'

'I mean it. Envy. Hate. Because of your hair. Ridiculous, but there, true.'

'Well, I don't know what to tell you. Maybe yours will grow back in blonde,' I suggest. 'It does that, sometimes, right? Grow back in completely different.'

She just shakes her head, gives me a knowing look.

'Yeah, well . . . mine's chemically processed now, too,' I remind her. 'Mine's all a lie. You'll have to find something else to hate me for.'

It's a shock to see her back. Or, almost back. The long straight black hair, the bangs. No ponytail, though, because the nadir is here to stay, time's up, she's mostly back in bed now, mostly reclined for good now, and it would make the back of her head hurt. She found it online, she tells me, the perfect reincarnation.

It was easy to order, she knows all about Virgin European and cuticle shaft by now, knows her cap size and her need for Comfy Grips. She shows me every tiny detail, the hand-knotted wefts and the latex scalp textured like actual skin. I expect to see a dandruff flake, a blocked pore, but no, it's perfect. And she was lucky, it was the last one the company had in stock and they sent it express.

'What do you think?' she asks, proud, hopeful.

I get a whiff of her, a fake sweetness on top of the other smells. She's wearing perfume, as if that will help. 'I suppose I'm a little hurt,' I say. 'That you went ahead without me. I thought we were a team.'

'Oh, honey,' she says. 'I couldn't ask you to keep questing with me. You've done way too much. You've been so patient, so amazing.'

'Well, it looks great. You look exactly like your old self,' I tell her. 'You look like you're sixteen.' She's pleased, in a weak but self-satisfied way, and I remember the day in chemistry, we had a midterm but we'd stayed out late the night before and hadn't studied, and she'd made up some story for our ageing, stubby teacher. I remember his rapt, understanding face, his devoted gaze as she told him whatever she'd told, tossing me into it, too, winning him over, me standing behind her and her thick black curtain of hair. She won us both an extension, bought us both more time. She was always able to get whatever she wanted, and I'd get the surplus by default. Just by hanging around her, just by waiting things out.

'So, I've been wanting to ask you something,' she says.

'Sure.'

'It might sound weird.'

'Go on. Ask me anything.'

'What do you hate me for?'

'What?' I say, startled. 'I don't hate you for anything.'

'I told you. I got it out of my system. So come on, I need to know. If you hate me for anything. If there's anything you've never told me.'

'There's nothing.'

'There must be something. Twenty years? Be honest.'

'Okay,' I say. 'I hate you for all of this shit.'

She laughs. 'That's too easy. We all hate me for that.'

Just then her husband comes in, bearing a tray of yoghurt and sliced fruit. A tight bud of a rose in a tiny crystal vase.

'Sweetheart, can you eat a little?'

'Sure, I'm hungry.' She catches his free hand, squeezes. 'She says I look like I did when we were sixteen.'

He smiles at her, but not at me. 'I bet that's true,' he says to her.

'It is. It's the truth,' I tell him. 'I'll show you a picture sometime.' I fluff my hand through the top of my hair, where it feels flat.

'Oh, I believe you.' He carefully rests the tray of food on the bed next to her, fussing so that he doesn't have to meet my eyes. I think about some way to get him to look at me, face me. I just have to wait, the moment'll come. He's being careful, but he won't be able to help himself. It's been so long. We've been so patient. So good. But there's a sudden loud blast of cartoon music from the other room, and little boy voices getting combative.

'Hey, you guys,' he yells, 'keep it down.'

'No, let them,' she says. 'Just let them.'

'You should take a nap soon.'

'I will, later.' She spoons yoghurt into her mouth. 'We're talking about stuff.'

'I'll clean up before I leave,' I tell him.

'No, that's okay, thanks, I'll get it,' he tells my direction over his shoulder. 'And you need some rest,' he says to her. He leans over, brushes the fake bangs back, kisses her on the forehead just below the start of fake scalp. Right in front of me. As if I'm not even there. He isn't avoiding me, I realise. I'm just not quite anything. I don't quite count.

'Yeah, I'm taking off soon,' I say to his retreating back. 'Don't worry.'

'Here.' She offers me a spoonful of yoghurt with a wavering hand. 'I really can't eat this. He's trying so hard, I don't want him to know.'

I take the spoon, hesitant to put my mouth where hers has been. 'What is this, vanilla,' I say. 'Ugh. Just eat what you can, I'll flush the rest.'

'He's a prince,' she says. 'He really is.'

'Yes,' I say.

'So we made love last night,' she tells me.

'Oh?' I say.

'I thought at first it was just guilt, or pity, you know?'

'Yeah, maybe.'

'But I really think it just hit him that there needed to be a last time. Where you *know* it's the last time. So you'll always have that.'

'You think that was the last time?'

'Yeah.' She takes a bite of a slice of nectarine; her fingers are shaky and she puts the rest down. 'It wasn't good the way it used to be good,' she says. 'I mean, it used to be *great*, you know?'

'Yes,' I say. 'I've heard.'

'But it was good for all the other reasons it stays good. I mean, it was awkward and uncomfortable, you know, it's been a long time, but then it had all the things you always hope will be there between you. Like it's just the two of you in this moment, this space, but in a way that will last. Something you'll always have. I hope *he'll* always have. I hope he'll remember that part of it forever and forget everything else. I think he's hoping for that, too. I think that's why he did it. It was good.' She laughs, sheepish. 'Or maybe it was just a pity fuck.'

'Yeah, maybe,' I say. I don't know how he could stand the smell of her, the chemical sweet trying so hard to cover up the chemical waste and rot.

'Or maybe it was just the wig.' She strokes her beautiful long black hair. 'You think?' she asks.

I see his mouth still pressed to her waxy, wasted face. I try for patience, for pity. For sparing her.

Do it, I hear in my ear. *Be her true and honest friend, give her whatever she wants.* She deserves it.

'You really want me to be honest?' I say. 'Really honest?'

'Yeah, of course. Thank you. What?'

I have her full attention.

'We slept together. A couple of times.'

She looks at me, her face blank.

'Months ago. Before all this.'

There's a raw twist and crumple to her features, and I feel a joyful rush, a jolt, the lunge for the ball you just know you're going to smash back hard and win the game with, the thing that'll let you win the prize, be victorious and serene.

'You were off at your mom's with the boys, and he thought we'd just rent a movie, get pizza. Like the three of us used to do—'

'I know,' she says.

'—except you weren't there, you were gone—'

'I know, stop—'

'—and he invited me over, and—'

'I *know*,' she repeats. 'Just *stop* it. Stop.'

I stop. 'What do you mean?'

'I don't want details,' she says. 'That's between the two of you.'

'What are you talking about?'

'He told me.'

'He told you.'

'Last night.' There's the crumple of her again, beneath the glossy bangs, then she takes a breath and her face settles back to smooth. 'I knew something's been wrong. I knew there was something. What you said before, about him going through stuff, too, remember? So I told him whatever it was, he better be looking at the clock, you know?'

'And he told you.'

'It wasn't easy. It wasn't pretty. *I* wasn't pretty. Believe me, you would *not* have wanted to be here for what was going on last night.'

'No.'

'But finally, finally, I was all right. It was horrible, but afterward, it was all right. It was good. The two of us. I think it's even why it was good.' She actually laughs. 'Well, that and the wig.'

'What about me?'

'Oh, honey.' She takes my hand. 'I was hoping you'd say something. That you'd be honest with me. That's what I wanted. I'm glad you told me. I've always been able to trust you that way, that you don't leave things unsaid. That's what I needed, now. You get to this place where, if it isn't real, forget it.' Her face is fully content and peaceful now. Her face is a plastic, placid mask. 'And hey,' she says. 'Don't think this is weird, but I even had the thought that maybe you two would get together. Afterwards.'

'What?' I say. 'Excuse me?'

'I know, weird, fucked up, but in a way it would make sense.'

'Are you kidding me?'

'Hon, honey, he'll need taking care of. And it would be all right with me. If that happened. Because it doesn't change anything. I want you to know that.'

Like some queen granting favours, tossing coins to her servant girl, bread to the peasants, giving her lesser jewels away to charity.

I see his sensitive, devoted hand ceaselessly on her leached-out skin, her toneless body. Caressing her glorious, extravagant, interminable hair. Stroking her, undyingly.

And it really, really should have been me.

'. . . Yeah, maybe this really did the trick,' I hear her say.

There's a chuckle. She's fussing with her wig, she's been talking this whole time.

'All the others were a lie. Trying to be someone else. This is really what I wanted.'

'This one is perfect,' I tell her. 'It's you. The perfect you.'

'I want to be wearing it, you know. Promise me?'

'I promise you.'

'And you have to check my eyebrows are all right.'

'I promise. The eyebrows, and I'll be sure you have it on.'

She examines a lock. 'I got yoghurt in it. I want it to be all pretty and clean. You'll make sure, okay? Even if it gets crazy?'

'Give it to me now. I'll wash it now. We have that special shampoo.' The clock is ticking, I think.

'You don't mind?'

'Please,' I say. 'It's what friends are for.'

'Would you close the door? The boys...' She fusses with her Comfy Grips, and gently slips the wig off with practised care. 'Going out in style,' she says.

She hands it over to me, and I picture the remote, yielding nuns surrendering their precious and painstaking sacrifice. She's all stripped down to scalp and skull now, illusionless, foetal and wizened. She's no Empress, no Cadillac, no Queen, just a drained sack of cells that went lethal and rank on her, and I'm the only one able to see it, spot the patches of sweat on the burgundy satin dress, really know the ugly, bald truth about her. She's hideous, but everyone else will eternally only see the beautiful fake. I imagine her lying serene in her casket, flushed clean and perfectly groomed, an abiding Nefertiti or Cleopatra.

Do it, be unabashed, be wild.

I take the wig into the bathroom with me, close the door. I run the water in the sink. I open the medicine cabinet still and forever announcing *I love you*, find the tweezers. I close the toilet lid and sit, cross one leg over the other, take her hair in my hand, her perfect and healthy and human black hair and I begin to tweeze. I pluck each thick glossy fake strand out by its fake root and let them drift hair by hair by hair down to the cold white tile floor.

Esprit de Corpse

Jean Lamb

I look up at the ceiling. It's still dirty. I can't believe he left my eyes open.

Or perhaps I can. He's capable of any cruelty.

The last thing I remember before this was the sickening crunch of my bones as a car went over them. Somehow I awoke in here.

I'm dead. I know I'm dead. Why am I still here? Perhaps it's because my body has been lovingly preserved with the reeking chemicals he put in it. I don't know. I just wish I could leave.

Especially now when I hear his footsteps. He leans over and gazes down on me. I hated him when I first knew him, and I hate him now. Especially now. He unbuckles his pants and takes pleasure in my helplessness. His hot breath smells of garlic and tobacco. It doesn't take him long.

Then someone makes a noise outside the room. He zips himself up with a satisfied look on his face. He quickly puts small cups over my eyeballs and pins my eyelids down over them.

I hear my husband's sobs. I try to cry out to him, but my mouth is sewed up. *Bill*, I think. *Bill, oh why can't you hear me? Why can he hear me and you can't?*

After a while, Bill leaves. Then he reopens my eyes, and smiles. 'You'll belong to me forever,' he says. 'I made sure of that. Too bad you didn't look both ways like your mama told you.'

225

I refuse to think anything then. If he can't hear me at all, perhaps he'll believe I'm truly gone. Better the dark ground than this.

He caresses my cheek. 'I know you're in there,' he says with a sigh.

The funeral is tomorrow, I think at him.

He just smiles again. Then he puts the cups back over my eyes.

The darkness is peaceful, even friendly, compared to what I see and endure in the light. I don't know how much time is passing. I ready myself to leave this prison somehow. There has to be a way out if only I can find it.

The light comes back. 'The funeral was yesterday,' he says with a smirk.

I was afraid of this. Who – or what – was buried in my place? He fondles me again. But I can't feel it as much as I did before. Perhaps my time for escape will come sooner than he thinks.

'Oh, no,' he says, and shakes his head angrily. 'You won't get away that easy!'

He walks off into another room and brings out a cart. He puts me on it and rolls it to the back. Then he opens a large door and a cloud of frozen air puffs out. He puts me into it. 'See how much you enjoy this! You'll be begging for company, even my company, before too long!'

But he's wrong. It's cold, and dark, and very peaceful here. Frost settles on me like the touch of the first snow of winter. Then I hear other voices. I am not the only body trapped here.

One of them is a ten-year-old girl. I know her – she was killed diving into a quarry last summer. *If only he'd leave the door open longer, I could go*, she cries plaintively.

Why would that work? I ask. Then she shows me with her mind where a small part of her body has finally gone rotten. Her shining soul is ready to fly out of her broken shell.

Time passes. Then I wish I could smile as I think of how to do it – how to help all of those in here. But I'll need patience. I have to do this right.

More time passes. At last I think it's been long enough. I call out mentally to get out of this awful place. This, of course, is a lie. I'm far happier here than with him, but he certainly doesn't know that.

I hear the clanking as he opens the door and removes my body. He touches me carefully. 'I'll have to let you thaw a bit,' he grumbles.

Don't wait too long, I think.

'So, you missed me after all,' he says. 'I told you in high school that I'd take better care of you than Bill ever would. Don't worry, I'm ready for you now.'

I rather hope he is. I slowly become less frozen. Soon he tests my skin and finds it more pliable. *Oh hurry, hurry*, I think. *I can hardly wait*.

He can't wait. He strips down bare and eagerly enters me. It's too bad he's not a cook. Anyone familiar with removing things from the inside of a supposedly defrosted turkey knows how frigid the hollow centre can be. Then the sudden moisture spurting from him quickly freezes him inside my chilly womb, like a tongue stuck to a pipe.

He tugs away but is trapped within me. If he can wait long enough, he'll go free. Unless a customer comes in, of course. I laugh inside as I think what will happen if he tries to pull himself away before then.

I wonder what he's going to do now.

He's never had much patience.

Contributor Biographies

Becky Bradford is a regular contributor of short stories, articles and book reviews for the creative writing website hagsharlotsheroines.com, and is currently writing the first draft of a novel. For the last few years she has been dividing her time between rural Andalucia, southern England and the west coast of Ireland.

Clare Colvin has published three novels, *The Mirror Makers*, *Masque of the Gonzagas*, and *A Fatal Season*. Her work has been translated into five European languages, and her short stories have appeared extensively in anthologies. Born in the UK, she grew up in South Africa, Lebanon, and India, and now lives in London. She writes on literary and arts subjects for several national newspapers and is opera critic for the *Sunday Express*. She is a tutor in creative writing at Birkbeck, University of London. Personal website: www.clarecolvin.com.

Madeline de Chambrey lives in Toronto, Canada. Her short stories have been anthologised in a number of collections, including *Confessions: Admissions of Sexual Guilt* and *Amazons: Sexy Tales of Strong Women*. For her erotic novels, such as *Wild Card,* she is Madeline Moore. In yet another guise, she writes TV and movie scripts. She is currently working on a new novel for Black Lace.

Stella Duffy is the author of ten novels, over thirty stories, and eight plays. Her novel *State of Happiness* was long-listed for the 2004 Orange Prize, and she is currently writing the screenplay for a feature film production. With Lauren Henderson she co-edited the anthology *Tart Noir*, from which her story 'Martha Grace' won the 2002 Crime Writers Association Short Story Award. She has appeared on BBC Radio 4 in sitcoms, plays and quizzes, and is a performer with comedy company Spontaneous Combustion, and Improbable. She is an occasional guest with the Comedy Store Players. She was born in London, grew up in New Zealand, and has lived in London since 1986.

Chris Dunning lives in Nottingham. This is his first published story although his work has been on BBC Radio Birmingham and the stage.

Tony Fennelly's first novel, *The Glory Hole Murders*, was nominated for an Edgar and since then her mysteries have been published in six languages in the US, Europe, and Asia. She lives in a townhouse in New Orleans and on a farm in Turkey Creek, Louisiana. Her website is www.tonyfennelly.com.

Niall Griffiths was born in Liverpool and now lives in Wales. He has published six novels, the most recent being *Runt*.

Vicki Hendricks is the author of noir novels *Miami Purity*, *Iguana Love*, *Voluntary Madness*, *Sky Blues*, and *Cruel Poetry*. She lives in Hollywood, Florida. Recently, she has contributed short stories to *Deadly Housewives*, *Dying For It*, and *Miami Noir*.

Tara Ison's first novel, *A Child Out of Alcatraz*, was a finalist for the *Los Angeles Times* Book Prize, and her short fiction and nonfiction have appeared in *Tin House*, *The Kenyon Review*, *The Mississippi Review*, and numerous other journals and anthologies. Her latest novel, *The List*, has recently been published. She lives in Los Angeles.

Rosie Jackson is the author of *Fantasy: The Literature of Subversion*; *The Eye of the Buddha and other Tales*; *Frieda Lawrence*; and *Mothers Who Leave*. She has taught literature at the University of East Anglia and Bristol UWE, and creative writing at Nottingham Trent University and in venues worldwide. Winner of the Writers Inc 2006 competition for her short story 'What the Water Gave Me', She currently writes fiction, poetry, reviews and a regular column for *Tears in the Fence*. She lives in Frome, Somerset, and her details and work can be found on www.divinewrite.org.uk.

Josie Kimber's short fiction has been published in the anthology *Typical Girls* and her short film work was shown as part of the *Bad Girls* exhibition at London's ICA. She has written art reviews for i-D magazine and performed her fiction at spoken word events. She contributes book reviews to *Flux* magazine and is writing her first novel. She currently lives in Brighton.

Jean Lamb's short stories have appeared in Renuciates of Darkover, Analog, Man/Kzin Wars VIII, and various other publications. Her story 'Galley Slave' made it to the Preliminary Ballot for the Nebula from its Analog publication. In addition to writing, she has also been a reviewer for Locus. She's married with two children and lives in Klamath Falls, Oregon.

Georgiana Nelsen's fiction has been published in various journals and e-zines. She practises business, publishing, and cyber law, and completing her first novel, *Occupied Territory*. She lives in Houston, Texas.

Danuta Reah, who also writes as Carla Banks, lives in Sheffield, the setting for her first four books *Only Darkness Silent Playgrounds Night Angels* and *Bleak Water*. Writing as Carla Banks she has published *The Forest of Souls*, and *Strangers*. In 2005, she won the Crime Writers Association Dagger for her short story, 'No Flies on Frank'. She writes full-time.

Dee Silman was brought up in the south of England but now lives in North Wales with her husband and two young daughters. Her short stories have been published in a variety of literary magazines and anthologies, most recently by *Mslexia* and *Honno*. She has had erotic fiction published by Black Lace and Cleis Press.

Umi Sinha was born in Bombay in 1952 and now lives in Brighton. In India she worked as a freelance editor and wrote children's comic books. She now teaches creative writing at the University of Sussex and is completing a novel set in India and England during the period of the British Raj. She is also a storyteller.